Dr
Warrior Daughters

A stirring collection of heroic fantasy stories from leading fantasy writers in which girls and women feature as warriors, healers, or simply as strong, independent people while boys and men are heroic in unexpected ways. Questing for adventure and romance, they come up against dragons, evil powers, magicians and the need for valour and wisdom.

Heroic, fairy-tale and science fantasy published in Lions and Tracks

Jessica Yates (Ed)

Dragons and Warrior Daughters

Fantasy Stories by Women Writers

COLLINS

LIONS · TRACKS

First published in Great Britain 1989 by Lions Tracks
8 Grafton Street, London W1X 3LA

Lions Tracks is an imprint of
the Children's Division, part of
the Collins Publishing Group

Printed in Great Britain,
by William Collins Sons & Co. Ltd, Glasgow

Acknowledgements

The publishers gratefully acknowledge permission to reprint copyright material to the following:

Macdonald & Co for *Dragonfield* from **Dragonfield and Other Stories** by Jane Yolen 1985, © 1985 by Jane Yolen; Tanith Lee for *Draco Draco* by Tanith Lee from **Beyond Lands of Never** ed. by Maxim Jakubowski, Unwin Unicorn 1984, © 1984 by Tanith Lee; Writers House Inc for *The Healer* by Robin McKinley from **Elsewhere Vol. 11** ed. by Terri Windling & Mark Alan Arnold, Ace Books 1982, © 1982 by Robin McKinley; Laura Cecil for *Dragon Reserve, Home Eight* by Diana Wynne Jones from **Warlock at the Wheel and Other Stories** Macmillan 1984, © Diana Wynne Jones; Carnell Literary Agency for *Crusader Damosel* by Vera Chapman from **The Fantastic Imagination 11** ed. by Robert H. Boyer & Kenneth J. Zahorski, Avon Books 1978, © 1978 by Vera Chapman; Don Congdon Associates for *Black God's Kiss* by C. L. Moore, first published in **Weird Tales** Oct 1934, copyright renewed 1962 by Catherine Reggie.

Every effort has been made to trace the owners of the copyright material in this book. In the event of any question arising as to the use of any material, the Editor will be pleased to make the necessary corrections in future editions of the book.

Contents

Dragonfield

Dragonfield

Jane Yolen

There is a spit of land near the farthest shores of the farthest islands. It is known as Dragonfield. Once dragons dwelt on the isles in great herds, feeding on the dry brush and fuelling their flames with the carcasses of small animals and migratory birds. There are no dragons there now, though the nearer islands are scored with long furrows as though giant claws had been at work, and the land is fertile from the bones of the buried behemoths. Yet though the last of the great worms perished long before living memory, there is a tale still told by the farmers and fisherfolk of the isles about that last dragon.

His name in the old tongue was Aredd and his colour a dull red. It was not the red of hollyberry or the red of the wild flowering trillium, but the red of a man's life blood spilled out upon the sand. Aredd's tail was long and sinewy, but his body longer still. Great mountains rose upon his back. His eyes were black and, when he was angry, looked as empty as the eyes of a shroud, but when he was calculating, they shone with a false jewelled light. His jaws were a furnace that could roast a whole bull. And when he roared, he could be heard like distant thunder throughout the archipelago.

Aredd was the last of his kind and untaught in the riddle-lore of dragons. He was but fierceness and fire, for he had hatched late from the brood. His brothers and sisters were all gone, slain in the famous Dragon Wars when even young dragons were spitted by warriors who had gone past fearing. But the egg that had housed Aredd had lain buried in the sand of Dragonfield years past the carnage, uncovered at last by an unnaturally high tide. And when he hatched, no one had remarked it. So the young worm had stretched and cracked the shell and emerged nose-first in the sand.

At the beginning he looked like any large lizard for he had not yet shed his eggskin, which was lumpy and whitish, like clotted cream. But he grew fast, as dragons will, and before the week was out he was the size of a small pony and his eggskin had sloughed off. He had, of course, singed and eaten the skin and so developed a taste for crackling. A small black-snouted island pig was his next meal, then a family of shagged cormorants flying island to island on their long migration south.

And still no one remarked him, for it was the time of great harvests brought about by the fertilization of the rich high tides, and everyone was needed in the fields: old men and women, mothers with their babes tied to their backs, young lovers who might have slipped off to the far isle to tryst. Even the young fishermen did not dare to go down to the bay and cast off while daylight bathed the plants and vines. They gave up their nets and lines for a full two weeks to help with the stripping, as the harvest was called then. And by night, of course, the villagers were much too weary to sail by moonlight to the spit.

Another week, then, and Aredd was a dull red and could trickle smoke rings through his nostrils, and he was the size of a bull. His wings, still crumpled and weak, lay untested along his sides, but his foreclaws, which had been as brittle as shells at birth, were now as hard as golden oak. He had sharpened them against the beach boulders, leaving scratches as deep as worm runnels. At night he dreamed of blood.

The tale of Aredd's end, as it is told in the farthest islands, is also the tale of a maiden who was once called Tansy after the herb of healing but was later known as Areddiana, daughter of the dragon. Of course it is a tale with a hero. That is why there are dragons, after all: to call forth heroes. But he was a hero in spite of himself and because of Tansy. The story goes thus:

There were three daughters of a healer who lived on the northern shore of Medd, the largest isle of the archipelago. Although they had proper names, after the older gods, they were always called by their herbal names.

Rosemary, the eldest, was a weaver. Her face was plain but honest-looking, a face that would wear well with time. Her skin was dark as if she spent her days out in the sun, though, in truth, she preferred the cottage's cold dirt floors and warm hearth. Her mouth was full but she kept it thin. She buffed the calluses on her hands to make them shine. She had her mother's grey eyes and her passion for work, and it annoyed her that others had not.

Sage was the beauty, but slightly simple. She was as golden as Rosemary was brown, and brushed her light-filled hair a full hundred strokes daily. When told to she worked, but otherwise preferred to stare out the window at the sea. She was waiting, she said, for her own true love. She had even put it in rhyme.

Glorious, glorious, over the sea,
My own true love will come for me.

She repeated it so often they all believed it to be true.

Tansy was no special colour at all; rather she seemed to blend in with her surroundings, sparkling by a stream, golden in the sunny meadows, mouse-brown within the house. She was the one who was a trouble to her mother: early walking and always picking apart things that had been knit up with great care just to see what made them work. So she was named after the herb that helped women in their times of trouble. Tansy. It was hoped that she would grow into her name.

*

"Where *is* that girl?" May-Ma cried.

Her husband, crushing leaves for a poultice, knew without asking which girl she meant. Only with Tansy did May-Ma's voice take on an accusatory tone.

"I haven't seen her for several hours, May-Ma," said Rosemary from the loom corner. She did not even look up but concentrated on the marketcloth she was weaving.

"That Tansy. She is late again for her chores. Probably dreaming somewhere. Or eating some new and strange concoction." May-Ma's hands moved on the bread dough as if preparing to beat a recalcitrant child. "Some day, mind you, some day she will eat herself past your help, Da."

The man smiled to himself. Never would he let such a thing happen to his Tansy. She had knowledge, precious, god-given, and nothing she made was past his talents for healing. Besides, she seemed to know instinctively how far to taste, how far to test, and she had a high tolerance for pain.

"Mind you," May Ma went on, pounding the dough into submission, "now, mind you, I'm not saying she doesn't have a Gift. But Gift or no, she has chores to do." Her endless repetitions had begun with the birth of her first child and had increased with each addition to the family until now, three live children later (she never mentioned the three little boys buried under rough stones at the edge of the garden), she repeated herself endlessly. "Mind you, a Gift is no excuse."

"I'm minding, May-Ma," said her husband, wiping his hands on his apron. He kissed her tenderly on the head as if to staunch the flow of words, but still they bled out.

"If she would remember her chores as well as she remembers dreams," May-Ma went on, "as well as she remembers the seven herbs of binding, the three parts to setting a broken limb, the . . ."

"I'm going, May-Ma," whispered her husband into the flood, and left.

He went outside and down a gentle path winding towards

the river, guessing that on such a day Tansy would be picking cress.

The last turn opened onto the river and never failed to surprise him with joy. The river was an old one, its bends broad as it flooded into the great sea. Here and there the water had cut through soft rock to make islets that could be reached by poleboat or, in the winter, by walking across the thick ice. This turning, green down to the river's edge, was full of cress and reeds and even wild rice carried from the Eastern lands by migrating birds.

"Tansy," he called softly, warning her of his coming.

A gull screamed back at him. He dropped his eyes to the hatchmarked tracks of shorebirds in the mud, waited a moment to give her time to answer, and then when none came, called again, "Tansy. Child."

"Da, Da, here!" It was the voice of a young woman, breathless yet throaty, that called back. "And see what I have found. I do not know what it is."

The reeds parted and she stepped onto the grass. Her skirts were kilted up, bunched at her waist. Even so they were damp and muddy. Her slim legs were coated with a green slime and there was a smear of that same muck along her nose and across her brow where she had obviously wiped away sweat or a troublesome insect. She held up a sheaf of red grassy weeds, the tops tipped with pink florets. Heedless of the blisters on her fingers, she gripped the stalk.

"What is it?" she asked. "It hurts something fierce, but I've never seen it before. I thought you might know."

"Drop it. Drop it at once, child. Where are your mitts?"

At his cry, she let the stalk go and it landed in the water, spinning around and around in a small eddy, a spiral of smoke uncurling from the blossoms.

He plucked her hand toward him and reached into his belt-bag. Taking out a cloth-wrapped packet of fresh aloe leaves, he broke one leaf in two and squeezed out the healing

14

oils onto her hands. Soon the redness around the blisters on her fingers were gone, though the blisters remained like a chain of tiny seed pearls.

"Now will you tell me what it is?" she asked, grinning up at him despite what he knew to be a terribly painful burn. There was a bit of mischief in her smile, too, which kept him from scolding her further about her gloves.

"I have never seen it before, only heard of it. I thought it but a tale. It is called fireweed or flamewort. You can guess why. The little blisters on the hand are in the old rhyme. It grows only where a great dragon lives, or so the spellbook says:

> Leaves of blood and sores of pearl,
> In the sea, a smoky swirl,
> Use it for your greatest need,
> Dragon's Bane and fireweed.

They used it somehow in the dragon wars. But child, look at your hands!"

She looked down for the first time and caught her breath as she saw the tiny, pearly sores. "One, two, three . . . why there must be fifteen blisters here," she said, fascinated. "Sores of pearl indeed. But what is its use?"

Her father shook his head and wrapped the aloe carefully. "I cannot imagine, since the sting of it is so fierce. And if the note about it be true, it will burn for near an hour once the florets open, burn with a hot steady flame that cannot be put out. Then it will crumble all at once into red ash. So you leave it there, steaming, on the water and come home with me. There is *no use* for dragon's bane, for there are no more dragons."

The fireweed had already lost its colour in the river, greying out, but still it sent up a curl of blue-white steam. Tansy found a stick and pushed it towards the stalk and where she touched, the weed flared up again a bright red. When she pulled back the stick, the colour of the weed faded as quickly as a blush.

The stick burned down towards Tansy's fingers and she dropped it into the river where it turned to ash and floated away.

"Dragon's bane," she whispered. "And I wonder why." She neglected to mention to her father that there was a large patch of the weed growing, hidden, in the reeds.

"Such questions will not win you favour at home," her father said, taking her unblistered hand in his. "Especially not with your dear May-Ma ready to do your chores. She will chide you a dozen times over for the same thing if we do not hurry home."

"My chores!" Tansy cried. Then she shrugged and looked at her father with wise eyes. "Even if I were home to do them, I would hear of it again and again. Poor May-Ma, she speaks to herself for none of the rest of us really talks to her." She pulled away from him and was gone up the path as if arrowshot.

He chuckled aloud and walked to the water's edge to pick some fresh peppermint and sweet woodruff for teas. The river's slow meandering was still noisy enough that he did not hear the strange chuffing sound of heavy new wings above him. It was only when the swollen shadow darkened the ground that he looked up and into the belly of a beast he had thought long extinct. He was so surprised, he did not have time to cry out or to bless himself before dying. The flames that killed him were neither long or especially hot, but fear and loathing added their toll. The healer was dead before his body touched earth. He never felt the stab of the golden claws as the dragon carried him back to its home on the far spit of land.

Only the singed open herb bag, its contents scattered on the path, bore testimony to the event.

They did not look for him until near dark. And then, in the dark, with only their small tapers for light, they missed the burned herb sack. It was morning before they found it and Sage had run off to their closest neighbours for help.

What help could be given? The healer was gone, snatched from the good earth he had so long tended. They could not explain the singed sack, and so did not try. They concentrated instead on his missing body. Perhaps he had fallen, one man suggested, into the river. Since he was not a fisherman, he could not swim. They expected his body to fetch up against an island shore within a few days. Such a thing had happened to men before. The fisherfolk knew where to look. And that was all the comfort the villagers had to lend. It was harvest, after all, and they could spare only the oldest women to weep and prepare funeral pies.

"And what kind of funeral is it?" May-Ma asked repeatedly. "Without a body, what kind of burial? He will be back. Back to laugh at our preparations. I know it. I know it here." She touched her breast and looked out to the garden's edge and the large, newly-cut stone overshadowing the three smaller ones. "He will be back."

But she was the only one to hold out such hope and to no one's surprise but May-Ma's, the healer did not return. The priest marked his passing with the appropriate signs and psalms, then returned to help with the harvest. The girls wept quietly: Rosemary by her loom, dampening the cloth; Sage by the window, gazing off down the path; Tansy alone in the woods. May-Ma sobbed her hopes noisily and the villagers, as befitting their long friendship with the healer, spoke of his Gift with reverence. It did not bring him back.

The healer's disappearance became a small mystery in a land used to small mysteries until after the harvest was in. And then Tam-the-Carpenter's finest draft horse was stolen. A week and a half later, two prize ewes were taken from Mother Comfy's fold. And almost two weeks after that, the latest of the cooper's twelve children disappeared from its cradle in the meadow when the others had left it for just a moment to go and pick wild trillium in the dell. A great fear descended upon the village then. They spoke of ravening beasts, of blood-crazed goblins, of a mad changeling beast-man roaming the woods, and looked at one another with suspicion. The priest ranted of retribution and world's end. But none of them considered dragons, for, as they knew full well, the last of the great worms had been killed in the dragon wars. And while none had actually seen a goblin or a beast-man, and while there had not been wild animals larger than a goldskin fox in the woods for twice two hundred years, still such creatures seemed likelier than dragons. Dragons, they knew with absolute and necessary conviction, were no more.

It was a fisherman who saw Aredd and lived to tell of it. In a passion one early morning he had gone over the side of his boat to untangle a line. It was a fine line, spun out over the long winter by his wife, and he was not about to lose it, for the mark of its spinning was still on his wife's forefinger and thumb. The line was down a great ways underwater and he had scarcely breath enough to work it free of a black root. But after three dives he had worked it loose and was surfacing again when he saw the bright water above him suddenly darken. He knew water too well to explain it, but held his breath longer and slowed his ascent until the darkness had passed by. Lucky it was, for when he broke through the foam, the giant body was gone past, its claws empty. All the fisherman saw clearly through water-filmed eyes was the great rudder of its red tail. He trod water by his boat, too frightened to pull himself in, and a minute later the dragon went over him again, its claws full of the innkeeper's prize bull, the one that had sired the finest calves in the countryside but was so fierce it had to be staked down day and night. The bull was still twitching and the blood fell from its back thicker than rain.

The fisherman slipped his hand from the boat and went under the water, both to cleanse himself of the blood and the fear. When he surfaced again, the dragon was gone. But the fisherman stayed in the water until the cold at last drove him out, his hands as wrinkled as his grandpap's from the long soaking.

He swam to the shore, forgetting both boat and line, and ran all the way back to the village leaving a wet trail. No one believed him until they saw the meadow from which the bull – chain and all – had been ripped. Then even the priest was convinced.

The healer's wife and her three daughters wept anew when they were told. And Tansy, remembering the patch of dragon's bane, blamed herself for not having guessed.

May-Ma raised her fist to the sky and screamed out the old curse on dragons, remembered from years of mummery played out at planting:

> *Fire and water on thy wing,*
> *The curse of god in beak and flight.*

The priest tried to take the sting of her loss away. The cooper's wife was inconsolable as well, surrounded by her eleven younglings. The village men sharpened their iron pitchforks and the old poisoned arrows that hung on the church's small apse walls were heated until the venom dripped. Tansy had to treat three boys for the flux who had put their fingers on the arrows and then on their lips. The beekeeper got down an old book that had traveled through his family over the years called *Ye Draconis: An Historie Unnaturalis*. The only useful information therein was: "An fully fledged draconis will suppe and digeste an bullock in fourteen days." They counted twelve days at best before the beast returned to feed again.

And then someone said, "We need a dragonslayer."

So the fisherman's son and the beekeeper's son and three other boys were sent off to see who they could find, though, as the priest thundered from the pulpit, "Beware of false heroes.

Without dragons there be no need of dragonslayers."

As the boys left the village, their neighbours gathered to bid them godspeed. The sexton rang Great Tom, the treble bell that had been cast in the hundredth year after the victory over dragons. On its side was the inscription: *I am Tom, when I toll there is fire, when I thunder there is victory.* The boys carried the sound with them down the long, winding roads.

They found heroes aplenty in the towns they visited. There were men whose bravery extended to the rim of a wine cup but, sober the morning after, turned back into ploughboys, farmers, and labourers who sneaked home without a by-your-leave. They found one old general who remembered ancient wounds and would have followed them if he had had legs, but the man who carted him to and from town was too frightened to push the barrow after them. And they found a farmer's strong daughter who could lift a grown ewe under each arm but whose father forbade her to go. "One girl and five boys together on the road?" he roared. "Would that be proper? After such a trip, no one would wed her." So though she was a head taller than her da, and forty pounds heavier, she wanted a wedding, so she stayed.

It was in a tosspot inn that the five village boys found the one they sought. They knew him for a hero the moment he stood. He moved like a god, the golden hair rippling down his back. Muscles formed like small mountains on his arms and he could make them walk from shoulder to elbow without the slightest effort. He was of a clan of gentle giants but early on had had a longing to see the world.

It did not occur to any one of the five why a hero should have sunk so low as to be cadging drinks by showing off his arms. It was enough for them that they had found him.

"Be you a hero?" breathed the fisherman's son, tracing the muscles with his eyes.

The blond man smiled, his teeth white and even. "Do I look like one?" he asked, answering question with question, making the muscles dance across his shoulders. "My name is Lancot."

The beekeeper's son looked dazzled. "That be a hero's name," he said with a sigh.

The boys shared their pennies and bought Lancot a mug of stew. He remembered things for them then: service to a foreign queen, a battle with a walking tree, three goblins spitted on his sword. (Their blood had so pitted the blade he left it on their common grave, which was why he had it not.) On and on through the night he spun out his tales and they doled out their coin in exchange. Each thought it a fair bargain.

In the morning they caught up with him several miles down the road, his pockets a-jangle with the coins they had paid for his tales – as well as the ones they thought they had gone to bed with. They begrudged him none of it. A hero is entitled.

"Come back with us, Lancot," begged the beekeeper's son, "and we can promise you a fine living."

"More coins than ten pockets could hold," added the fisherman's son, knowing it for a small boast.

They neglected to mention the dragon, having learned that one small lesson along the way.

And the hero Lancot judged them capable of five pockets at best. Still, five was better than none, and a fine village living was better than no living at all. There was bound to be at least one pretty girl there. He was weary of the road, for the world had turned out to be no better than his home – and no worse. So he shook his head, knowing that would make his golden hair ripple all down his back. And he tensed his muscles once more for good measure. They deserved *something* for their coin.

"He is almost like . . . a god," whispered one of the boys.

Lancot smiled to himself and threw his shoulders back. He looked straight ahead. He knew he was no god. He was not even, the gods help him, a hero. Despite his posture and his muscles, he was a fraud. Heroes and gods were never afraid and he was deadly afraid every day of his life. It was so absurd that he found himself laughing most of the time for, only by holding himself upright and smiling his hero smile, by making others party to his monstrous fraud, could he keep most of the fears at bay.

And so they arrived home, the fisherman's son, the beekeeper's son, and the three other boys alternately trailing the golden-haired hero and leading him.

They were greeted by a sobbing crowd.

The dragon, it seems, had carried off the church bell ten days before. The sexton, who had been in the act of ringing matins, had clung to the rope and had been carried away as well. Great Tom had dropped upside-down with a final dolorous knell into the bay, where it could still be seen. Little fish swam round its clappers. The sexton had not been found.

With all the sobbing and sighing, no one had noticed that the hero Lancot had turned the colour of scum on an ocean wave. No one, that is, except Tansy, who noticed everything, and her sister Sage, who thought that gray-white was a wonderful tone for a hero's skin. "Like ice," she whispered to herself, "like the surface of a lake in winter, though his eyes are the colour of a summer sky." And Rosemary, who thought he looked big enough and strong enough to train to the farm, much as a draft horse is measured for the plough.

As there was no inn and May-Ma had first claim on heroes, her husband having been the great worm's earliest meal, Lancot was put up at the healer's cottage. He eyed the three daughters with delight.

Their first dinner was a dismal affair. The healer's wife spoke of raw vengeance, Rosemary of working, Sage of romance, and Tansy of herbs. Lancot spoke not at all. In this place of dragons he knew he dared not tell his tales.

But finally Tansy took pity on his silence and asked him what, besides being a hero, he liked to do.

22

It being a direct question, Lancot had to answer. He thought a bit. Playing a hero had taken up all his adult time. At last he spoke, "When I was a boy . . ."

Sage sighed prettily, as if being a boy were the noblest occupation in the world.

"When I was a boy," Lancot said again, "I liked to fly kites."

"A useless waste of sticks and string," said Rosemary.

Sage sighed.

But as May-Ma cleared the table, Tansy nodded. "A link with earth and sky," she said. "As if you, too, were flying."

"If we were meant to fly," reminded Rosemary, "we would have been born with a beak . . ."

Sage laughed, a tinkling sound.

"And a longing for worms. Yes, I know," interrupted Tansy. "But little worms are useful creatures for turning the soil. It is only the great worms who are our enemies."

Rosemary's mouth thinned down.

Lancot said uneasily, "Kites . . ." then stopped. Dinner was over and the need for conversation was at an end.

In the morning the boys, backed up by their fathers, came to call. Morning being a hero's time, they came quite early. Lancot was still asleep.

"I will wake him," volunteered Sage. Her voice was so eager the fisherman's son bit his lip, for he had long loved her from afar.

Sage went into the back room and touched the sleeping hero on the shoulder. Lancot turned on the straw mattress but did not open his eyes.

"Never mind," said Rosemary urgently when Sage returned without him. "I shall do it."

She strode into the room and clapped her hands loudly right behind his left ear. Lancot sat up at once.

"Your followers are here," she snapped. "Tramping in mud

and knocking the furniture about." She began to fluff up the pillow before the print of Lancot's head even had time to fade.

Rectantly he rose, splashed drops of cold water on his cheeks, and went to face the boys.

"Do we go today?" asked the fisherman's son, quick to show his eagerness to Sage.

"Is it swords or spears?" asked the innkeeper's son.

"Or the poisoned arrows?"

"Or rocks?"

"Or . . ."

"Let me think," said Lancot, waving them into silence. "A dragon needs a plan."

"A plan," said all the boys and their fathers at once.

"Come back tomorrow and I will have a plan," said Lancot. "Or better yet, the day *after* tomorrow."

The boys nodded, but the beekeeper spoke timidly.

"The day after tomorrow will be too late. The great worm is due to return to feed. The sexton was . . ." he swallowed noisily, ". . . a puny man." Unconsciously his hand strayed to his own ample waist.

Lancot closed his eyes and nodded as if he were considering a plan, but what he was really thinking about was escape. When he opened his eyes again, the boys and their fathers were gone. But Rosemary was holding the broom in a significant manner, and so Lancot put his head down as if in thought and strode from the house without even worrying about breaking his fast.

He turned down the first wooded path he came to, which was the path that wound down towards the river. He scarcely had time for surprise when the wood opened into the broad, meandering waterway, dotted with little isles, that at the edge of sight opened into the sea. Between him and the river was a gentle marsh of reeds and rice. Clustered white florets sat like tiny clouds upon green stems. There was no boat.

"There you are," said Tansy, coming out of the woods behind him. "I have found some perfect sticks for a kite and borrowed paper from the priest. The paper has a recipe for mulberry wine on it, but he says he has much improved the ingredients and so could let me have it. And I have torn up Da's old smock for ribbons and plaited vines for a rope."

"A kite?" Lancot said wonderingly. He stared at the girl, at her river-blue eyes set in a face that seemed the colour of planed wood. Yesterday she had seemed no great beauty, yet here in the wood, where she reflected the colours of earth, water, sky, she was beautiful, indeed. "A kite?" he asked again, his thoughts on her.

"Heroes move in mysterious ways," Tansy said, smiling. "And since you mentioned kites, I thought perhaps kites were teasing into your mind as part of your plan."

"My plan," Lancot repeated vaguely, letting his eyes grow misty as if in great thought. He was having trouble keeping his mind on heroics.

Suddenly he felt a touch on his hand, focused his eyes, and saw that Tansy had placed her green-stained fingers on his. *Her hands are like a wood sprite's*, he thought suddenly.

"Being a hero," Tansy said, "does not mean you need to be without fear. Only fools lack fear and I believe you to be no fool."

He dared to look at her and whispered, "No hero either." And having admitted it, he sank down on his heels as if suddenly free of shackles that had long held him upright.

Tansy squatted next to him. "I am no hero either," she said. "To run away is by far the most sensible thing that either of us could do. But that will not stop this great worm from devouring my village and, ultimately, our world. The very least the two of us poor, frightened un-heroes can do is to construct a plan."

They sat for a long moment in silence, looking at one another. The woods stilled around them. Then Lancot smiled and, as if on a signal, the birds burst into full throat again.

Little lizards resumed their scurrying. And over the water, sailing in lazy circles, a family of cormorants began their descent.

"A kite," said Lancot. His eyes closed with sudden memory. "I met a mage once, with strange high cheekbones and straw-coloured hair. He spoke in a language that jangled the ear, and he told me that in his tongue the word for kite is *drache*, dragon."

Tansy nodded slowly. "Correspondences," she said. "It is the first rule of herbalry. Like calls to like. Like draws out like." She clapped her hands together. "I *knew* there was a reason that you spoke of kites."

"Do you mean that a kite could kill a dragon? *The* dragon?" Lancot asked. "Such a small, flimsy toy?"

Tansy laced her fingers together and put her chin down on top of her hands. "Not all by itself," she said. "But perhaps there is some way that we could manipulate the kite . . ."

"*I* could do that!" said Lancot.

"And use it to deliver a killing blow," Tansy finished.

"But there is no way a kite could carry a spear or bend a bow or wield a sword." Lancot paused. "You do not mean to fly *me* up on the kite to do that battle." He forgot to toss his hair or dance his muscles across his shoulders, so great was his fear.

Tansy laughed and put her hands on his knee. "Lancot, I have not forgotten that you are no hero. And I am no kite handler."

He furrowed his brow. "*You* will not go up the kite string. I forbid it."

"I am not yours to forbid," Tansy said quietly. "But I am no hero either. What I had in mind was something else."

He stood then and paced while Tansy told him of her plan. The river rilled over rocks to the sea, and terns scripted warnings in the sky. Lancot listened only to the sound of Tansy's voice, and watched her fingers spell out her thoughts.

When she finished he knelt by her side.

"I will make us a great kite," he said. "A *drache*. I will need paint besides, red as blood and black as hope."

"I thought hope a lighter colour," exclaimed Tansy.

"Not when one is dealing with dragons," he said.

The cooper supplied the paint. Two precious books of church receipts were torn apart for the paper because Lancot insisted that the kite be dragon-size. The extra nappies belonging to the missing babe, the petticoats of six maidens, and the fisherman's son's favourite shirt were torn up for binding. And then the building began.

Lancot sent the boys into the woods for spruce saplings after refusing to make his muscles dance. They left sullenly with his *caveat* in their ears: "As the dragon is mighty, yet can sail without falling through the air, so must the wood of our kite likewise be strong yet light."

Tansy, overhearing this, nodded and murmured, "Correspondences," under her breath.

And then the hero, on his knees, under the canopy of trees, showed them how to bend the wood, soaking it in water to make it flex, binding it with the rags. He ignored the girls who stood behind him to watch his shoulders ripple as he worked.

The fisherman's son soon got the hang of it, as did the cooper's eldest daughter. Rosemary was best, grumbling at the waste of good cloth, but also proud that her fingers could so nimbly wrap the wood.

They made rounded links, the first twice as large as a man, then descending in size to the middle whose circumference was that of Great Tom's bow. From there the links became smaller till the last was a match for the priest's dinner plate.

"We could play at rings," suggested Sage brightly. Only the fisherman's son laughed.

All the while Tansy sat, crosslegged, plaiting a rope. She

used the trailing vines that snaked down from the trees and added horse hair that she culled from the local herd. She borrowed hemp and line from the fisherman's wife, but she did the braiding herself, all the while whispering a charm against the unknitting of bones.

It took a full day, but at last the links were made and stacked and Lancot called the villagers to him. "Well done," he said, patting the smallest boy on the head. Then he sent the lot of them home.

Only Tansy remained behind. "That was indeed well done," she said.

"It was *easy* done," he said. "There is nothing to fear in the making of a kite. But once *it* is finished, I will be gone."

"A hero does what a hero can," answered Tansy. "We ask no more than that." But she did not stop smiling, and Lancot took up her smile as his own.

They walked along the path together towards the house, but strange to say, they were both quite careful not to let their hands meet or to let the least little bit of their clothing touch. They only listened to the nightjar calling and the erratic beating of their own timid hearts.

The next morning, before the sun had picked out a path through the interlacing of trees, the villagers had assembled the links into the likeness of a great worm. Lancot painted a dragon's face on the largest round and coloured in the rest like the long, sinewy body and tail.

The boys placed the poisoned arrowheads along the top arch of the links like the ridge of a dragon's neck.

The girls tied sharpened sticks beneath, like a hundred unsheathed claws.

Then the priest blessed the stick-and-paper beast, saying:

> *Fly with the hopes of men to guide you,*

Fly with the heart of a hero to goad you,
Fly with the spirit of God to guard you,
Blessings on you, beak and tail.

Tansy made a hole in the *drache*'s mouth, which she hemmed with a white ribbon from her own hope chest. Through that hole she strung a single long red rope. To one end of the rope she knotted a reed basket, to the other she looped a handle.

"What is the basket for?" asked May-Ma. "Why do we do this? Where will it get us? And will it bring dear Da back home?"

Rosemary and Sage comforted her, but only Tansy answered her. "It is the hero's plan," she said.

And with that May-Ma and all the villagers, whose own questions had rested in hers, had to be content.

Then with all the children holding the links, they marched down to the farthest shore. There, on the strand, where the breezes shifted back and forth between one island and the next, they stretched out the great kite, link after link, along the sand.

Lancot tested the strings, straightening and untwisting the line. Then he wound up the guy string on Rosemary's shuttle. Looking up into the sky, one hand over his eyes, he saw that for miles there were no clouds. Even the birds were down. It was an elegant slate on which to script their challenge to the great worm.

"Links up!" he cried. And at that signal, the boys each grabbed a large link, the girls the smaller ones, and held then over their heads.

"Run from me," Lancot cried.

And the children began to run, pulling the great guy rope taut between them as they went.

Meanwhile Lancot and the village men held fast to the unwinding end, tugging it up and over their own heads.

Then the wind caught the links, lifting them into the air, till the last, smallest part of the tail was up. And the beekeeper's littlest daughter, who was holding it, was so excited, she forgot to let go and was carried up and away.

"I will catch you," cried the fisherman's son to her, and she let go after a bit and fell into his arms. Sage watched admiringly, and touched him on the arm, and he was so red with hope he let the child tumble out of his hands.

The wind fretted and goaded the kite, and the links began to swim through the air, faster and higher, in a sinuous dance; up over their outstretched hands, over the tops of trees, until only the long red rope curling from the mouth lay circling both ends on the ground.

"Make it fast," commanded Lancot, and the men looped the great guy around the trunk of an old, thick willow, once, twice, and then a third time for luck. Then the fisherman knotted the end and the priest threw holy water on it.

"And now?" asked Rosemary.

"And now?" asked the priest.

"And now?" echoed the rest of the villagers.

"And now you must all run off home and hide," said Lancot, for it was what Tansy had rehearsed with him. "The dragon will be here within the day."

"But what is the basket for?" asked May-Ma. "And why do we do this? And where will it get us? And will it bring your dear Da back?" This last she asked to Tansy, who was guiding her down the path.

But there were no answers and so no comfort in it. All the villagers went home. Tansy alone returned to find Lancot pacing by the shore.

"I thought you would be gone," she said.

"I will be." His voice was gruff, but it broke between each word.

"Then the next work is mine," said Tansy.

"I will help." His eyes said there would be no argument.

He followed her along the shoreline till they came to the place where the river flowed out, the blue-white of the swift-running water meeting the lapis of the sea. Tansy turned upstream, wading along the water's edge. That left Lancot either the deeper water or the sand. He chose the water.

Tansy questioned him with a look.

He shrugged. "I would not have you fall in," he said.

"I can swim," she answered.

"I cannot."

She laughed and skipped onto the sand. Relieved, Lancot followed.

Suddenly Tansy stopped. She let slip the pocket of woven reeds she had tied at her waist. "Here," she said pointing.

Between the sturdy brown cattails and the spikes of wild rice was a strangely sown pattern of grassy weeds, bloody red in colour, the tops embroidered with florets of pearl and pink.

"*That* is dragon's bane?" Lancot asked. "That pretty bouquet? *That* is for our greatest need?" He snorted and bent and brushed a finger carelessly across one petal. The flower seared a bloody line across his skin. "Ow!" he cried and stuck a finger in his mouth.

"Best put some aloe on that," Tansy said, digging around in her apron pocket.

Lancot shook his head. Taking his finger from his mouth he said quickly, "No bother. It is just a little sting." Then he popped the finger back in.

Tansy laughed. "I have brought my mitts this time. Fireweed burns only flesh. I, too, have felt that sting." She held up her hand and he could see a string of little rounded, faded scars across her palm. "Dragons are made of flesh – under the links of mail."

Lancot reached out with his burned finger and touched each scar gently, but he did not say a word.

Taking her mitts from a deep apron pocket, Tansy drew them on. Then she grasped the fireweed stems with one hand, the flowers with the other, and snapped the blossoms from the green stalk. Little wisps of smoke rose from her mitts, but did

31

not ignite. She put each cluster into her bag.

Lancot merely watched, alert, as if ready to help.

At last the bag was pouched full of flowers.

"It is enough," Tansy said, stripping the mitts from her hands.

Back at the beach, Tansy lowered the flying basket carefully and stuffed it full of the bane. As she hauled on the rope, sending the basket back aloft, a steady stream of smoke poured through the wicker, a hazy signal written on the cloudless sky.

"Now we wait," said Tansy.

"Now we wait *under cover*," said Lancot. He led her to a nearby narrow gulch and pulled branches of willow across from bank to bank. Then he slipped under the branches, pulling Tansy after.

"Will we have to wait long?" Tansy mused, more to herself than to Lancot.

Before he could answer, they heard a strange loud chuffing, a foreign wind through trees, and smelled a carrion stink. And though neither of them had ever heard that sound before or smelled that smell, there was no mistaking it.

"Dragon," breathed Lancot.

"*Vermifax major*," said Tansy.

And then the sky above them darkened as the great mailed body, its stomach links scratched and bloodstained from lying on old bones, put out their sun.

Instinctively, they both cringed beneath the lacy willow leaves until the red rudder of tail sailed over. Tansy even forgot to breathe, so that when the worm was gone from sight and only the smell lingered, she drew a deep breath and nearly choked on the stench. Lancot clapped his hand so hard over her mouth he left four marks on the left side of her face and a red thumbprint on the right cheek bone. Her only protest was to place her hand gently on his wrist.

"Oh, Tansy, forgive me, I am sorry I hurt you." Lancot bit his lip. "My strength is greater than I supposed."

"I am not sorry," she answered back. "This . . ." she brushed her fingers across her face, "this is but a momentary pain. If that great beast had heard me and had hurt you, the pain would go on and on and on forever."

At that moment they heard a tremendous angry scream of defiance and a strange rattling sound.

"The dragon must have seen our kite," whispered Tansy. "And like all great single beasts, he kills what he cannot court."

Lancot shifted a willow branch aside with great care, and they both blinked in the sudden light of sky. High above them the red dragon was challenging the *drache*, voice and tail making statements that no self-respecting stranger would leave unanswered. But the kite remained mute.

The dragon screamed again and dived at the kite's smallest links, severing the last two. As the links slipped through the air, twisting and spiralling in the drafts made by the dragon's wings, the beast turned on the paper-and-stick pieces and swallowed them in a single gulp. Then, with a great surprised belch, the worm vomited up the pieces again. Crumpled, broken, mangled beyond repair, they fell straight down into the sea.

The dragon roared again, this time snapping at the head of the kite. The roar was a mighty wind that whipped the kite upward, and so the dragon's jaws closed only on the rope that held the basket of fireweed, shredding the strand. The basket and half the rope fell lazily through the air and, with a tiny splash, sank beneath the waves. At once, a high frantic hissing bubbled up through the water, and the sea boiled with the bane.

"It's gone," Tansy whispered. "The bane. It's gone." Without giving a thought for her own safety, she clambered out of the gulch and, bent over, scuttled to the trees, intent on fetching more of the precious weed. The dragon, concentrating on its skyborne foe, never saw her go.

But Lancot did, his hand reaching out too late to clutch the

33

edge of her skirt as it disappeared over the embankment. "Tansy, no!"

She made no sign she had heard, but entered the trees and followed the stream quickly to the muddle of water and reeds that held the rest of the bane. Wading in, she began to snatch great handfuls of the stuff, heedless of the burns, until she had gathered all there was to find. Then she struggled ashore and raced back. Her wet skirts tangled in her legs as she ran.

Lancot, caught in a panic of indecision, had finally emerged from their hiding place and stared alternately at the sky and the path along the sea. When Tansy came running back, hands seared and smoking but holding the fireweed, he ran to her.

"I have gathered all there is," she said, only at the last letting her voice crack with the pain.

Lancot reached for the weed.

"No," Tansy whispered hoarsely, "take the mitts from my pocket." She added miserably, "I was in such a hurry, I forgot to put them on. And then I was in too much pain to do other."

Lancot grabbed the mitts from her pocket and forced them onto his large hands. Then he took the weed from her. She hid her burned hands behind her back.

"How will I get these up to the dragon?" asked Lancot suddenly, for the question had not occurred to either of them before.

They turned as one and stared at the sky.

It was the dragon itself that gave them the answer then, for, as they watched, it grabbed a great mouthful of the kite and raged at it, pulling hard against the line that tethered the *drache* to the tree. The willow shook violently with each pull.

Lancot smiled down at Tansy. "You are no hero," he said. "Your hands are too burned for that. And I am no hero, either. But . . ." His voice trembled only slightly, "as a boy I fetched many kites out of trees." And before Tansy could stop him, he kissed her forehead, careful of the bane he carried, and whispered into her hair, "And put some *hallow* on those palms."

34

"Aloe," she said, but he did not hear her.

Lancot transferred the bane to one mitt, slipped the mitt off his other hand, and began to shinny one-handed up the guy rope that was anchored to the underside of the kite. If the dragon, still wrestling with the *drache*, felt the extra weight, it made not the slightest sign.

Twice the dragon pulled so furiously that Lancot slipped off. And then, when he was halfway up the rope, there was a huge sucking sound. Slowly the willow was pulled up, roots and all, out of the earth. And the dragon, along with the kite, the string, Lancot, and the tree, flew east towards the farthest isles.

Tansy, screaming and screaming, watched them go.

As they whipped through the air, Lancot continued his slow crawl up the rope. Once or twice the fireweed brushed his cheek and he gritted his teeth against the pain. And once a tiny floret touched his hair, and the single strand sizzled down to his scalp. The smell of that was awful. But he did not drop the weeds nor did he relinquish his hold on the guy. Up and up he inched as the dragon, its limp paper prey in its claws, pulled them towards its home.

They were closing in on the farthest island, a sandy lozenge-shape resting in the blue sea, when Lancot's bare hand touched the bottom of the kite and the cold golden nail of the dragon's claw. He could feel his heart hammering hard against his chest and the skin rippled faster along his shoulders and neck than ever he could have made the muscles dance. He could feel the wind whistling past his bared teeth, could feel the tears teasing from his eyes. He remembered Tansy's voice saying, "I can swim," and his own honest reply. Smiling ruefully, he thought, *I shall worry about that anon.* Then he slipped his arms around the dragon's leg, curved his legs up and around, until he could kneel. He dared not look down again.

He stood and at last the dragon seemed to take notice of

him. It clenched and unclenched its claw. The kite and tree fell away, tumbling – it seemed – forever till they plunged into the sea, sending up a splash that could be seen from all the islands.

Lancot looked up just in time to see the great head of the beast bend curiously around to examine its own feet. It was an awkward move in the air, and for a moment worm and man plummeted downward.

Then the dragon opened its great furnace jaws, the spikes of teeth as large as tree trunks, as sharp as swords.

Lancot remembered his boyhood and the games of sticks and balls. He snatched up the fireweed with his ungloved hand and, ignoring the sting of it, flung the lot into the dragon's maw.

Surprised, the dragon swallowed, then straightened up and began to roar.

Lancot was no fool. He put the mitt over his eyes, held his nose with his burned hand, and jumped.

On shore, Tansy had long since stopped screaming to watch the precarious climb. Each time Lancot slipped she felt her heart stutter. She prayed he might drop off before the dragon noticed, until she remembered he could not swim.

When he reached the dragon's foot, Tansy was wading into the water, screaming once again. Her aloe-smeared hands had left marks on her skirts, on her face.

And when the tree and kite fell, she felt her hopes rise until she saw that Lancot was not with them. She prayed then, the only prayer she could conjure up, the one her mother had spoken:

> Fire and water on thy wing,
> The curse of god in beak and flight.

It seemed to her much too small a prayer to challenge so great and horrible a beast.

And then the dragon turned on itself, curling round to look at Lancot, and they began to tumble towards the sea.

At that point Tansy no longer knew what prayers might work. "Fly," she screamed. "Drop," she screamed.

No sooner had she called out the last than the dragon straightened out and roared so loudly she had to put her hands over her ears, heedless of the aloe smears in her hair. Then as she watched, the great dragon began to burn. Its body seemed touched by a red aureole and flames flickered the length of its body, from mouth to tail. Quite suddenly, it seeemd to go out, guttering like a candle, from the back forward. Black scabs fell from its tail, its legs, its back, its head. It turned slowly around in the air, as if each movement brought pain, and Tansy could see its great head. Only its eyes held life till the very end when, with a blink, the life was gone. The dragon drifted, floated down onto a sandbar, and lay like a mountain of ash. It was not a fierce ending but rather a gigantic sigh, and Tansy could not believe how unbearably sad it made her feel, as if she and the dragon and Lancot, too, had been cheated of some reward for their courage. She thought, quite suddenly, of a child's balloon at a fair pricked by a needle, and she wept.

A hand on her shoulder recalled her to the place. It was the fisherman's son.

"Gone then?" he asked. He meant the dragon.

But knowing Lancot was gone as well, Tansy began sobbing anew. Neither her mother nor her sisters nor the priest nor all the celebrations that night in the town could salve her. She walked down to the water's edge at dusk by herself and looked out over the sea to the spit of land where the ash mound that had been the dragon was black against the darkening sky.

The gulls were still. From behind her a solitary owl called its place from tree to tree. A small breeze teased into the willows, setting them to rustling. Tansy heard a noise near her and shrugged further into herself. She would let no one pull her out of her misery, not her mother nor her sisters nor all the children of the town.

"I could use a bit of *hallow* on my throwing hand," came a voice.

"Aloe," she said automatically before she turned.

"It's awfully hard to kill a hero," said Lancot with a smile.

"But you can't swim."

"It's low tide," he said. "And I *can* wade."

Tansy laughed.

"It's awfully hard to kill a hero," so said Lancot. "But we ordinary fellows, we do get hurt. So I could use a bit of *hallow* on my hand."

She didn't mind the smear of aloe on her hair and cheek. But that came later on, much later that night. And it seemed to the two of them that what they did then was very heroic indeed.

There is a spit of land near the farthest shores of the farthest islands. It is known as Dragonfield. Once dragons dwelt on the isles in great herds, feeding on the dry bush and fuelling their flames with the carcasses of small animals and migratory birds. There are no dragons there now, though the nearer islands are scored with long furrows as though giant claws had been at work, and the land is fertile from the bones of the buried behemoths. There is a large mount of ash-coloured rock that appears and disappears in the ebb and flow of the tide. No birds land on that rock, and seals avoid it as well. The islanders call it Worm's Head, and once a year they row out to it and sail a great kite from its highest point, a kite which they then set afire and let go into the prevailing winds. Some of the younger mothers complain that one day that kite will burn down a house and they have agitated to end the ceremony. But as long as the story of Tansy and the hero is told, the great kites will fly over the rock, of that I am sure.

Draco, Draco

Draco, Draco

Tanith Lee

You'll have heard stories, sometimes, of men who have fought and slain dragons. These are all lies. There's no swordsman living ever killed a dragon, though a few swordsmen dead that tried.

On the other hand, I once travelled in company with a fellow who got the name of 'dragon-slayer'.

A riddle? No. I'll tell you.

I was coming from the North back into the South, to civilisation as you may say, when I saw him sitting by the roadside. My first feeling was envy, I admit. He was smart and very clean for someone in the wilds, and he had the South all over him, towns and baths and money. He was crazy, too, because there was gold on his wrists and in one ear. But he had a sharp grey sword, an army sword, so maybe he could defend himself. He was also younger than me, and a great deal prettier, but the last isn't too difficult. I wondered what he'd do when he looked up from his daydream and saw me, tough, dark and sour as a twist of old rope, clopping down on him on my swarthy little horse, ugly as sin, that I love like a daughter.

Then he did look up and I discovered.

"Greetings, stranger. Nice day, isn't it?"

He stayed relaxed as he said it, and somehow you knew from that he really could look after himself. It wasn't he thought I was harmless, just that he thought he could handle me if I tried something. Then again, I had my box of stuff alongside. Most people can tell my trade from that, and the aroma of drugs and herbs. My father was with the Romans, in fact he was probably the last Roman of all, one foot on the ship to go home, the rest of him with my mother up against the barnyard wall. She said he was a camp physician and maybe that was so. Some idea of doctoring grew up with me, though nothing great or grand. An itinerant apothecary is welcome almost anywhere, and can even turn bandits civil. It's not a wonderful life, but it's the only one I know.

I gave the young soldier-dandy that it was a nice day. I added he'd possibly like it better if he hadn't lost his horse.

"Yes, a pity about that. You could always sell me yours."

"Not your style."

He looked at her. I could see he agreed. There was also a momentary idea that he might kill me and take her, so I said, "And she's well known as mine. It would get you a bad name. I've friends round about."

He grinned, good-naturedly. His teeth were good, too. What with that, and the hair like barley, and the rest of it – well, he was the kind who usually gets what he wants. I was curious as to which army he had hung about with to gain the sword. But since the Eagles flew, there are kingdoms everywhere, chiefs, war-leaders, Roman knights, and every tide brings an invasion up some beach. Under it all, too, you can feel the earth, the actual ground, which had been measured, and ruled with fine roads, the land which had been subdued but never tamed, beginning to quicken. Like the shadows that come with the blowing out of a lamp. Ancient things, which are in my blood somewhere, so I recognise them.

But he was like a new coin that hadn't got dirty yet, nor learned much, though you could see your face in its shine, and cut yourself on its edge.

His name was Caiy. Presently we came to an arrangement and he mounted up behind me on Negra. They spoke a smatter of Latin where I was born, and I called her that before I knew her, for her darkness. I couldn't call her for her hideousness, which is her only other visible attribute.

The fact is, I wasn't primed to the country round that way at all. I'd had word, a day or two prior, that there were Saxons in the area I'd been heading for. And so I switched paths and was soon lost. When I came on Caiy, I'd been pleased with the road, which was Roman, hoping it would go somewhere useful. But, about ten miles after Caiy joined me, the road petered out in a forest. My passenger was lost, too. He was going South, no surprise there, but last night his horse had broken loose and bolted, leaving him stranded. It sounded unlikely, but I wasn't inclined to debate on it. It seemed to me someone might have stolen the horse, and Caiy didn't care to confess.

There was no way round the forest, so we went in and the road died. Being summer, the wolves would be scarce and the bears off in the hills. Nevertheless, the trees had a feel I didn't take to, sombre and still, with the sound of little streams running through like metal chains, and birds that didn't sing but made purrings and clinkings. Negra never baulked nor complained – if I'd waited to call her, I could have done it for her courage and warm-heartedness – but she couldn't come to terms with the forest, either.

"It smells," said Caiy, who'd been kind enough not to comment on mine, "as if it's rotting. Or fermenting."

I grunted. Of course it did, it was, the fool. But the smell told you other things. The centuries, for one. Here were the shadows that had come back when Rome blew out her lamp and sailed away, and left us in the dark.

Then Caiy, the idiot, began to sing to show up the birds who wouldn't. A nice voice, clear and bright. I didn't tell him to leave off. The shadows already knew we were there.

When night came down, the black forest closed like a cellar door.

We made a fire and shared my supper. He'd lost his rations with his mare.

42

"Shouldn't you tether that – your horse," suggested Caiy, trying not to insult her since he could see we were partial to each other. "My mare was tied, but something scared her and she broke the tether and ran. I wonder what it was," he mused, staring in the fire.

About three hours later, we found out.

I was asleep, and dreaming of one of my wives up in the far North, and she was nagging at me, trying to start a brawl, which she always did for she was taller than me, and liked me to hit her once in a while so she could feel fragile, feminine and mastered. Just as she emptied the beer jar over my head, I heard a sound up in the sky like a storm that was not a storm. And I knew I wasn't dreaming any more.

The sound went over, three or four great claps, and the tops of the forest reeling, and left shuddering. There was a sort of quiver in the air, as if sediment were stirred up in it. There was even an extra smell, dank, yet tingling. When the noise was only a memory, and the bristling hairs began to subside along my body, I opened my eyes.

Negra was flattened to the ground, her own eyes rolling, but she was silent. Caiy was on his feet, gawping up at the tree tops and the strands of starless sky. Then he glared at me.

"What in the name of the Bull was that?"

I noted vaguely that the oath showed he had Mithraic allegiances, which generally meant Roman. Then I sat up, rubbed my arms and neck to get human, and went to console Negra. Unlike his silly cavalry mare she hadn't bolted.

"It can't," he said, "have been a bird. Though I'd have sworn something flew over."

"No, it wasn't a bird."

"But it had wings. Or – no, it couldn't have had wings the size of that."

"Yes it could. They don't carry it far, is all."

"Apothecary, stop being so damned provoking. If you know, out with it! Though I don't see how you can know. And don't

43

tell me it's some bloody woods demon I won't believe in."

"Nothing like that," I said. "It's real enough. Natural, in its own way. Not," I amended, "that I ever came across one before, but I've met some who did."

Caiy was going mad, like a child working up to a tantrum. *"Well?"*

I suppose he had charmed and irritated me enough I wanted to retaliate, because I just quoted some bastard nonsensical jabber-Latin chant at him:

> *Bis terribilis –*
> *Bis appellare –*
> *Draco! Draco!*

At least, it made him sit down.

"What?" he eventually said.

At my age I should be over such smugness. I said, "It was a dragon."

Caiy laughed. But he had glimpsed it, and knew better than I did that I was right.

Nothing else happened that night. In the morning we started off again and there was a rough track, and then the forest began to thin out. After a while we emerged on the crown of a moor. The land dropped down to a valley, and on the other side there were sunny smoky hills and a long streamered sky. There was something else, too.

Naturally, Caiy said it first, as if everything new always surprised him, as if we hadn't each of us, in some way, been waiting for it, or something like it.

"This place stinks."

"Hn."

"Don't just grunt at me, you blasted quack doctor. It does, doesn't it? Why?"

"Why do you think?"

He brooded, pale gold and citified, behind me. Negra tried to paw the ground, and then made herself desist.

44

Neither of us brave humans had said any more about what had interrupted sleep in the forest, but when I'd told him no dragon could fly far on its wings, for from all I'd ever heard they were too large and only some freakish lightness in their bones enabled them to get airborne at all, I suppose we had both taken it to heart. Now here were the valley and the hills, and here was this reek lying over everything, strange, foul, alien, comparable to nothing, really. Dragon smell.

I considered. No doubt, the dragon went on an aerial patrol most nights, circling as wide as it could, to see what might be there for it. There were other things I'd learnt. These beasts hunt nocturnally, like cats. At the same time, a dragon is more like a crow in its habits. It will attack and kill, but normally it eats carrion, dead things, or dying and immobilised. It's light, as I said, it has to be to take the skies, but the lack of weight is compensated by the armour, the teeth and talons. Then again, I'd heard of dragons that breathed fire. I've never been quite convinced there. It seems more likely to me such monsters only live in volcanic caves, the mountain itself belching flame and the dragon taking credit for it. Maybe not. But certainly, this dragon was no fire-breather. The ground would have been scorched for miles; I've listened to stories where that happened. There were no marks of fire. Just the insidious pervasive stench that I knew, by the time we'd gone down into the valley, would be so familiar, so soaked into us, we would hardly notice it any more, or the scent of anything else.

I awarded all this information to my passenger. There followed a long verbal delay. I thought he might just be flabbergasted at getting so much chat from me, but then he said, very hushed, "You truly believe all this, don't you?"

I didn't bother with the obvious, just clucked to Negra, trying to make her turn back the way we'd come. But she was unsure and for once unco-operative, and suddenly his strong hand, the nails groomed even now, came down on my arm.

"Wait, Apothecary. If it *is* true – "

"Yes, yes," I said. I sighed. "You want to go and challenge it, and become a hero." He held himself like marble, as if I were speaking of some girl he thought he loved. I didn't see why I should waste experience and wisdom on him, but then. "No man ever killed a dragon. They're plated, all over, even the underbelly. Arrows and spears just bounce off – even a pilum. Swords clang and snap in half. Yes, yes," I reiterated, "you've heard of men who slashed the tongue, or stabbed into an eye. Let me tell you, if they managed to reach that high and actually did it, then they just made the brute angry. Think of the size and shape of a dragon's head, the way the pictures show it. It's one hell of a push from the eye into the brain. And you know, there's one theory the eyelid is armoured, too, and can come down faster than *that*."

"Apothecary," he said. He sounded dangerous. I just knew what he must look like. Handsome, noble and insane.

"Then I won't keep you," I said. "Get down and go on and the best of luck."

I don't know why I bothered. I should have tipped him off and ridden for it, though I wasn't sure Negra could manage to react sufficiently fast, she was that edgy. Anyway, I didn't, and sure enough next moment his sword was at the side of my throat, and so sharp it had drawn blood.

"You're the clever one," he said, "the know-all. And you do seem to know more than I do, about this. So you're my guide, and your scruff-bag of a horse, if it even deserves the name, is my transport. Giddy-up, the pair of you."

That was that. I never argue with a drawn sword. The dragon would be lying up by day, digesting and dozing, and by night I could hole up someplace myself. Tomorrow Caiy would be dead and I could leave. And I would, of course, have seen a dragon for myself.

After an hour and a half's steady riding – better once I'd persuaded him to switch from the sword to poking a dagger against my ribs, less tiring for us both – we came around a stand of woods, and there was a village. It was the savage Northern kind, thatch and wattle and turf banks, but big for all that, a good mile of it, not all walled. There were walls this end, however, and men on the gate, peering at us.

Caiy was aggrieved because he was going to have to ride up to them pillion, but he knew better now than to try managing Negra alone. He maybe didn't want to pretend she was his horse in any case.

As we pottered up the pebbled track to the gate, he sprang off and strode forward, arriving before me, and began to speak.

When I got closer I heard him announcing, in his dramatic, beautiful voice.

" – And if it's a fact, I swear by the Victory of the Light that I will meet the thing and kill it."

They were muttering. The dragon smell, even though we were used to it, sodden with it, seemed more acid here. Poor Negra had been voiding herself from sheer terror all up the path. With fortune on our side, there would be somewhere below ground, some cave or dug out place, where they'd be putting their animals out of the dragon's way, and she could shelter with the others.

Obviously, the dragon hadn't always been active in this region. They'd scarcely have built their village if it had. No, it would have been like the tales. Dragons live for centuries. They can sleep for centuries, too. Unsuspecting, man moves in, begins to till and build and wax prosperous. Then the dormant dragon wakes under the hill. They're like the volcanoes I spoke of, in that. Which is perhaps, more than habitat, why so many of the legends say they breathe fire when they wake.

The interesting thing was, even clouded by the dragon stink, initially, the village didn't seem keen to admit to anything.

Caiy, having made up his mind to accept the dragon – and afraid of being wrong – started to rant. The men at the gate were frightened and turning nasty. Leading Negra now, I approached, tapped my chest of potions and said:

47

"Or, if you don't want your dragon slain, I can cure some of your other troubles. I've got medicines for almost everything. Boils, warts. Ear pains. Tooth pains. Sick eyes. Women's afflictions. I have here – "

"Shut up, you toad-turd," said Caiy.

One of the guards suddenly laughed. The tension sagged.

Ten minutes after, we had been let in the gate and were trudging through the cow-dung and wild flowers – neither of which were to be smelled through the other smell – to the headman's hall.

It was around two hours after that when we found out why the appearance of a rescuing champion-knight had given them the jitters.

It seemed they had gone back to the ancient way, propitiation, the scapegoat. For three years, they had been making an offering to the dragon, in spring, and at midsummer, when it was likely to be most frisky.

Anyone who knew dragons from a book would tell them this wasn't the way. But they knew their dragon from myth. Every time they made sacrifice, they imagined the thing could understand and appreciate what they'd done for it, and would therefore be more amenable.

In reality, of course, the dragon had never attacked the village. It had thieved cattle off the pasture by night, elderly or sick cows at that, and lambs that were too little and weak to run. It would have taken people, too, but only those who were disabled and alone. I said, a dragon is lazy and prefers carrion, or what's defenceless. Despite being big, they aren't so big they'd go after a whole tribe of men. And though even forty men together undoubtedly couldn't wound a dragon, they could exhaust it, if they kept up a rough-house. Eventually it would keel over and they could brain it. You seldom hear of forty men going off in a band to take a dragon, however. Dragons are still ravelled up with night fears and spiritual mysteries, and latterly with an Eastern superstition of a mighty

48

demon who can assume the form of a dragon which is invincible and – naturally – breathes sheer flame. So, this village, like many another, would put out its sacrifice, one girl tied to a post, and leave her there, and the dragon would have her. Why not? She was helpless, fainting with horror – and young and tender into the bargain. Perfect. You never could convince them that, instead of appeasing the monster, the sacrifice encourages it to stay. Look at it from the dragon's point of view. Not only are there dead sheep and stray cripples to devour, but once in a while a nice juicy damsel on a stick. Dragons don't think like a man, but they do have memories.

When Caiy realised what they were about to do, tonight, as it turned out, he went red then white, exactly as they do in a bardic lay. Not anger, mind you. He didn't comprehend any more than they did. It was merely the awfulness of it.

He stood up and chose a stance, quite unconsciously impressive, and assured us he'd save her. He swore to it in front of us all, the chieftain, his men, me. And he swore it by the Sun, so I knew he meant business.

They were scared, but now also childishly hopeful. It was part of their mythology again. All mythology seems to take this tack somewhere, the dark against the light, the Final Battle. It's rot, but there.

Following a bit of drinking to seal the oath, they cheered up and the chief ordered a feast. Then they took Caiy to see the chosen sacrifice.

Her name was Niemeh, or something along those lines.

She was sitting in a little lamplit cell off the hall. She wasn't fettered, but a warrior stood guard beyond the screen, and there was no window. She had nothing to do except weave flowers together, and she was doing that, making garlands for her death procession in the evening.

When Caiy saw her, his colour drained away again.

He stood and stared at her, while somebody explained he was her champion.

Though he got on my nerves, I didn't blame him so much this time. She was about the most beautiful thing I ever hope to see. Young, obviously, and slim, but with a woman's shape, if you have my meaning, and long hair more fair even than Caiy's, and green eyes like sea pools and a face like one of the white flowers in her hands, and a sweet mouth.

I looked at her as she listened gravely to all they said. I remembered how in the legends it's always the loveliest and the most gentle gets picked for the dragon's dinner. You perceive the sense in the gentle part. A girl with a temper might start a ruckus.

When Caiy had been introduced and once more sworn by the Sun to slay the dragon and so on, she thanked him. If things had been different, she would have blushed and trembled, excited by Caiy's attention. But she was past all that. You could see, if you looked, she didn't believe anyone could save her. But though she must have been half dead already of despair and fright, she still made space to be courteous.

Then she glanced over Caiy's head straight at me, and she smiled so I wouldn't feel left out.

"And who is this man?" she asked.

They all looked startled, having forgotten me. Then someone who had warts recalled I'd said I could fix him something for warts, and told her I was the apothecary.

A funny little shiver went through her then.

She was so young and so pretty. If I'd been Caiy I'd have stopped spouting rubbish about the dragon. I'd have found some way to lay out the whole village, and grabbed her, and gone. But that would have been a stupid thing to do, too. I've enough of the old blood to know about such matters. She was the sacrifice and she was resigned to it; more, she didn't dream she could be anything else. I've come across rumours, here and there, of girls, men too, chosen to die, who escaped. But the fate stays on them. Hide them securely miles off, across water, beyond tall hills, still they feel the geas weigh like lead upon their souls. They kill themselves in the end, or go mad. And this girl, this Niemeh, you could see it in her. No, I would never have abducted her. It would have been no use. She was convinced she must die, as if she'd seen it written in light on a stone, and maybe she had.

She returned to her garlands, and Caiy, tense as a bowstring, led us back to the hall.

Meat was roasting and more drink came out and more talk came out. You can kill anything as often as you like, that way.

It wasn't a bad feast, as such up-country things go. But all through the shouts and toasts and guzzlings, I kept thinking of her in her cell behind the screen, hearing the clamour and aware of this evening's sunset, and how it would be to die . . . as she would have to. I didn't begin to grasp how she could bear it.

By late afternoon they were mostly sleeping it off, only Caiy had had the sense to go and sweat the drink out with soldiers' exercises in the yard, before a group of sozzled admirers of all sexes.

When someone touched my shoulder, I thought it was Warty after his cure, but no. It was the guard from the girl's cell, who said very low, "She says she wants to speak to you. Will you come, now?"

I got up and went with him. I had a spinning minute, wondering if perhaps she didn't believe she must die after all, and would appeal to me to save her. But in my heart of hearts I guessed it wasn't that.

There was another man blocking the entrance, but they let me go in alone, and there Niemeh sat, making garlands yet, under her lamp.

But she looked up at me, and her hands fell like two more white flowers on the flowers in her lap. "I need some medicine, you see," she said. "But I can't pay you. I don't have anything. Although my uncle – "

"No charge," I said hurriedly.

She smiled. "It's for tonight."

"Oh," I said.

"I'm not brave," she said, "but it's worse than just being afraid. I know I shall die. That it's needful. But part of me wants to live so much – my reason tells me one thing but my body won't listen. I'm frightened I shall panic, struggle and scream and weep – I don't want that. It isn't right. I have to consent, or the sacrifice isn't any use. Do you know about that?"

"Oh, yes," I said.

"I thought so. I thought you did. Then . . . can you give me something, a medicine or herb – so I shan't feel anything? I don't mean the pain. That doesn't matter. The gods can't blame me if I cry out then, they wouldn't expect me to be beyond pain. But only to make me not care, not want to live so very much."

"An easy death."

"Yes." She smiled again. She seemed serene and beautiful. "Oh, yes."

I looked at the floor.

"The soldier. Maybe he'll kill it," I said.

She didn't say anything.

When I glanced up, her face wasn't serene any more. It was brimful of terror. Caiy would have been properly insulted.

"Is it you can't give me anything? Don't you have anything? I was sure you did. That you were sent here to me to – to help, so I shouldn't have to go through it all alone – "

"There," I said, "it's all right. I do have something. Just the thing. I keep it for women in labour when the child's slow and hurting them. It works a treat. They go sort of misty and far

52

off, as if they were nearly asleep. It'll dull pain, too. Even –
any kind of pain."

"Yes," she whispered, "I should like that." And then she
caught my hand and kissed it. "I knew you would," she said,
as if I'd promised her the best and loveliest thing in all the
earth. Another man, it would have broken him in front of her.
But I'm harder than most.

When she let me, I retrieved my hand, nodded reassuringly,
and went out. The chieftain was awake and genial enough, so
I had a word with him. I told him what the girl had asked. "In
the East," I said, "it's the usual thing, give them something to
help them through. They call it Nektar, the drink of the gods.
She's consented," I said, "but she's very young and scared,
delicately bred too. You can't grudge her this." He acquiesced
immediately, as glad as she was, as I'd hoped. It's a grim affair,
I should imagine, when the girl shrieks for pity all the way up
to the hills. I hadn't thought there'd be any problem. On the
other hand, I hadn't wanted to be caught slipping her potions
behind anyone's back.

I mixed the drug in the cell where she could watch. She was
interested in everything I did, the way the condemned are nearly
always interested in every last detail, even how a cobweb hangs.

I made her promise to drink it all, but none of it until they
came to bring her out. "It may not last otherwise. You don't
want it to wear off before – too early."

"No," she said. "I'll do exactly what you say."

When I was going out again, she said, "If I can ask them
for anything for you, the gods, when I meet them . . ."

It was in my mind to say: Ask them to go stick – but I
didn't. She was trying to keep intact her trust in recompense,
immortality. I said, "Just ask them to look after you."

She had such a sweet, sweet mouth. She was made to love
and be loved, to have children and sing songs and die when
she was old, peacefully, in her sleep.

And there would be others like her. The dragon would be

given those, too. Eventually, it wouldn't just be maidens, either. The taboo states it has to be a virgin so as to safeguard any unborn life. Since a virgin can't be with child – there's one religion says different, I forget which – they stipulate virgins. But in the end any youthful woman, who can reasonably be reckoned as not with child, will do. And then they go on to the boys. Which is the most ancient sacrifice there is.

I passed a very young girl in the hall, trotting round with the beer-dipper. She was comely and innocent, and I recollected I'd seen her earlier and asked myself, Are you the next? And who'll be next after you?

Niemeh was the fifth. But, I said, dragons live a long while. And the sacrifices always get to be more frequent. Now it was twice a year. In the first year it had been once. In a couple more years it would happen at every season, with maybe three victims in the summer when the creature was most active.

And in ten more years it would be every month, and they'd have learned to raid other villages to get girls and young men to give it, and there would be a lot of bones about, besides, fellows like Caiy, dragon-slayers dragon slain.

I went after the girl with the beer-dipper and drained it. But drink never did comfort me much.

And presently, it would be time to form the procession and start for the hills.

It was the last gleaming golden hour of day when we set off.

The valley was fertile and sheltered. The westering light caught and flashed in the trees and out of the streams. Already there was a sort of path stamped smooth and kept clear of undergrowth. It would have been a pleasant journey, if they'd been going anywhere else.

There was sunlight warm on the sides of the hills, too. The sky was almost cloudless, transparent. If it hadn't been for the tainted air, you would never have thought anything was wrong.

But the track wound up the first slope and around, and up again, and there, about a hundred yards off, was the flank of a bigger hill that went down into shadow at its bottom, and never took the sun. That underside was bare of grass, and eaten out in caves, one cave larger than the rest and very black, with a strange black stillness, as if light and weather and time itself stopped just inside. Looking at that, you'd know at once, even with sun on your face and the whole lucid sky above.

They'd brought her all this way in a Roman litter which somehow had become the property of the village. It had lost its roof and its curtains, just a kind of cradle on poles, but Niemeh had sat in it on their shoulders, motionless, and dumb. I had only stolen one look at her, to be sure, but her face had turned mercifully blank and her eyes were opaque. What I'd given her started its work swiftly. She was beyond us all now. I was only anxious everything else would occur before her condition changed.

Her bearers set the litter down and lifted her out. They'd have to support her, but they would know about that, girls with legs gone to water, even passed out altogether. And I suppose the ones who fought and screamed would be forced to sup strong ale, or else concussed with a blow.

Everyone walked a little more, until we reached a natural palisade of rock. This spot provided concealment, while over-looking the cave and the ground immediately below it. There was a stagnant dark pond caught in the gravel there, but on our side, facing the cave, a patch of clean turf with a post sticking up, about the height of a tall man.

The two warriors supporting Niemeh went on with her towards the post. The rest of us stayed behind the rocks, except for Caiy.

We were all garlanded with flowers. Even I had had to be, and I hadn't made a fuss. What odds? But Caiy wasn't garlanded. He was the one part of the ritual which, though arcanely acceptable, was still profane. And that was why, even though they would let him attack the dragon, they had nevertheless brought the girl to appease it.

There was some kind of shackle at the post. It wouldn't be iron, because anything fey has an allergy to sable metals, even so midnight a thing as a dragon. Bronze, probably. They locked one part around her waist and another round her throat. Only the teeth and claws could get her out of her bonds now, piece by piece.

She sagged forward in the toils. She seemed unconscious at last, and I wanted her to be.

The two men hurried back, up the slope and into the rock cover with the rest of us. Sometimes the tales have the people rush away when they've put out their sacrifice, but usually the people stay, to witness. It's quite safe. The dragon won't go after them with something tasty chained up right under its nose.

Caiy didn't remain beside the post. He moved down towards the edge of the polluted pond. His sword was drawn. He was quite ready. Though the sun couldn't get into the hollow to fire his hair or the metal blade, he cut a grand figure, heroically braced there between the maiden and Death.

At the end, the day spilled swiftly. Suddenly all the shoulders of the hills grew dim, and the sky became the colour of lavender, and then a sort of mauve amber, and the stars broke through.

There was no warning.

I was looking at the pond, where the dragon would come to drink, judging the amount of muck there seemed to be in it. And suddenly there was a reflection in the pond, from above. It wasn't definite, and it was upside down, but even so my heart plummeted through my guts.

There was a feeling behind the rock, the type you get, they tell me, in the battle lines, when the enemy appears. And mixed with this, something of another feeling, more maybe like the inside of some god's house when they call on him, and he seems to come.

56

I forced myself to look then, at the cave mouth. This, after all, was the evening I would see a real dragon, something to relate to others, as others had related such things to me.

It crept out of the cave, inch by inch, nearly down on its belly, cat-like.

The sky wasn't dark yet, a Northern dusk seems often endless. I could see well, and better and better as the shadow of the cave fell away and the dragon advanced into the paler shadow by the pond.

At first, it seemed unaware of anything but itself and the twilight. It flexed and stretched itself. There was something uncanny, even in such simple movements, something evil. And timeless.

The Romans know an animal they call Elephantus, and I mind an ancient clerk in one of the towns describing this beast to me, fairly accurately, for he'd seen one once. The dragon wasn't as large as elephantus, I should say. Actually not that much higher than a fair-sized cavalry gelding, if rather longer. But it was sinuous, more sinuous than any snake. The way it crept and stretched and flexed, and curled and slewed its head, its skeleton seemed fluid.

There are plenty of mosaics, paintings. It was like that, the way men have shown them from the beginning. Slender, tapering to the elongated head, which is like a horse's, too, and not like, and to the tail, though it didn't have that spade-shaped sting they put on them sometimes, like a scorpion's. There were spines, along the tail and the back-ridge, and the neck and head. The ears were set back, like a dog's. Its legs were short, but that didn't make it seem ungainly. The ghastly fluidity was always there, not grace, but something so like grace it was nearly unbearable.

It looked almost the colour the sky was now, slatey, bluish-grey, like metal but dull; the great overlapping plates of its scales had no burnish. Its eyes were black and you didn't see them, and then they took some light from somewhere, and they flared like two flat coins, cat's eyes, with nothing – no brain, no soul – behind them.

It had been going to drink, but had scented something more interesting than dirty water, which was the girl.

The dragon stood there, static as a rock, staring at her over the pond. Then gradually its two wings, that had been folded back like fans along its sides, opened and spread.

They were huge, those wings, much bigger than the rest of it. You could see how it might be able to fly with them. Unlike the body, there were no scales, only skin, membrane, with ribs of external bone. Bat's wings, near enough. It seemed feasible a sword could go through them, damage them, but that would only maim, and all too likely they were tougher than they seemed.

Then I left off considering. With its wings spread like that, unused – like a crow – it began to sidle around the water, the blind coins of eyes searing on the post and the sacrifice.

Somebody shouted. My innards sprang over. Then I realised it was Caiy. The dragon had nearly missed him, so intent it was on the feast, so he had had to call it.

"Bis terribilis – Bis appellare – Draco! Draco!"

I'd never quite understood that antic chant, and the Latin was execrable. But I think it really means to know a dragon exists is bad enough, to call its name and summon it – call twice, twice terrible – is the notion of a maniac.

The dragon wheeled. It – *flowed*. Its elongated horse's-head-which-wasn't was before him, and Caiy's sharp sword slashed up and down and bit against the jaw. It happened, what they say – sparks shot glittering in the air. Then the head split, not from any wound, just the chasm of the mouth. It made a sound at him, not a hissing, a sort of *hroosh*. Its breath would be poisonous, almost as bad as fire. I saw Caiy stagger at it, and then one of the long feet on the short legs went out through the gathering dark. The blow looked slow and harmless. It threw Caiy thirty feet, right across the pond. He fell at the entrance to the cave, and lay quiet. The sword was still in his hand. His grip must have clamped down on it involuntarily. He'd likely bitten his tongue as well, in the same way.

The dragon looked after him, you could see it pondering whether to go across again and dine. But it was more attracted by the other morsel it had smelled first. It knew from its scent this was the softer more digestible flesh. And so it ignored Caiy, leaving him for later, and eddied on towards the post, lowering its head as it came, the light leaving its eyes.

I looked. The night was truly blooming now, but I could see, and the darkness didn't shut my ears; there were sounds, too. You weren't there, and I'm not about to try to make you see and hear what I did. Niemeh didn't cry out. She was senseless by then, I'm sure of it. She didn't feel or know any of what it did to her. Afterwards, when I went down with the others, there wasn't much left. It even carried some of her bones into the cave with it, to chew. Her garland was lying on the ground since the dragon had no interest in garnish. The pale flowers were no longer pale.

She had consented, and she hadn't had to endure it. I've seen things as bad that had been done by men, and for men there's no excuse. And yet, I never hated a man as I hated the dragon, a loathing, deadly, sickening hate.

The moon was rising when it finished. It went again to the pond, and drank deeply. Then it moved up the gravel back towards the cave. It paused beside Caiy, sniffed him, but there was no hurry. Having fed so well, it was sluggish. It stepped into the pitch-black hole of the cave, and drew itself from sight, inch by inch, as it had come out, and was gone.

Presently Caiy pulled himself off the ground, first to his hands and knees, then on to his feet.

We, the watchers, were amazed. We'd thought him dead, his back broken, but he had only been stunned, as he told us afterwards. Not even stunned enough not to have come to, dazed and unable to rise, before the dragon quite finished its feeding. He was closer than any of us. He said it maddened him – as if he hadn't been mad already – and so, winded and part stupefied as he was, he got up and dragged himself into the dragon's cave after it. And this time he meant to kill it for sure, no matter what it did to him.

Nobody had spoken a word, up on our rocky place, and no one spoke now. We were in a kind of communion, a trance. We leaned forward and gazed at the black gape in the hill where they had both gone.

Maybe a minute later, the noises began. They were quite extraordinary, as if the inside of the hill itself were gurning and sharling. But it was the dragon, of course. Like the stink of it, those sounds it made were untranslatable. I could say it looked this way comparable to an elephantus, or that way to a cat, a horse, a bat. But the cries and roars – no. They were like nothing else I've heard in the world, or been told of. There were, however, other noises, as of some great heap of things disturbed. And stones rattling, rolling.

The villagers began to get excited or hysterical. Nothing like this had happened before. Sacrifice is usually predictable.

They stood, and started to shout, or groan and invoke supernatural protection. And then a silence came from inside the hill, and silence returned to the villagers.

I don't remember how long it went on. It seemed like months.

Then suddenly something moved in the cave mouth.

There were yells of fear. Some of them took to their heels, but came back shortly when they realised the others were rooted to the spot, pointing and exclaiming, not in anguish but awe. That was because it was Caiy, and not the dragon, that had emerged from the hill.

He walked like a man who has been too long without food and water, head bowed, shoulders drooping, legs barely able to hold him up. He floundered through the edges of the pond and the sword trailed from his hand in the water. Then he tottered over the slope and was right before us. He somehow raised his head then, and got out the sentence no one had ever truly reckoned to hear.

"It's – dead," said Caiy, and slumped unconscious in the moonlight.

They used the litter to get him to the village, as Niemeh didn't need it any more.

We hung around the village for nearly ten days. Caiy was his merry self by the third, and since there had been no sign of the dragon, by day or night, a party of them went up to the hills, and, kindling torches at noon, slunk into the cave to be sure.

It was dead all right. The stench alone would have verified that, a different perfume than before, and all congealed there, around the cave. In the valley, even on the second morning, the live dragon smell was almost gone. You could make out goats and hay and mead and unwashed flesh and twenty varieties of flowers.

I myself didn't go in the cave. I went only as far as the post. I understood it was safe, but I just wanted to be there once more, where the few bones that were Niemeh had fallen through the shackles to the earth. And I can't say why, for you can explain nothing to bones.

There was rejoicing and feasting. The whole valley was full of it. Men came from isolated holdings, cots and huts, and a rough-looking lot they were. They wanted to glimpse Caiy the dragon-slayer, to touch him for luck and lick the finger. He laughed. He hadn't been badly hurt, and but for bruises was as right as rain, up in the hayloft half the time with willing girls, who would afterwards boast their brats were sons of the hero. Or else he was blind drunk in the chieftain's hall.

In the end, I collected Negra, fed her apples and told her she was the best horse in the land, which she knows is a lie and not what I say the rest of the time. I had sound directions now, and was planning to ride off quietly and let Caiy go on as he desired, but I was only a quarter of a mile from the village when I heard the splayed tocking of horse's hooves. Up he galloped beside me on a decent enough horse, the queen of the chief's stable, no doubt, and grinning, with two beer skins.

I accepted one, and we continued, side by side.

"I take it you're sweet on the delights of my company," I said at last, an hour after, when the forest was in view over the moor.

"What else, Apothecary? Even my insatiable lust to steal your gorgeous horse has been removed. I now have one of my very own, if not a third as beautiful." Negra cast him a sidelong look as if she would like to bite him. But he paid no attention. We trotted on for another mile or so before he added, "And there's something I want to ask you, too."

I was wary, and waited to find out what came next.

Finally, he said, "You must know a thing or two in your trade about how bodies fit together. That dragon, now. You seemed to know all about dragons."

I grunted. Caiy didn't cavil at the grunt. He began idly to describe how he'd gone into the cave, a tale he had flaunted a mere three hundred times in the chieftain's hall. But I didn't cavil either, I listened carefully.

The cave entry-way was low and vile, and soon it opened into a cavern. There was elf-light, more than enough to see by, and water running here and there along the walls and over the stony floor.

There in the cavern's centre, glowing now like filthy silver, lay the dragon, on a pile of junk such as dragons always accumulate. They're like crows and magpies in that, also, shiny things intrigue them and they take them to their lairs to paw possessively and to lie on. The rumours of hoards must come from this, but usually the collection is worthless, snapped knives, impure glass that had sparkled under the moon, rusting armlets from some victim, and all of it soiled by the devil's droppings, and muddled up with split bones.

When he saw it like this, I'd bet the hero's reckless heart failed him. But he would have done his best, to stab the dragon in the eye, the root of the tongue, the vent under the tail, as it clawed him in bits.

"But you see," Caiy now said to me, "I didn't have to."

This, of course, he hadn't said in the hall. No. He had told the village the normal things, the lucky lunge and the brain pierced, and the death throes, which we'd all heard plainly enough. If anyone noticed his sword had no blood on it, well, it had trailed in the pond, had it not?

"You see," Caiy went on, "it was lying there comatose one minute, and then it began to writh about, and to go into a kind of spasm. Something got dislodged off the hoard-pile – a piece of cracked-up armour, I think, gilded – and knocked me silly again. And when I came round, the dragon was all sprawled about, and dead as yesterday's roast mutton."

"Hn" I said. "*Hm.*"

"The point being," said Caiy, watching the forest and not me, "I must have done something to it with the first blow, outside. Dislocated some bone or other. You told me their bones have no marrow. So to do that might be conceivable. A fortunate stroke. But it took a while for the damage to kill it."

"Hn*n.*"

"Because," said Caiy, softly, "you do believe I killed it, don't you?"

"In the legends," I said, "they always do."

"But you said before that, in reality, a man can't kill a dragon."

"One did," I said.

"Something I managed outside then. Brittle bones. That first blow to its skull."

"Very likely."

Another silence. Then he said:

"Do you have any gods, Apothecary?"

"Maybe."

"Will you swear me an oath by them, and then call me 'dragon-slayer'? Put it another way. You've been a help. I don't like to turn on my friends. Unless I have to."

His hand was nowhere near that honed sword of his, but the sword was in his eyes and his quiet, oh-so-easy voice. He had his reputation to consider, did Caiy. But I've no reputation at all. So I swore my oath and I called him dragon-slayer, and when our roads parted my hide was intact. He went off to glory somewhere I'd never want to go.

Well, I've seen a dragon, and I do have gods. But I told them, when I swore that oath, I'd almost certainly break it, and my gods are accustomed to me. They don't expect honour and chivalry. And there you are.

Caiy never killed the dragon. It was Niemeh, poor lovely loving gentle Niemeh who killed it. In my line of work, you learn about your simples. Which cure, which bring sleep, which bring the long sleep without awakening. There are some miseries in this blessed world can only end in death, and the quicker death the better. I told you I was a hard man. I couldn't save her, I gave you reasons why. But there were all those others who would have followed her. Other Niemeh's. Other Caiy's, for that matter. I gave her enough in the cup to put out the life of fifty strong men. It didn't pain her, and she didn't show she was dead before she had to be. The dragon devoured her, and with her the drug I'd dosed her with. And so Caiy earned the name of dragon-slayer.

And it wasn't a riddle.

And no, I haven't considered making a profession of it. Once is enough with any twice-terrible thing. Heroes and knights need their impossible challenges. I'm not meant for any bard's romantic song, a look will tell you that. You won't ever find me in the Northern hills calling "Draco! Draco!"

Falcon's Mate

Falcon's Mate

Pat McIntosh

"Poor Thula," said Aneka from her big leather-curtained horse-litter. "Is your headache any better?"

That, oddly enough, decided me. My headache was definitely her fault. I made some answer, and reined in my horse to let the big litter lurch through the archway into the inn-yard, nodding to her cousin where he sat his raw-boned bay horse bawling instructions at the pack-drivers. He ignored me.

"Do you go up," I said to Aneka. "I'll stable my horse."

"Gelen says they serve in half an hour," she said, jumping down in a swirl of embroidered petticoats. I nodded and led my big grey Dester into the stable. Unsaddling and brushing him down with soothing, accustomed movements, I considered the matter.

If she had drugged my wine, it was with a purpose. I could think of two, but dismissed one. I had lived among girls of my own age or younger since I was seven: if she had done it out of sheer mischief, Aneka of all girls would have shown it, by secret smiles and giggles. And yet the other was incredible. Three nights running, the door had been locked, the key under my pillow, the open window at least four fathoms above ground with nothing to tie a rope to: Master Gelen took these precautions, not I think out of suspicion but simply to safeguard valuable merchandise. And when I woke in the morning, Aneka had been sound asleep, sprawled on her bed with the covers kicked back and her nightshift under her arms, an abandoned pose which did not suggest a fond farewell at the door, and replacing the key under my pillow.

And yet, three mornings running, I had woken with a mouth

like the floor of a birdcage, and a cleaver in my skull.

"Perhaps he can fly," I said to Dester. He snorted, and nudged me impatiently. I returned to my task, and determined on two things before I had finished. In the first place, Aneka would have my wine tonight, and I hers: and in the second, I would watch all night with my sword drawn.

Aneka was delighted when I arrived with my sword balanced on top of my saddlebags.

"What are you going to do?" she demanded. "Will you practise? Has it a name?"

"Her name is *Fenala*," I said rather shortly. I had forgotten until I drew the blade, that it was not my own familiar one of blue Southron steel; that lay on Fenala's breast in the tomb beside the village temple, away beyond Rhawn Dys. "She needs to be oiled," I said. This was partly true. "There isn't room to practise here."

"Show me!" said Aneka, kneeling beside me in three petticoats and no shoes. "There's writing! What does it say?"

I turned the blade on my knee, and spelled out the ancient letters with difficulty.

"Niachan len dova," I read at length. "A friend has two edges."

"A friend has two edges," she repeated, "what does it mean?"

"I don't know," I said. "It's a very old sword. You'd better dress, it's nearly dinner time."

She leapt up with a squeal that started my headache again, and seized another petticoat. I set down the sword, and began to remove my travel-stained clothes. They had brought warm water to wash with; Aneka had used most of it, as usual.

"Can you read?" she demanded through the final petticoat.

"Well, of course I can," I said. "And write. They teach us, in the Order."

"Oh, of course, the Order," she said. "Mama says reading's unfeminine."

67

"You surprise me," I said, rather drily. She lifted her brown-and-gold dress and pulled it over her head; it matched her hair, which was braided down her back after the custom of Rhawn Dys. I thought for the manyth time what a pity it was she should go to Dervir, where the ladies went powdered and corseted, in dresses ever richer than their neighbours'.

"I expect my husband wouldn't like it if I could read," she said complacently, smoothing the dress down. I reached for my clean shirt. "Don't you want to be married, Thula? Although I expect it's a bit late now, I mean, you're twenty-one." She made it sound as if I would soon be fifty.

"There was a girl left at thirty to get married," I said, a little defensively. She made round eyes.

"My sister was younger than me when she married," she said. "Mama says a man should be twice your age when you marry. Did that girl marry a man of sixty?"

"I doubt it," I said, rather sharply, doing up my tunic.

"My husband's thirty-two," she said, brushing out her hair. "Gelen says he's very handsome, but I think he should be a bit younger, say about twenty-seven."

Something in her tone made me say, "Do you want to marry him?"

In the mirror her lips moved, but the sound was drowned by a banging at the door.

"Ladies!" shouted the cousin. "Are you ready?"

"Nearly!" squeaked Aneka, braiding her hair with rapid expert fingers. Snatching a ribbon she wound it quickly round the ends and knotted it, and I straightened my tunic, stuck my dagger in my belt where it belonged and opened the door.

"We are ready, goodsir," I said; he bowed, averting his eyes from my trousered legs, and offered his arm to Aneka. Curtsying, she accepted its support. I followed them down the stairs, wondering if I had seen right. In the mirror, Aneka's answer to my question had looked very like *No*.

After dinner we played the game of Siege. It is a board

game, where one player defends a corner of the board against the other, the number of the pieces depending on the skill of the players. It is more common in the Eastlands than here in the West; they often use it as a ritual means of making temple-offerings. I beat Aneka, and after a long game her cousin. As he cleared the pieces he said quietly, "You and Aneka should have another game, mistress. I am sure she will win this one."

"Are you?" I said.

"So am I!" said Aneka, overhearing. "Come on, Thula! It's barely dark. Moonrise isn't for hours yet. You won our last match, so you lose a man, and it's my turn to defend."

I set up the pieces reluctantly. I was tired, and the cousin seemed to be expecting me to give her the game. Against a player like Aneka this is not easy: she played badly, but she was astute enough to see when I made foolish moves deliberately. And, since the game is sacred to the Moon, it was scarcely proper to reduce it to an amusement for a merchant's spoiled daughter in this way. I won. Aneka was annoyed, and showed it.

"We're playing another one," she said. "And I'm going to win."

"It's bedtime," I said, "and I've played three games in a row. Leave it till tomorrow night, Aneka."

"No," she said, "because tomorrow – " She paused, and changed what she was going to say. "Tomorrow you'll be fresh again and now you're tired. I'm sure I will win!"

I was indeed tired, and my headache had returned. It was a long game, but at last Aneka said,

"In three moves, Thula, I've got you!"

"You have?" I said, startled. She crowed with delight.

"Yes, I have! See, my captain moves there, and this soldier here, and this one here, and you can't block any of them, and then I'm in the castle."

Master Gelen crossed the room to see the board, and said,

"That's right, Aneka. That's the Falcon's Mate. I taught it you, remember."

"So it is," she marvelled. "And you said only a clever player could use it properly!"

"Now you have your revenge," I said, "and I agree it was cleverly done, are we going to bed?"

There was a jug of wine and two glasses set on the kist between the beds. To make things easy, I went to the window and leaned out. The courtyard was five fathoms down, and sheer; only a fly could climb the wall. I turned, and Aneka was sitting on her bed, sipping wine. I went and sat down too, and then said,

"Your hair's a funny colour. I wonder if it's going grey."

"Grey?" she said. "No! It can't be!" She set down her wine, some of it slopping over, and ran to the nearest box, delving in frantic haste for a mirror. I put my glass in the ring hers had made, and took hers in my hand; she got out the mirror and began peering anxiously, using the mirror over the wash-stand to see the back of her head.

"Perhaps it's just the light," I said, reassuringly. "Or the dust. Your colour hair does look funny in candle-light sometimes."

"Well it looks all right now," she said. "You frightened me."

In ten minutes she was asleep, half undressed. I finished the task, with difficulty, and covered her up; then I went to the window again, and on a sudden impulse took my naked sword and wedged it across the aperture, the sharper edge outward. Then I took my dagger in my hand, blew out the candle, and sat crosslegged on my bed to wait for dawn. Or was I waiting for moonrise?

And what would come then anyway? I began to feel that perhaps I was acting foolishly. I comforted myself with the thought that if I was, no one would know, except perhaps Aneka, and went over the facts again. I had thought this was a good way to cross the old Mountains safely and be paid for doing it: there are lone war-maids but I am not one of them and Fenala was too recently dead for my own company to be a good thing. We had never been lovers, as I believe some pairs are, but we had been inseparable since I was eight and she nine and the gap made by her death –

I dragged myself sharply from that train of thought. It led, as I well knew, to endless fits of weeping, and this was no time for tears. I had wept enough to fill an ocean, those weeks at the Temple in Rhawn Dys while I waited for another pair to come in, or a lone girl like me who wanted company. Then Mother Superior had sent for me, and described this task: Enys ma Doarrh ma Enys required a chaperone-bodyguard for his daughter, ten gold pieces to me and ten to the Order if she reached her husband as she left her father's house. It had seemed simple enough when I accepted.

Through the window I could see stars. They moved slowly past my sword, and at length the moon rose and threw silver on the wall. I began to feel numb, and tried to move, and could not. Panic rose in my throat as I tried unavailing to move so much as an eyelid. For what seemed an eternal year I struggled, and then a voice spoke.

"Aneka," it said. "Are you watching, little love? She will not wake, I have a keeping-spell on her. Are you watching, Aneka?"

I would have spoken, but I could not. Aneka never moved. Wings swished, and a great dark shape floated across the patch of sky.

"Aneka," said the voice. "It's Fenist – the moon has risen. Wake and let me in, love, for she has barred the window. Are you waking, Aneka?"

Still I could not answer him and Aneka never moved. Again the wings swished, and the dark shape was at the window. Talons scrabbled on the sill, square-tipped wings beat and fluttered, a small sound of pain came on the night air.

"Aneka!" he said, desperately now. "Her sword at the window cuts me to the bone! Aneka, this night of all nights, wake and let me in, for I bleed here in the darkness – *Aneka!*"

I truly think, if I could have stirred, I would have risen and let him in; but he had bespelled me, and Aneka never moved. There was a silence, in which I heard breathing surely harsher than a bird's, and something splashed on the sill. Then he said,

"Aneka, I called you three times, and you did not answer, and tonight I was to bear you away. If you will not come to me by your will, you shall come by mine."

The dark wings, edged with moonlight, moved in the patch of sky, swished into the distance and were gone. And I was left waiting, numb with grief as with his spell. The pleading in his voice had touched my heart; just so had I pleaded with Fenala, to wake and turn to me and answer me, and she never moved.

I pulled myself together. That was no solitary warmaid, but a shape-shifter who had seduced an innocent maid destined for another man, instructed her to make me sleep, maybe even gave her the stuff to put in my wine. And what had they been doing while I slept – ? I made an involuntary movement to reject the thought, and discovered I could move again. Jumping up I ran to the window and got my sword in. There was blood on the blade, still warm, and great drops of it gleaming faintly in the moonlight lying on the sill.

I cleaned my sword and sheathed it, and undressed slowly and lay down. But for a long time I could not sleep. Two voices rang in my head. One was Fenist's, the shape-shifter's:

"If you do not come to me by your will, you shall come by mine."

The other was my own, reading the words on my sword. A friend has two edges, it said. How should a person have two edges? Should a sword be my only friend? Certainly, if one got involved with people one got involved in problems . . .

The thunder that woke me diminished, and became Master

Gelen banging on the door. I answered something, and he went away; and I got out of bed. Aneka lay heavily asleep, as if she had not stirred all night. My eye lit on my sword, propped beside the bed, and the events of the night rushed into my mind. Mother of mares, I prayed, give me strength to dissemble. I cannot lie, and you know it . . . I bent to shake Aneka awake.

There was no chance to dissemble. She roused slowly, but I saw the point at which she realised she had missed him. She leapt out of bed, despite the way it must have pained her head, and ran to the window and flung it wide. She stared out, east and then west at the Mountains looming closer, and then her gaze fell on the dried blood on the sill. She froze for a moment: then she began to scream.

We were late leaving. Aneka was still in hysterics, although by now these were mercifully reduced to a dry sobbing and occasional moans of "Traitor!" I had not attempted to argue, but concentrated on getting her into the litter. The cousin's enquiries I had stopped with a significant glance at the moon, just vanishing behind the Mountains. It was plausible enough: he was scarcely likely to know when her last moon-day had been. Since half the column of pack-horses had already moved off, her boxes were heaved into the litter beside her, and she lay sobbing among them with the curtains closed. I felt for her, but I could see no other course than to take her to her husband and hope she could be taught enough to fool him on his wedding night. We rode out of the inn-yard, and up the dusty road that led to the North Pass: the two big horses bearing the litter made good speed and I riding beside them on my grey Dester kept them up.

The pack-train reached the approaches to the pass before noon. The road rose up in coils about the grey dusty heights, bare of grass and heather. We rose more slowly now, but by mid-afternoon we had crossed the first, false summit and as the road wound we caught occasional glimpses of the High House, where we would spend the night. The road itself was narrow:

the column had long since shuffled into single file and I was riding ahead of the litter, the last dozen or so pack-horses behind it, when Aneka put her head out and informed me, with the icy adolescent dignity, that she wished to go behind a bush.

"There aren't any here," I said. "It'll have to be a rock." I reined back and halted the litter, and the pack-horses picked their way past, the drivers grumbling as the horses slithered in the stony ground. Aneka emerged from the litter and found a suitable rock: when she emerged from behind it, sometime later, the tail of the column was well out of sight and the head was already appearing round the curve beyond. As she climbed back into the litter a shadow crossed the sun, and I could have sworn I heard the swish of wings, but when I looked up the sky was clear and empty. I whipped up the two big horses, and they achieved a lumbering trot. We thudded up to the corner and round it, into a cutting where the road widened to its original size. My Dester shied, and tossed his head, unwilling to go on.

"What is it, stupid?" I asked him, urging him on with knees and heels, using the whip in both hands alternately, on him and on the litter-horses. He squealed and half reared, swinging round into the lead horse. There was a rumbling and crashing of thunder above us, and suddenly the defile before us was full of rocks, great boulders, pebbles, earth and a choking dust that rose above everything. The lead horse, already alarmed by Dester, screamed in panic and tried to back and run away both at once. The other horse backed too, and somehow, I don't know how, the next thing was the two litter-horses bolting back down the road away from me, the litter jerking and swaying between them, Aneka's shrill screams floating back above the drumming hooves. I finally got control of Dester and turned him after the litter, at a less breakneck pace – nothing excites a runaway like being chased. Then a last mutter and rumble came above me, and another few boulders crashed down. I think a pebble or something got Dester on the quarters, because he squealed again, and leapt forward: I stayed on by some miracle, and found I was clinging to the pommel while he went down the road after the litter as if there were wings on his big feet.

I still don't know where we went. After the litter, yes, but that left the road soon. I was too busy staying on and trying to get control to look at the scenery. When Dester tired I finally got control, and drove him on at the trot although he wanted to stop and get his breath back. We were on a track, and up ahead was the litter, on a sort of knoll beyond an overhang. It was intact and securely fastened to both horses, who stood with heads down, sides heaving. Aneka was still moaning inside it. I was concentrating on that, which is why the man who jumped me from the overhang took me quite by surprise. I marked him, with teeth and nails, and I had nearly got the upper hand when his companion came running up and struck me over the head. Sparks flared, and I fell into night.

I woke in torchlight. It flickered and leapt beyond my closed eyelids, and above the crackle of the pine were small sounds, rustling and breathing. My head hurt. I wondered vaguely why, and then remembered –

"Aneka?" I said, opening my eyes. She appeared beside me, looking only relieved, though the tearstains still showed.

"Does it hurt?" she said. "Your head."

I put up my hand and felt gingerly. A lump where the neck muscles join the skull stabbed pain when I touched it. No blood.

"I'll live," I said. "Where are we? What happened?"

"I don't know," she said. "Thula, I'm frightened!"

"Tell me what happened after I was laid out," I suggested, and sat up with caution. I was on a high, well-draped bed: about us were kists and a cupboard, and a curtain that swung in the draught and probably covered a garde-robe. The window was shuttered: a high fireplace gaped blackly across the room.

"How did we get here?" I prodded. She sat on the bed beside me.

"They threw you in on top of me," she said obediently. "They wouldn't speak to me, I don't understand what they said to each other. I didn't see where we went, I was trying to wake you. Then they made me get out in the courtyard here and two of them carried you, and one took my arm, and we came here. And I couldn't wake you. So I went to sleep," she finished.

That made me giggle. It hurt, so I stopped abruptly. Aneka gave me a dignified look and added, "There's some food."

With a glass of wine and a chicken wing I felt better. I prowled round the room eating, relieved to find my legs would bear me. I could see no way out. I kept remembering the words of Aneka's lover: *If you do not come to me by your will, you shall come by mine.* What could I do, with Aneka to take care of? I had to get her to her husband in Maer-Cuith, but how should we escape from here?

The door flung open. Aneka drew breath as if to scream: I reached for my dagger, but the second man had a crossbow, wound and loaded and pointing at me. The first bowed to Aneka and took her wrist; the second stood aside into the room; the third came in and took my arm, and he had a knife in his other hand. Aneka said "Thula – !"

"It's all right," I said. "I don't think they're going to hurt you."

We were led down the wheel stair, the crossbow at the back of my neck. At the foot of the stair a boy with a torch bobbed and stared at Aneka, then turned and went off along a corridor, into the deeps of the castle. We were led after, our escorts never letting go, the crossbower padding softly behind me on felt-soled boots. Through many corridors we went, and up more stairs, till I began to think of rabbit-warrens. Then we halted at a door. Aneka's guide knocked and spoke harshly. The door was opened, and we stepped into a glare of torches and candles. Aneka stood in front of me maybe three seconds; then she gave a great cry of "Fenist! Oh, Fenist!" She ran forward, and I was prodded into the room. The door closed.

And in front of me Aneka knelt by a bed heaped with furs. The light of many candles fell on her head, and on the hand that came from among the furs and lay on her neck like a caress. I walked round the bed, the crossbow following as I moved, until I could see her face. She was bent over the man in the bed, kissing him quickly with light practised movements. He was whispering, the words half lost against her face, over and over: "Aneka, my dear love, my heart's delight, Aneka . . ."

I watched with the half-dozen men in the room, for some time. At length I stepped forward, despite the insistent crossbow at my side, and put my hand on her shoulder. She looked round, startled, and the man's eyes rose to mine. I looked away from the challenge in them, and said gently,

"Aneka, you're promised. Remember? You're betrothed to Alevr ma Julden of Dervir – "

"I made no promises!" she said. "I signed no contracts. Women are not chattels, Thula, to be bargained for like diamonds and cinnamon, you should know that!"

"She is mine," said the man among the furs. I straightened, and this time met the hawk's eyes squarely.

"Goodsir, I swore a convenant with her father, that she would reach her husband's house as she left her father's, or not at all. I swore to defend her honour as my own. My honour is a small thing – " His eyes mocked me and I added hastily, "except to me, but the Order loses twenty crescents and honour as well."

"I'll give you forty," he said. The eyes danced; under his beaked nose the cruel mouth suddenly smiled entrancingly. "There is the matter that she hasn't reached me as she left her father's house, but I'll forget that in the circumstances."

"I should kill her," I said. At my feet Aneka shrank into the crook of her lover's arm.

"And how far would you go from here if you did?" He was watching me with a certain amount of sympathy. "Mistress, how would her life be in the women's quarters of Alevr ma Julden's house?"

I remembered, dimly, my mother's life, before I was given to the Order. Scents and rustling gowns, other ladies coming and going, and the echo of my father's voice making her freeze like a rabbit hearing a fox. The man was watching me.

"Just so," he said, reading my expression. "Here she will be mistress of my castle and councillor of my people. I may even teach her to read." He kissed the end of her nose, and turned back to stare at me, like a hawk hovering, for a long moment. Then the hawk swooped.

"I'm damned if I'll lie here," he said moving stiffly among the furs, "helping you argue down your conscience. Obik, fetch me the board yonder! Mistress, I'll play you three games of Siege. If I win three, Aneka decides your fate and hers. If I win two, you may go free and no more said. If you win two, you may try if you can persuade Aneka to go with you."

"And if I win three?" I said. He laughed, and winced as if it hurt him.

"You won't," he said confidently.

"But *you* will, love," said Aneka. "I beat her last night, and you can beat me."

He kissed her again, and brought the other arm out of the furs to wave me to a seat across the board. White linen on the brown skin made Aneka gasp.

"Oh, Fenist, I thought – " She looked at his arm, and then pulled back the furs. More linen was swathed about his belly where the ribs stopped. She stared for a moment, then tucked the furs round him again and raised her eyes to my face.

"You did that," she said. I knew suddenly that it would not be good to lose three games. And I had thought she liked me . . .

"In the line of duty," said Fenist. "I bear no grudges. I was foolish, perhaps." He inspected the pieces laid out on the board. "My move to start, mistress? So – King's Captain, advance three paces."

I looked up, startled, but he had turned back to Aneka. That move opened the most famous of the ritual games, and was rarely used otherwise. Perhaps I was imagining things . . . ? I replied with the following move – King's Captain to the corner turret. He looked back at the click of the piece on the board, and moved his Queen's Soldier two squares left without hesitating. Across the squared board his eyes met mine, unreadable. When I made pretence to consider before moving the Queen's Knight in support of my King's Captain, he smiled gently, and shifted carefully among the furs. I stared at the board, not seeing it. This was ritual play, and I was to win. Why?

"So I go free," I said, setting up the pieces for the second game. He smiled again, and nodded.

"So you go free, mistress. Your move to start."

I hesitated, hand over the board. If I won, I could try to persuade Aneka to leave, and honour her father's promise. If I lost I might still win the next one. I lifted my Queen, still hesitating. If she merely moved in support of her King, set at the front of the siege from the beginning, that was an ambiguous start. But if she moved to the attack . . .

"So," I said. "Queen to the corner turret."

His smile showed that he appreciated the move.

"Very symbolic," he said. "So is my move. King to the corner turret."

A cold finger stroked my backbone. This was free play, and I was playing with either a master or a fool. Somehow, looking at the narrow, intent face, I could not think the Lord Fenist a fool. But they teach us well, in the Order, before they send us out in the world. I moved my King to support my Queen.

This game took longer. Aneka and his soldiers watched in silence, unmoving. We two did not stir, except to reach over the board, moving the ebony and ivory pieces. The only sound was the click of the men on the board and the hiss and crackle of the torches on the wall, and the slow breathing of my opponent.

"Mate," he said at last. "In three moves, not so?"

"Five," I said.

"Well, five," he conceded reluctantly. "Obik! Wine for the ladies.'

I stretched, and realised my head was aching. He watched me, the cruel mouth smiling under his hawk's beak of a nose.

"Will you not admit me the third game?" he said. "Admit you are outplayed?"

I had been considering doing just that.

"No," I said. He laughed, and winced. I drank wine, and set up the pieces. "You lose a man," I said. "I defend, so you move first."

He considered a moment. Then he moved – King's Soldier right three paces. Another opening rarely used outside the rituals, and this time he was to win. I looked at the board, and then at him. the next move to this game was Queen's Soldier to the rampart, two paces. I considered for more than a moment; then I lifted my Queen.

"Queen to the corner turret," I said clearly, and set her down. His hand had been hovering already over his Queen's Soldier, to move it in support of the other piece; at my words he looked back sharply from Aneka's upturned face. One comprehensive glance and he began laughing, his hand to his side.

"Oh, don't love – !" said Aneka anxiously. "Fenist, please don't, you'll make it bleed!"

"I know," he said, still laughing weakly. "Oh, you show your teeth, mistress! Well here is your answer. King to the corner turret."

That game took longest of the three. Aneka and the soldiers watched in silence; the only sounds were the click of the men on the ebony and ivory board, and the hiss and crackle of the torches, and the slow breathing of my opponent. It took the longest, and it was won by the least margin.

"Mate," he said at length. "In three moves, with these three men. King's Captain moves there, this soldier here, this one here, and I hold the castle."

"I can see," I said. "No need to spell it out. Falcon's Mate."

"No," he said, frowning. "No need." He lay back among the furs, grey-faced. I stood up, saying,

"Goodsir, when do I go free?"

"In the morning," he said. "I'll give you food, and a spare horse." His speech was slurred; Aneka, bending hastily over him, was the only one who caught his next words, before he slid into sleep. She straightened; across the bed piled with furs her eyes met mine, unloving.

"You lose hard," she repeated. She looked round at the men. "Go house her as my lord would wish," she said. "The place we were in will do."

I turned at the door, despite the crossbow once more insistent at my shoulder.

"Aneka," I said. She was still watching me. "What does it say on my sword?"

She stared at me, remembering slowly.

"A friend has two edges," she said at last. There was another silence; then she crossed the room. The crossbower stood aside for her, and she leaned up and kissed my cheek, and then turned back to her sleeping lord.

"Goodnight, Aneka," I said.

"Goodbye, my friend," she said. "It's nearly dawn."

So I rode alone, down from the Old Mountains into Amyn on the road south-west, with forty gold crescents close packed in one saddle-bag as Aneka's bride price, and ten in the other as my wages, since it would be unwise to try to collect from Alevr ma Julden. And my conscience was unquiet, for the game of Siege, sacred to the Moon, should not be used as I had used it. The difference is subtle, between one losing and another winning, and whatever he might think, Lord Fenist, Fenist the Falcon, had not won the last game. I had lost it. There are many more games written down than are ever used in the rituals.

The Healer

The Healer

Robin McKinley

The child was born just as the first faint rays of dawn made their way through the cracks between the shutters. The lantern-wick burned low. The new father bowed his head over his wife's hand as the midwife smiled at the mite of humanity in her arms. Black curls framed the tiny face; the child gave a gasp of shock, then filled its lungs for its first cry in this world; but when the little mouth opened, no sound came out. The midwife tightened her hands on the warm wet skin as the baby gave a sudden writhe, and closed its mouth as if it knew that it had failed at something expected of it. Then the eyes stared up into the midwife's own, black, and clearer than a newborn's should be, and deep in them such a look of sorrow that tears rose in the midwife's own eyes.

"The child does not cry," the mother whispered in terror, and the father's head snapped up to look at the midwife and the baby cradled in her arms.

The midwife could not fear the sadness in this baby's eyes; and she said shakily, "No, the baby does not cry, but she is a fine girl nonetheless," and the baby blinked, and the look was gone. The midwife washed her quickly, and gave her into her mother's eager, anxious arms, and saw the damp-curled, black-haired head of the young wife bend over the tiny curly head of the daughter. Her smile reminded the midwife of the smiles of many other new mothers, and the midwife smiled herself, and opened a shutter long enough to take a few deep breaths of the new morning air. She closed it again firmly, and chased the father out of the room so that mother and child might be bathed properly, and the bedclothes changed.

*

They named her Lily. She almost never cried; it was as though she did not want to call attention to what she lacked, and so at most her little face would screw itself into a tiny red knot, and a few tears would creep down her cheeks, but she did not open her mouth. She was her parents' first child, and her mother hovered over her, and she suffered no neglect for her inability to draw attention to herself.

When Lily was three years old, her mother bore a second child, another daughter; when she was six and a half, a son was born. Both these children came into the world howling mightily. Lily seemed to find their wordless crying more fascinating than the grownups' speech; and when she could she loved to sit beside the new baby and play with it gently, and make it chuckle at her.

By the time her little brother was taking his first wobbly steps it had become apparent that Lily had been granted the healer's gift. A young cow or skittish mare would foal more quietly with her head in Lily's lap; children with fever did not toss and turn in their beds if Lily sat beside them; and it was usually in Lily's presence that the fevers broke, and the way back to health began.

When she was twelve she was apprenticed to the midwife who had birthed her.

Jolin by then was a strong handsome woman of forty-five or so. Her husband had died when they had had only two years together, and no children; and she had decided that she preferred to live alone as a healer after that. But it was as the midwife she was best known, for her village was a healthy one; hardly anyone ever fell from a horse and broke a leg or caught a fever that her odd-smelling draughts could not bring down. "I'll tell you, young one," she said to Lily, "I'll teach you everything I know, but if you stay here you won't be needing it; you'll spend the time you're not birthing babies sewing little sacks of herbs for the women to hang in the wardrobes and tuck among the linens. Can you sew properly?" Lily nodded, smiling; but Jolin looked into her black eyes and saw the same sorrow there that she had first seen twelve years ago. She said abruptly; "I've heard you whistling. You can whistle more like the birds than the birds do. There's no reason you can't talk with those calls; we'll put meanings to the different ones, and we'll both learn 'em. Will you do that with me?"

Lily nodded eagerly, but her smile broke, and Jolin looked away.

Five years passed; Jolin had bought her apprentice a horse the year before, because Lily's fame had begun to spread to neighbouring towns, and she often rode a long way to tend the sick. Jolin still birthed babies, but she was happy not to have to tend stomach-aches at midnight any more, and Lily was nearly a woman grown, and had surpassed her old teacher in almost all Jolin had to offer her. Jolin was glad of it, for it still worried her that the sadness stayed deep in Lily's eyes and would not be lost or buried. The work meant much to each of them; for Jolin it had eased the loss of a husband she loved, and had had for so little time she could not quite let go of his memory; and for Lily, now, she thought it meant that which she had never had.

Of the two of them, Jolin thought, Lily was the more to be pitied. Their village was one of a number of small villages, going about their small concerns, uninterested in anything but the weather and the crops, marriages, births and deaths. There was no one within three days' ride who could read or write, for Jolin knew everyone; and the birdcall-speech that she and her apprentice had made was enough for crops and weather, births and deaths, but Jolin saw other things passing swiftly over Lily's clear face, and wished there was a way to let them free.

At first Jolin had always accompanied Lily on her rounds,

but as Lily grew surer of her craft somehow she also grew able to draw what she needed to know or to borrow from whomever she tended; and Jolin could sit at home and sew her little sacks of herbs and prepare the infusions Lily would need, and tend the several cats that always lived with them, and the goats in the shed and the few chickens in the coop that survived the local foxes.

When Lily was seventeen, Jolin said: "You should be thinking of marrying." She knew at least two lads who followed Lily with their eyes and were clumsy at their work when she was near, though Lily seemed unaware of them.

Lily frowned and shook her head.

"Why not?" Jolin said. "You can be a healer as well. I was. It takes a certain kind of man – " she sighed " – but there are a few. What about young Armar? He's a quiet, even-handed sort, who'd be proud to have a wife that was needed by half the countryside. I've seen him watching you." She chuckled. "And I have my heart set on birthing your first baby."

Lily shook her head more violently, and raised her hands to her throat.

"You can learn to whistle at him as you have me," Jolin said gently, for she saw how the girl's hands shook. "Truly, child, it's not that great a matter; five villages love you and not a person in 'em cares you can't talk."

Lily stood up, her eyes full of the bitter fire in her heart, and struck herself on the breast with her fist, and Jolin winced at the weight of the blow; she did not need to hear the words to know that Lily was shouting at her: *I do!*

Lily reached her twentieth year unmarried, although she had had three offers, Armar among them. The crop of children in her parents' home had reached seven since she had left them eight years ago; and all her little brothers and sisters whistled birdcalls at her when she whistled to them. Her mother called her children her flock of starlings; but the birds themselves would come and perch on Lily's outstretched fingers, but on no one else's.

Lily was riding home from a sprained ankle in a neighbouring village, thinking about supper, and wondering if Karla had had her kittens yet when she realized she was overtaking another traveller on the road. She did not recognize the horse, and reined back her own, for she dreaded any contact with strangers; but the rider had already heard her approach and was waiting for her. Reluctantly she rode forward. The rider threw back the hood of his cloak as she approached and smiled at her. She had never seen him before; he had a long narrow face, made longer by lines of sorrow around his mouth. His long hair was blond and grey mixed, and he sat his horse as if he had been sitting on horseback for more years past than he would wish to remember. His eyes were pale, but in the fading twilight she could not see if they were blue or grey.

"Pardon me, lady," he greeted her, "but I fear I have come wrong somewhere. Would you have the goodness to tell me where I am?"

She shook her head, looking down at the long quiet hands holding his horse's reins, then forced herself to look up, meeting his eyes. She watched his face for comprehension as she shook her head again, and touched two fingers to her mouth and her throat; and said sadly to herself, *I cannot tell you anything, stranger. I cannot talk.*

The stranger's expression changed indeed, but the comprehension she expected was mixed with something else she could not name. Then she heard his words clearly in her mind, although he did not move his lips. *Indeed, but I can hear you, lady.*

Lily reached out, not knowing that she did so, and her fingers closed on a fold of the man's cloak. He did not flinch from her touch, and her horse stood patiently still, wanting his warm

88

stall and his oats, but too polite to protest. *Who – who are you?* she thought frantically; *what are you doing to me?*

Be easy, lady. I am – here there was an odd flicker – *a mage, of sorts; or once I was one. I retain a few powers. I –* and his thought went suddenly blank with an emptiness that was much more awful than that of a voice fallen silent – *I can mindspeak. You have not met any of – us – before?*

She shook her head.

There are not many. He looked down into the white face that looked up at him and felt an odd creaky sensation where once he might have had a heart.

Where are you going? she said at last.

He looked away; she thought he stared at the horizon as if he expected to see something he could hastily describe as his goal.

I do not mean to question you, she said; *forgive me, I am not accustomed to – speech – and I forget my manners.*

He smiled at her, but the sad lines around his mouth did not change. *There is no lack of courtesy,* he replied; *only that I am a wanderer, and I cannot tell you where I am going.* He looked up again, but there was no urgency in his gaze this time. *I have not travelled here before, however, and even a – wanderer – has his pride; and so I asked you the name of this place.*

She blushed that she had forgotten his question, and replied quickly, the words leaping into her mind, *the village where I live lies just there, over the little hill. Its name is Rhungill. That way –* she turned in her saddle – *is Teskip, where I am returning from; this highway misses it, it lay to your right, beyond the little forest as you rode this way.*

He nodded gravely. *You have always lived in Rhungill?*

She nodded; the gesture felt familiar, but a bubble of joy beat in her throat that she need not halt with the nod. *I am the apprentice of our healer.*

He was not expecting to hear himself say: *Is there an inn in your village, where a wanderer might rest for the night?* In the private

89

part of his mind he said to himself: there are three hours till sunset; there is no reason to stop here now. If there are no more villages, I have lain by a fire under a tree more often than I have lain in a bed under a roof for many years past.

Lily frowned a moment and said, *No-o, we have no inn; Rhungill is very small. But there is a spare room – it is Jolin's house, but I live there too – we often put people up, who are passing through and need a place to stay. The villagers often send us folk.* And because she was not accustomed to mindspeech, he heard her say to herself what she did not mean for him to hear: *let him stay a little longer.*

And so he was less surprised when he heard himself answer: *I would be pleased to spend the night at your healer's house.*

A smile, such as had never before been there, bloomed on Lily's face; her thoughts tumbled over each other and politely, he did not listen, nor let her know that he might have. She let her patient horse go on again, and the stranger's horse walked beside.

They did not speak. Lily found that there were so many things she would like to say, to ask, that they overwhelmed her; and then a terrible shyness closed over her, for fear that she would offend the stranger with her eagerness, with the rush of pent-up longing for the particulars of conversation. He held his silence as well, but his reasons stretched back over many wandering years; although once or twice he did look in secret at the bright young face beside him, and again there was the odd, uncomfortable spasm beneath his breastbone.

They rode over the hill and took a narrow, well-worn way off the highway. It wound into a deep cutting, and golden grasses waved above their heads at either side. Then the way rose, or the skies fell away, and the stranger looked around him at pastureland with sheep and cows grazing earnestly and solemnly across it; and then at empty meadows; and then there was a small stand of birch and ash and willow, and a small thatched house with a strictly-tended herb garden around it, laid out in a maze of squares and circles and borders and low hedges. Lily swung off her small gelding at the edge of the garden and whistled; a high thin cry that told Jolin she had brought a visitor.

Jolin emerged from the house smiling. Her hair, mostly grey now, with lights of chestnut brown, was in a braid; and tucked into the first twist of the hair at the nape of her neck was a spray of yellow and white flowers. They were almost a halo, nearly a collar.

"Lady," said the stranger, and dismounted.

This is Jolin, Lily said to him. *And you* – she stopped, confused, shy again.

"Jolin," said the stranger, but Jolin did not think it odd that he knew her name, for often the villagers sent visitors on with Lily when they saw her riding by, having supplied both their names first. "I am called Sahath."

Lily moved restlessly; there was no birdcall available to her for this eventuality. She began the one for "talk," and broke off. Jolin glanced at her, aware that something was troubling her.

Sahath, said Lily, *tell Jolin* – and her thought paused, because she could not decide, even to herself, what the proper words for it were.

But Jolin was looking at their guest more closely, and a tiny frown appeared between her eyes.

Sahath said silently to Lily: *she guesses*.

Lily looked up at him: standing side by side he was nearly a head taller than she. *She – ?*

Jolin had spent several years travelling in her youth, travelling far from her native village and even far from her own country; and on her travels she had learned more of the world than most of the other inhabitants of Rhungill, for they were born and bred to live their lives on their small land-plots, and any sign of wanderlust was firmly suppressed. Jolin, as a healer and so a little unusual, was permitted wider leeway than any of the rest of Rhungill's daughters, but her worldly knowledge was something she rarely admitted and still more rarely demonstrated. But one of the things she had learned as she and her mother drifted from town to town, dosing children and heifers, binding the broken limbs of men and pet cats, was to read the mage-mark.

"Sir," she said now, "what is one such as you doing in our quiet and insignificant part of the world?" Her voice was polite but not cordial; for mages, while necessary for some work beyond the reach of ordinary mortals, often brought with them trouble as well; and an unbidden mage was almost certainly trouble. This too she had learned when she was young.

Sahath smiled sadly. "I carry the mark, lady, it is true, but no mage am I." Jolin, staring at him, holding her worldly knowledge just behind her eyes where everything he said must be reflected through it, read truth in his eyes. "I was one once, but no longer."

Jolin relaxed, and if she need not fear this man she could pity him: for to have once been a mage and to have lost that more than mortal strength must be as heavy a blow as any man might receive and yet live; and she saw the lines of sorrow in his face.

Lily stood staring at the man with the sad face, for she knew no more of mages than a child knows of fairy tales: she would as easily have believed in the existence of tigers or of dragons, of chimeras or of elephants; and yet Jolin's face and voice were serious. A mage. This man was a mage – or had been one – and he could speak to her. It was more wonderful than elephants.

Sahath said: "Some broken pieces of my mage-truth remain to me, and one of these Lily wishes me to tell you: that I can speak to her – mind to mind."

Lily nodded eagerly, and seized her old friend and mentor's hands in hers. She smiled, pulled her lips together to whistle "it is true" and her lips drew back immediately again to the smile. Jolin tried to smile back into the bright young face before her: there was a glow there which had never been there before, and Jolin's loving heart turned with jealousy and – fear reawakened. For this man, with his unreasonable skills, even if he were no proper mage, might be anyone in his own heart. Jolin loved Lily as much as any person may love another. What, she asked herself in fear, might this man do to her, in her innocence, her pleasure in the opening of a door so long closed to her, and open now only to this stranger? Mages were not to be trusted on a human scale of right and wrong, reason and unreason. Mages were sworn to other things. Jolin understood that they were sworn to – goodness, to rightness; but often that goodness was of a high, far sort that looked very much like misery to the smaller folk who had to live near it.

As she thought these things, and held her dearer-than-daughter's hands in hers, she looked again at Sahath. "What do you read in my mind, mage?" she said, and her voice was harsher than she meant to permit it, for Lily's sake.

Sahath dropped his eyes to his own hands; he spread the long fingers as if remembering what once they had been capable of. "Distrust and fear," he said after a moment; and Jolin was the more alarmed that she had had no sense of his scrutiny. No mage-skill she had, but as a healer she heard and felt much that common folk had no ken of.

Lily's eyes widened, and she clutched Jolin's hands. Sahath felt her mind buck and shudder like a frightened horse, for the old loyalty was very strong. It was terrible to her that she might have to give up this wonderful, impossible thing even sooner than the brief span of an overnight guest's visit that she had promised herself – or at least freely hoped for. Even his mage's wisdom was awed by her strength of will, and the strength of her love for the aging, steady-eyed woman who watched him. He felt the girl withdrawing from him, and he did not follow her, though he might have; but he did not want to know what she was thinking. He stood where he was, the two women only a step or two distant from him; and he felt alone, as alone as he had felt once before, on a mountain, looking at a dying army, knowing his mage-strength was dying with them.

"I – " he said, groping, and the same part of his mind that had protested his halting so long before sundown protested again, saying, why do you defend yourself to an old village woman who shambles among her shrubs and bitter herbs, mouthing superstitions? But the part of his mind that had been moved by Lily's strength and humility answered: because she is right to question me.

"I am no threat to you in any way I control," he said to Jolin's steady gaze, and she thought still he talks like a mage, with the mage logic, to specify that which he controls. Yet perhaps it is not so bad a thing, some other part of her mind said calmly, that any human being, even a mage, should know how little he may control.

"It – it is through no dishonour that I lost the – the rest of my mage-strength." The last words were pulled out of him, like the last secret drops of the heart's blood of a dragon, and Jolin heard the pain and pride in his voice, and saw the blankness in his eyes; yet she did not know that he was standing again on a mountain, feeling all that had meant anything to him draining away from him into the earth, drawn by the ebbing life-force of the army he had opposed. One of the man's long-fingered hands had stretched toward the two women as he spoke; but as he said *mage-strength* the hand went to his forehead. When it dropped to his side again there were white marks that stood a moment against the skin, where the fingertips had pressed too hard.

Jolin put one arm around Lily's shoulders and reached her other hand out delicately, to touch Sahath's sleeve. He looked up again at the touch of her fingers. "You are welcome to stay with us, Sahath."

Lily after all spoke to him very little that evening; as if, he thought, she did not trust herself; although she listened eagerly to the harmless stories he told them of other lands and peoples he had visited; and she not infrequently interrupted him to ask for unimportant details. He was careful to answer everything she asked as precisely as he could; once or twice she laughed at his replies, although there was nothing overtly amusing about them.

In the morning when he awoke, only a little past dawn, Lily was already gone. Jolin gave him breakfast and said without looking at him, "Lily has gone gathering wild herbs; dawn is best for some of those she seeks." Sahath saw in her mind that Lily had gone by her own decision; Jolin had not sent her, nor tried to suggest the errand to her.

He felt strangely bereft, and he sat, crumbling a piece of sweet brown bread with his fingers and staring into his cup of herb tea. He recognized the infusion; chintanth for calm, morrar for clear-mindedness. He drank what was in the cup and poured himself more. Jolin moved around the kitchen, putting plates and cups back into the cupboard.

He said abruptly: "Is there any work a simple man's strength might do for you?"

There was a rush of things through Jolin's mind: her and Lily's self-sufficiency, and their pleasure in it; another surge of mistrust for mage-cunning – suddenly and ashamedly put down – this surprised him, as he stared into his honey-clouded tea, and it gave him hope. Hope? he thought. He had not known hope since he lost his mage-strength; he had nearly forgotten its name. Jolin stood gazing into the depths of the cupboard, tracing the painted borders of vines and leaves and flowers with her eye; and now her thoughts were of things that it would be good to have done, that she and Lily always meant to see to, and never quite had time for.

When Lily came home in the late morning, a basket over her arm, Sahath was working his slow way with a spade down the square of field that Jolin had long had in her mind as an extension of her herb garden. Lily halted at the edge of the freshly turned earth, and breathed deep of the damp sweet smell of it. Sahath stopped to lean on his spade, and wiped his forehead on one long dark sleeve. *It is near dinnertime*, said Lily hesitantly, fearful of asking him why he was digging Jolin's garden; but her heart was beating faster than her swift walking could explain.

He ate with them, a silent meal, for none of the three wished to acknowledge or discuss the new balance that was already growing among them. Then he went back to his spade.

He did a careful, thorough job of the new garden plot; two days it took him. When he finished it he widened the kitchen garden. Then he built a large new paddock for Lily's horse – and his own; the two horses had made friends at once, and stood head to tail in the shade at the edge of the tiny turn-out that flanked the small barn. When they were first introduced to their new field, they ran like furies around it, squealing and plunging at one another. Jolin came out of the house to see what the uproar was about. Sahath and Lily were leaning side by side on the top rail of the sturdy new fence; Jolin wondered what they might be saying to each other. The horses had enough of being mad things, and ambled quietly over to ask their riders for handouts. Jolin turned and reentered the house.

On the third day after his arrival Jolin gave Sahath a shirt and trousers, lengthened for their new owner; the shirt-tail and cuffs were a wide red band sewn neatly onto the original yellow cloth; the trousers were green, and each leg bore a new darker green hem. No mage had ever worn such garb. He put them on. At the end of the week Lily gave him a black and green – the same coarse green of the trouser-hems – jacket. He said, *thank you, lady*, and she blushed and turned away. Jolin watched them, and wondered if she had done the right thing, not to send him away when she might have; wondered if he knew that Lily was in love with him. She wondered if a mage might know anything of love, anything of a woman's love for a man.

He propped up the sagging cow shed where the two goats lived, and made the chicken-coop decently fox-proof. He built bird houses and feeders for the many birds that were Lily's friends; and he watched her when he thought she did not notice, when they came to visit, perching on her hands and shoulders and rubbing their small heads against her face. He listened to their conversations, and knew no more of what passed than Jolin did of his and Lily's.

He had never been a carpenter, any more than he had been a gardener, but he knew his work was good, and he did not care where the skill came from. He knew he could look at the things he wished to do here and understand how best to do them, and that was enough. He slept the nights through peacefully and dreamlessly.

A few days after the gift of the jacket Jolin said to him, "The leather worker of our village is a good man and clever. He owes us for his wife's illness last winter; it would please – us – if you would let him make you a pair of boots." His old boots, accustomed to nothing more arduous than the chafing of stirrup and stirrup-leather, had never, even in their young days, been intended for the sort of work he was lately requiring of them. He looked at them ruefully, stretched out toward the fire's flickering light, the dark green cuffs winking above them, and Karla's long furry red tail curling and uncurling above the cuffs.

He went into the village the next day. He understood, from the careful but polite greetings he received that the knowledge of Jolin's new hired man had gone before him; and he also understood that no more than his skill with spade and hammer had gone into the tale. There was no one he met who had the skill to recognize a mage-mark, nor was there any suspicion,

97

besides the wary observation of a stranger expected to prove himself one way or another, that he was anything more or less than an itinerant labourer. The boot-maker quietly took his measurements and asked him to return in a week.

Another week, he thought, and was both glad and afraid. It was during that week that he finished the paddock for the horses. He wanted to a build a larger shed to store hay; for there was hay enough in the meadowland around Jolin's house to keep all the livestock – even a second horse, he thought distantly – all the winter, if there were more room for it than the low loft over the small barn.

In a week he went back to fetch his boots: they were heavy, hard things, a farmer's boots, and for a moment they appalled him, till he saw the beauty of them. He thanked their maker gravely, and did not know the man was surprised by his tone: farmers, hired men, took their footgear for granted; he had long since learned to be proud of his craft for its own sake. And so he was the first of the villagers to wonder if perhaps there was more to Jolin's hired man – other than the fact, well mulled over all through Rhungill, that Jolin had never before in over twenty years been moved to hire anyone for more than a day's specific job – than met the eye. But he had no guess of the truth.

Sahath asked the boot-maker if there was someone who sold dry planking, for he had all but used Lily and Jolin's small store of it, till now used only for patching up after storms and hard winter weather. There were several such men, and because the leather-worker was pleased at the compliment Sahath paid him, he recommended one man over the others. Sahath, unknowing, went to that man, who had much fine wood of just the sort Sahath wanted; but when he asked a price the man looked at him a long moment and said, "No charge, as you do good work for them; you may have as much as you need as you go on for them. There are those of us know what we owe them." The man's name was Armar.

Sahath went in his heavy boots to the house he had begun in secret to call home. He let no hint of the cost to his pride his workman's hire of sturdy boots had commanded; but still Jolin's quick eyes caught him staring at the calluses on his long-fingered hands, and guessed something of what he was thinking.

A week after he brought his boots home he began the hay shed. He also began to teach Lily and Jolin their letters. He had pen and paper in his saddlebags, and a wax tablet that had once been important in a mage's work. When he first took it out of its satchel he had stood long with it in his hands; but it was silent, inert, a tool like a hammer was a tool and nothing more. He brought it downstairs, and whittled three styluses from bits of firewood.

"If you learn to write," he said, humbly, to Jolin, "Lily may speak to you as well as she may speak to any wandering – mage." It was all the explanation he gave, laying the pale smooth tablet down on the shining golden wood of the table; and Jolin realized, when he smiled uncertainly at her and then turned to look wistfully at Lily, that he did love her dearer-than-daughter, but that nothing of that love had passed between them. Jolin had grown fond of the quiet, weary man who was proving such a good landsman, fond enough of him that it no longer hurt her to see him wearing her husband's old clothes which she herself had patched for his longer frame, and so she thought, why does he not tell her? She looked at them as they looked at each other, and knew why, for the hopelessness was as bright in their eyes as the love. Jolin looked away unhappily, for she understood too that there was no advice she could give them that they would listen to. But she could whisper charms that they permit themselves to see what was, and not blind themselves with blame for what they lacked. Her lips moved.

Each evening after that the two women sat on either side of him and did their lessons as carefully as the students of his mage-master had ever done theirs, although they had been learning words to crack the world and set fire to the seas. Sahath copied the letters of the alphabet out plainly and boldly, onto a piece of stiff parchment, and Jolin pinned it to the front of the cupboard, where his two students might look at it often during the day.

Spring turned to summer, and Sahath's boots were no longer new, and he had three more shirts and another pair of trousers. The last shirt and trousers were made for him, not merely made over, and the first shirt had to be patched at the elbows. The goats produced two pairs of kids, which would be sold at the fall auction in Teskip. Summer began to wane, and Sahath began to wander around the house at twilight, after work and before supper, staring at the bottles of herbs, the basket of scraps from which Jolin made her sachets; and outside in the garden, staring at the fading sun and the lengthening shadows.

Jolin thought, with a new fear at her heart, he will be leaving us soon. What of Lily? And even without thought of Lily she felt sorrow.

Lily too watched him pacing, but she said nothing at all; and what her thoughts were neither Jolin nor Sahath wished to guess.

One evening when Lily was gone to attend a sick baby, Sahath said, with the uneasy abruptness Jolin had not heard since he had asked one morning months ago if there was any work for a simple man's strength: "It is possible that I know someone who could give Lily her voice. Would you let her travel away with me, on my word that I would protect her dearer than my own life?"

Jolin shivered, and laid her sewing down in her lap. "What is this you speak of?"

Sahath was silent a moment, stroking grey tabby Annabelle. "My old master. I have not seen him since I first began – my travels; even now I dread going back . . ." So much he could say after several months of farmer's labour and the companionship of two women. "He is a mage almost beyond the knowing of the rest of us, even his best pupils." He swallowed, for he had been one of these. "But he knows many things. I – I know Lily, I think, well enough to guess that her voice is something my master should be able to give her."

Jolin stared unblinking into the fire till the heat of it drew tears. "It is not my decision. We will put it to Lily. If she wishes to go with you, then she shall go."

Lily did not return till the next morning, and she found her two best friends as tired and sleepless-looking as she felt herself, and she looked at them with surprise. "Sahath said something last night that you need to hear," said Jolin; but Sahath did not raise his heavy eyes from his tea-cup.

"His – mage-master – may be able to give you your voice. Will you go with him, to seek this wizard?"

Lily's hands were shaking as she set her basket on the table. She pursed her lips, but no sound emerged. She licked her lips nervously and whistled: "I will go."

They set out two days later. It was a quiet two days; Lily did not even answer the birds when they spoke to her. They left when dawn was still grey over the trees. Jolin and Lily embraced for a long time before the older woman put the younger one away from her and said, "You go on now. Just don't forget to come back."

Lily nodded, then shook her head, then nodded again and smiled tremulously.

"I'll tell your parents you've gone away for a bit, never fear."

Lily nodded once more, slowly, then turned away to mount her little bay horse. Sahath was astride already, standing a little away from the two women, staring at the yellow fingers of light pushing the grey away; he looked down startled when Jolin touched his knee. She swallowed, tried to speak, but no words came, and her fingers dug into his leg. He covered her hand with his and squeezed; when she looked up at him he smiled, and finally she smiled back; then turned away and left them. Lily watched the house door close behind her dearest friend, and sat immobile, staring at the place where Jolin had disappeared, till Sahath sent his horse forward. Lily awoke from her reverie, and sent the little bay after the tall black horse. Sahath heard the gentle hoofbeats behind him, and turned to smile encouragement; and Lily, looking into his face, realized that he had not been sure, even until this moment, if she would follow him or not. She smiled in return, a smile of reassurance. Words, loose and flimsy as smoke, drifted into Sahath's mind: *I keep my promises.* But he did not know what she had read in his face, and he shook his head to clear it of the words that were not meant for him.

No villager would have mistaken Sahath for a workman now, in the dark tunic and cloak he had worn when he first met Lily, riding his tall black horse; the horse alone was too fine a creature for anyone but a man of rank. For all its obvious age, for the bones of its face showed starkly through the skin, it held its crest and tail high, and set its feet down as softly as if its master were made of eggshells. Lily, looking at the man beside her on his fine horse, and looking back to the pricked ears of her sturdy, reliable mount, was almost afraid of her companion, as she had been afraid when he first spoke in her mind, and as she had not been afraid again for many weeks.

Please, Sahath said now. *Do not fear me: I am the man who hammered his fingers till they were blue and black, and cursed himself for clumsiness till the birds fled the noise; and stuck his spade into his own foot and yelped with pain. You know me too well to fear me.*

Lily laughed, and the silent chime of her laughter rang in his mind as she tipped her chin back and grinned at the sky.

And I am the girl who cannot spell.

You do very well.

Not half as well as Jolin.

Jolin is special.

Yes. And their minds fell away from each other, and each disappeared into private thoughts.

They rode south and west. Occasionally they stopped in a town for supplies, but they slept always under the stars, for Lily's dread of strangers and Sahath's uneasiness that any suspicion rest on her for travelling thus alone with him: and he a man past his prime and she a beauty. Their pace was set by Lily's horse, who was willing enough, but unaccustomed to long days of travelling; though it was young and Sahath's horse was old. But it quickly grew hard, and when they reached the great western mountains both horses strode up the slopes without trouble.

It grew cold near the peaks, but Sahath had bought them fur cloaks at the last town; no one lived in the mountains. Lily looked at hers uncertainly, and wished to ask how it was Sahath always had money for what he wished to buy. But she did not quite ask, and while he heard the question anyway, he chose not to answer.

They wandered among the mountain crests, and Lily became totally confused, for sometimes they rode west and south and sometimes east and north; and then there was a day of fog, and the earth seemed to spin around her, and even her stolid practical horse had trouble finding its footing. Sahath said, *There is only a little more of this until we are clear*, and Lily thought he meant something more than the words simply said; but again she did not ask. They dismounted and led the horses, and Lily timidly reached for a fold of Sahath's sleeve, for the way was wide enough that they might walk abreast. When he felt her fingers he seized her hand in his, and briefly he raised it to his lips and kissed it, and then they walked on hand in hand.

That night there was no sunset, but when they woke in the morning the sky was blue and cloudless, and they lay in a hollow at the edge of a sandy shore that led to a vast lake; and the mountains were behind them.

They followed the shore around the lake, and Lily whistled

to the birds she saw, and few of them dropped out of the sky to sit on Lily's head and shoulders and chirp at her.

What do the birds say to you? said Sahath, a little jealously.

Oh – small things, replied Lily, a little at a loss; she had never tried to translate one friend for another before. *It is not easy to say. They say this is a good place, but –* she groped for a way to explain *– different.*

Sahath smiled. *I am glad of the good and I know of the different, for we are almost to the place we seek.*

They turned away from the lake at last, onto a narrow track; but they had not gone far when a meadow opened before them. There were cows and horses in the meadow; they raised their heads to eye the strangers as they passed. Lily noticed there was no fence to enclose the beasts, although there was an open stable at the far edge of the field; this they rode past. A little way farther and they came to an immense stone hall with great trees closed around it, except for a beaten space at its front doors. This space was set round with pillars, unlit torches bound to their tops. A man sat alone on one of the stone steps leading to the hall doors; he was staring idly into nothing, but Lily was certain that he knew of their approach – and had known since long before he had seen or heard them – and was awaiting their arrival.

Greetings, said Sahath, as his horse's feet touched the bare ground.

The man brought his eyes down from the motes of air he had been watching and looked at Sahath and smiled. *Greetings,* he replied, and his mindspeech sounded in Lily's head as well as Sahath's. Lily clung to Sahath's shadow and said nothing, for the man's one word *greetings* had echoed into immeasurable distances, and she was dizzy with them.

This is my master, Sahath said awkwardly, and Lily ducked her head once and glanced at the man. He caught her reluctant eye and smiled, and Lily freed her mind enough to respond:

Greetings.

That's better, said the man. His eyes were blue, and his hair was blond and curly; if it were not for the aura of power about him that hung shivering like a cloak from his head and shoulders he would have been an unlikely figure for a mage-master.

What did you expect, came his thought, amused, *an ancient with a snowy beard and piercing eyes – in a flowing black shroud and pointed cap?*

Lily smiled in spite of herself. *Something like that.*

The man laughed: it was the first vocal sound any of the three had yet made. He stood up. He was tall and narrow, and he wore a short blue tunic over snug brown trousers and tall boots. Sahath had dismounted, and Lily looked at the two of them standing side by side. For all the grey in Sahath's hair, and the heavy lines in his face, she could see the other man was much the elder. Sahath was several inches shorter than his master, and he looked worn and ragged from travel, and Lily's heart went out in a rush to him. The blond man turned to her at once: *You do not have to defend him from me*; and Sahath looked between them puzzled. And Lily, looking into their faces, recognized at last the mage-mark, and knew that she would know it again if she ever saw it in another face. And she was surprised that she had not recognized it as such long since in Sahath's face, and she wondered why; and the blond man flicked another glance at her, and with the glance came a little gust of amusement, but she could not hear any words in it.

After a pause Sahath said, *You will know why we have come.*

I know. Come; you can turn your horses out with the others; they will not stray. Then we will talk.

The hall was empty but for a few heavy wooden chairs and a tall narrow table at the far end, set around a fireplace. Lily looked around her, tipping her head back till her neck creaked in protest, lagging behind the two men as they went purpose-fully toward the chairs. She stepped as softly as she might, and her soft-soled boots made no more noise than a cat's paws; yet as she approached the centre of the great hall she stopped and shivered, for the silence pressed in on her as if it were a guardian. *What are you doing here? Why have you come to this place?* She wrapped her arms around her body, and the silence seized her the more strongly: *How dare you walk the hall of the mage-master?*

Her head hurt; she turned blindly back toward the open door and daylight, and the blue sky. Almost sobbing, she said to the silence: *I come for vanity, for vanity, I should not be here, I have no right to walk in the hall of the mage-master.*

But as she stretched out her hands toward the high doors, a bird flew through them: a little brown bird that flew in swoops, his wings closing briefly against his sides after every beat; and he perched on one of her out-flung hands. He opened his beak, and three notes fell out; and the guardian silence withdrew slightly, and Lily could breathe again. He jumped from Lily's one hand to the other and she, awed, cupped her hands around him. He cocked his head and stared at her with one onyx-chip eye and then the other. The top of his head was rust-coloured, and there were short streaks of cinnamon at the corner of each black eye. He offered her the same three notes, and this time she pursed her lips and gently gave them back to him. She had bent her body over her cupped hands, and now she straightened up, and after a pause of one breath, threw her head back, almost as if she expected it to strike against something; but whatever had been there had fled entirely. The bird hopped up her wrist to her arm, to her shoulder; and then he flew up, straight up, without swooping, till he perched on the sill of one of the high windows, and he tossed his three notes back down to her again. Then two more small brown birds flew through the doors, and passed Lily so closely that her hair stirred with the wind of their tiny wings; and they joined their fellow on the window sill. There were five birds after them, and eight after that; till the narrow sills of the tall windows were full of them and of their quick sharp song. And Lily turned away from the day-filled doorway, back to the dark chairs at the farther end of the hall, where the men awaited her.

The blond man looked long at her as she came up to him; but it was not an unkind look. She smiled timidly at him, and he put out a hand and touched her black hair. *There have been those who were invited into my hall who could not pass the door.*

Sahath's face was pale. *I did not know that I brought her —*

Into danger? finished the mage-master. *Then you have forgotten much that you should have remembered.*

Sahath's face had been pale, but at the master's words it went white, corpse-white, haggard with memory. *I have forgotten everything.*

The mage-master made a restless gesture. *That is not true; it has never been true; and if you wish to indulge in self-pity you must do it somewhere other than here.*

Sahath turned away from the other two, slowly, as if he were an old, old man; and if Lily had had any voice she would have cried out. But when she stepped forward to go to him, the master's hand fell on her shoulder, and she stopped where she stood, although she ached with stillness.

Sahath, the master went on more gently, *you were among the finest of any of my pupils. There was a light about you that few of the others could even see from their dullness, though those I chose to teach were the very best. Among them you shone like a star.*

Lily, the master's hand still on her shoulder, began to see as he spoke a brightness form about Sahath's hands, a shiningness, an almost-mist about his feet, that crept up his legs, as if the master's words lay around him, built themselves into a wall or a ladder to reach him, for the master's wisdom to climb, and to creep into his ear.

Sahath flung out a hand and brightness flickered and flaked away from it, and a mote or two drifted to Lily's feet. She stooped, and touched the tips of two fingers to them, the mage-master's hand dropping away from her shoulder as she knelt. She raised her hand, and the tips of her first and third fingers glimmered.

I was the best of your pupils once, Sahath said bitterly, and the bitterness rasped at the minds that heard him. *But I did not learn what I needed most to learn; my own limits. And I betrayed myself, and your teaching, my master, and I have wandered many years since then, doing little, for little there is that I am able to do. With my mage-strength gone, my learning is of no use, for all that I know is the use of mage-strength.* He spread his hands, straightening the fingers violently as though he hated them; and then he made them into fists and shook them as if he held his enemy's life within them.

And more flakes of light fell from him and scattered, and Lily crept, on hands and knees, nearer him, and picked them up on the tips of her fingers, till all ten fingers glowed; and the knees of her riding dress shone, and when she noticed this she lay her hands flat on the stone floor, till the palms and the finger-joints gleamed. As she huddled, bent down, her coil of hair escaped its last pins and the long braid of it fell down, and its tip skittered against the stones, and when she raised her head again the black braid-tip was star-flecked.

The mage-master's eyes were on the girl as he said: *You betrayed nothing, but your own sorrow robbed you by the terrible choice you had to make, standing alone on that mountain. You were too young to have had to make that choice; I would have been there had I known, but I was too far away, and I saw what would happen too late. You saw what had to be done, and you had the strength to do it — that was your curse. And when you had done it, you left your mage-strength where you stood, for the choice had been too hard a one, and you were sickened with it. And you left, and I — I could not find you, for long and long* . . . there was a weight of sorrow as bitter as Sahath's in his thought, and Lily sat where she was, cupping her shining hands in her lap and looking up at him, while his eyes still watched her. She thought, but it was a very small thought: *The silence was right — I should not be here.*

It was a thought not meant to be overheard, but the blond man's brows snapped together and he shook his head once, fiercely; and she dropped her eyes to her starry palms, and yet she was comforted.

I did not leave my mage-strength, said Sahath, still facing away from his master, and the girl sitting at his feet; but as his arms dropped to his sides, the star-flakes fell down her back and across her spreading skirts.

I am your master still, the blond man said, and his thought was mild and gentle again, *And I say to you that you turned your back on it and me and left us. Think you that you could elude me — me? — for so long had you not the wisdom I taught you — and the strength to make yourself invisible to my far-seeing? I have not known what came to you since you left that mountain with the armies dying at its feet, till you spoke of me to two women in a small bright kitchen far from here. In those long years I have known nothing of you but that you lived, for your death you could not have prevented me from seeing.*

In the silence nothing moved but the tiny wings of birds.

Sahath turned slowly around.

Think you so little of the art of carpentry that you believe any man who holds a hammer in his hand for the first time may build a shed that does not fall down, however earnest his intentions — and however often he bangs his thumb and curses?

Lily saw Sahath's feet moving toward her from the corner of her eye, and lifted her face to look at him, and he looked down at her, dazed. *Lily* – he said, and stooped, but the mage-master was there before him, and took Lily's hands, and drew her to her feet. Sahath touched the star-flakes on her shoulders, and then looked at his hands, and the floor around them where the star-flakes lay like fine sand. "I – " he said, and his voice broke.

The mage-master held Lily's hands still, and now he drew them up and placed them, star-palms in, against her own throat; and curled her fingers around her neck, and held them there with his own long-fingered hands. She stared up at him, and his eyes reminded her of the doors of his hall, filled with daylight; and she felt her own pulse beating in her throat against her hands. Then the master drew his hands and hers away, and she saw that the star-glitter was gone from her palms. He dropped her hands, smiling faintly, and stepped back.

The air whistled strangely as she sucked it into her lungs and blew it out again. She opened her mouth and closed it, raised one hand to touch her neck with her fingers, yet she could find nothing wrong. She swallowed, and it made her throat tickle; and then she coughed. As she coughed she looked down at the dark hem of her riding dress; the star-flakes were gone from it too, and the dust of them had blown away or sunk into the floor. She coughed again, and the force of it shook her whole body, and hurt her throat and lungs; but then she opened her mouth again when the spasm was past and said, "Sahath." It was more a croak, or a bird's chirp, than a word; but she looked up, and turned towards him, and said "Sahath" again, and it was a word this time. But as her eyes found him she saw the tears running down his face.

He came to her, and she raised her arms to him; and the mage-master turned his back on them and busied himself at the small high table before the empty hearth. Lily heard the chink of cups as she stood encircled by Sahath's arms, her dark head on his dark-cloaked shoulder, and the taste of his tears on her lips. She turned at the sound, and looked over her shoulder; the master held a steaming kettle in his hands, and she could smell the heat of it, although the hearth was as black as before. Sahath looked up at his old teacher when Lily stirred; and the mage-master turned toward them again, a cup in each hand. Sahath laughed.

The mage-master grinned and inclined his head. "School-boy stuff, I know," but he held the cups out toward them nonetheless. Lily reached out her left hand and Sahath his right, so that their other two hands might remain clasped together.

Whatever the steaming stuff was it cleared their heads and smoothed their faces, and Lily said, "Thank you," and smiled joyfully. Sahath looked at her and said nothing, and the blond man looked at them both, and then down into his cup. "You know this place," the mage-master said presently, raising his eyes again to Sahath's shining face; "You are as free in it now as you were years ago, when you lived here as my pupil." And he left them, setting his cup down on the small table and striding away down the hall, out into the sunlight. His figure was silhouetted a moment, framed by the stone doorsill; and then he was gone. The small brown birds sang farewell.

It was three days before Lily and Sahath saw him again. For those three days they wandered together through the deep woods around the master's hall, feeling the kindly shade curling around them; or lifting their faces to the sun when they walked along the shores of the lake. Lily learned to sing and to shout. She loved to stand at the edge of the lake, her hands cupped around her mouth, that her words might fly as far as they could across the listening water; but though she waited till the last far whisper had gone, she never had an answer. Sahath also taught her to skip small flat stones across the silver surface; she had never seen water wider than a river before, and the rivers of her acquaintance moved on about their business much too swiftly for any such game. She became a champion rock-skipper, anything less than eight skittering steps across the water before the small missile sank, and she would shout and stamp with annoyance, and Sahath would laugh at her. His stones always fled lightly and far across the lake.

"You're *helping* them," she accused him.

"And what if I am?" he teased her, grinning.

"It's not *fair*."

III

The grin faded, and he looked at her thoughtfully. He picked up another small flat stone and balanced it in his hand. "You want to lift it as you throw it – lift it up again each time it strikes the water . . ." He threw, and the rock spun and bounded far out toward the centre of the lake; they did not see where it finally disappeared.

Sahath looked at Lily. "You try."

"I – " But whatever she thought of saying, she changed her mind, found a stone to her liking, tossed it once or twice up and down in her hand, and then flicked it out over the water. They did not notice the green-crested black bird flying low over the lake, for they were counting the stone's skips; but on the fourteenth skip the bird seized the small spinning stone in its talons, rose high above the water, and set out to cross the lake.

At last the bird's green crest disappeared, and they could not make out one black speck from the haze that seemed always to muffle the farther shore.

The nights they spent in each other's arms, sleeping in one of the long low rooms that opened off each side of the mage-master's hall, where there were beds and blankets as if he had occasion to play host to many guests. But they saw no one but themselves.

The fourth morning they awoke and smelled cooking; instead of the cold food and kindling they had found awaiting their hunger on previous days, the mage-master was there, bent over a tiny red fire glittering fiercely out of the darkness of the enormous hearth at the far end of the great hall. He was toasting three thick slices of bread on two long slender sticks. When they approached him he gravely handed the stick with two slices on it to Lily. They had stewed fruit with their toast, and milk from one of the master's cows, with the cream floating in thick whorls on top.

"It is time to decide your future," said the mage-master, and Lily sighed.

"Is it true that Sahath might have cured me – himself – at any time – without our having come here at all?" Her voice was still low and husky as if with disuse, but the slightly anxious tone of the query removed any rudeness it might have otherwise held.

The blond man smiled. "Yes and no. I think I may claim some credit as an – er – catalyst."

Sahath stirred in his chair, for they were sitting around the small fire, which snapped and hissed and sent a determined thread of smoke up the vast chimney.

"Sahath always was pig-headed," the master continued. "It was something of his strength and much of his weakness."

Sahath said, "And what comes to your pig-headed student now?"

"What does he wish to come to him?" his old teacher responded, and both men's eyes turned to Lily.

"Jolin is waiting for – us," Lily said. The *us* had almost been a *me*: both men had seen it quivering on her lips, and both noticed how her voice dropped away to nothing when she said *us* instead.

The mage-master leaned forward and poked the fire thoughtfully with his toasting stick; it snarled and threw a handful of sparks at him. "There is much I could teach you," he said tentatively. Lily looked up at him, but his eyes were on the fire, which was grumbling to itself; then she looked at Sahath by her side. "No," said the master. "Not just Sahath: both of you. There is much strength in you, Lily; too much perhaps for the small frame of a baby to hold, and so your voice was left behind. You've grown into it since; I can read it in your face.

"And Sahath," he said, and raised his eyes from the sulky fire to his old pupil's face. "You have lost nothing but pride and sorrow – and perhaps a little of the obstinacy. I – there is

113

much use for one such as you. There is much use for the two of you." He looked at them both, and Lily saw the blue eyes again full of daylight; and when they were turned full on her she blinked.

"I told Jolin I would not forget to come back," she said, and her voice was barely above a whisper. "I am a healer; there is much use for me at my home."

"I am a healer too," said the mage-master, and his eyes held her, till she broke from him by standing up and running from the hall; her feet made no more noise than a bird's.

Sahath said: "I have become a farmer and a carpenter, and it suits me; I am become a lover, and would have a wife. I have no home but hers, but I have taken hers and want no other. Jolin waits for us: for both of us; and I would we return to her together." Sahath stood up slowly; the master sat, the stick still in his hands, and watched him till he turned away and slowly followed Lily.

I hold no one against his will, the master said to his retreating back; *but your lover does not know what she is refusing, and you do know. You might – some day – tell her why it is possible to make rocks fly.*

On the next morning Lily and Sahath departed from the stone hall and the mist-obscured lake. The mage-master saw them off. He and Sahath embraced; and Lily thought, watching, that Sahath looked younger and the master older than either had five days before. The master turned to her, and held out his hands, but uncertainly. She thought he expected her not to touch them, and she stepped forward and seized them strongly, and he smiled down at her, the morning sun blazing in his yellow hair. "I would like to meet your Jolin," he said; and Lily said impulsively, "Then you must visit us."

The master blinked; his eyes were as dark as evening, and Lily realized that she had surprised him. "Thank you," he said.

"You will be welcome in our home," she replied; and the daylight seeped slowly into his eyes again. "What is your name?" she asked, before her courage failed her.

"Luthe," he said.

Sahath had mounted already; Lily turned from the mage-master and mounted her horse, who sighed when her light weight settled in the saddle; it had had a pleasant vacation, knee-deep in sweet grass at the banks of the lake. Lily and Sahath both looked down at the man they had come so far to see; he raised a hand in farewell. Silently he said to them: *I am glad to have seen you again, Sahath, and glad to have met you, Lily.*

Lily said silently back: *We shall meet again perhaps.*

The mage-master made no immediate answer, and they turned away, and their horses walked down the path that bordered the clearing before the hill; and just as they stepped into the shade of the trees his words took shape in their minds: *I think it very likely.* Lily, riding second, turned to look back before the trees held him from view; his face was unreadable below the burning yellow hair.

They had an easy journey back, no rain fell upon them and no wind chilled them, and the mountain fog seemed friendly and familiar, with nothing they need fear hidden within it, and the birds still came to Lily when she whistled to them.

They were rested and well, and anxious to be home, and they travelled quickly. It was less than a fortnight after Lily had seen the mage-master standing before his hall to bid them farewell that they turned off the main road from the village of Rhungill into a deep cutting that led into the fields above Jolin's house. As Lily's head rose above the tall golden grasses she could see the speck of colour that was Jolin's red skirt and blue apron, standing quietly on the doorstep of the house, with the white birches at one side, and her herb garden spread out at her feet.

Lily's horse, pleased to be home at last, responded eagerly to a request for speed, and Sahath's horse cantered readily at its heels. They drew up at the edge of the garden, where Jolin had run to meet them. Lily dismounted hastily and hugged her.

"You see, we remembered to come back," she said.

Dragon Reserve, Home Eight

Dragon Reserve, Home Eight

Diana Wynne Jones

Where to begin? Neal and I had had a joke for years about a little green van coming to carry me off – this was when I said anything more than usually mad – and now it was actually happening. Mother and I stood at my bedroom window watching the van bouncing up the track between the dun green hills, and neither of us smiled. It wasn't a farm van, and most of our neighbours visit on horseback anyway. Before long, we could see it was dark green with a silver dragon insigne on the side.

"It *is* the Dragonate," Mother said. "Siglin, there's nothing I can do." It astonished me to hear her say that. Mother only comes up to my shoulder, but she held her land and our household, servants, Neal and me, and all three of her husbands, in a hand like iron, *and* she drove out to plough or harvest if one of my fathers was ill. "They said the dragons would take you," she said. "I should have seen. You think Orm informed on you?"

"I know he did," I said. "It was my fault for going into the Reserve."

"I'll blood an axe on him," Mother said, "one of these days. But I can't do it over this. The neighbours would say he was quite right." The van was turning between the stone walls of the farmyard now. Chickens were squirting and flapping out of its way and our sheepdog pups were barking their heads off. I could see Neal upon the wash-house roof watching yearningly. It's a good place to watch from because you can hide behind the chimney. Mother saw Neal too. "Siglin," she said, "don't let on Neal knows about you."

"No," I said. "Nor you either."

"Say as little as you can, and wear the old blue dress – it makes you look younger," Mother said, turning towards the door. "You might just get off. Or they might just have come about something else," she added. The van was stopping outside the front door now, right underneath my window. "I'd best go and greet them," Mother said, and hurried downstairs.

While I was forcing my head through the blue dress, I heard heavy boots on the steps and a crashing knock at the door. I shoved my arms into the sleeves, in too much of a hurry even to feel indignant about the dress. It makes me look about twelve and I am nearly grown up! At least, I was fourteen quite a few weeks ago now. But Mother was right. If I looked too immature to have awakened, they might not question me too hard. I hurried to the head of the stairs while I tied my hair with a childish blue ribbon. I knew they had come for me, but I had to *see*.

They were already inside when I got there, a whole line of tall men tramping down the stone hallway in the half-dark, and Mother was standing by the closed front door as if they had swept her aside. What a lot of them, just for me! I thought. I got a weak, sour feeling and could hardly move for horror. The man at the front of the line kept opening the doors all down the hallway, calm as you please, until he came to the main parlour at the end. "This room will do nicely," he said. "Out you get, you." And my oldest father, Timas, came shuffling hurriedly out in his slippers, clutching a pile of accounts and looking scared and worried. I saw Mother fold her arms. She always does when she is angry.

Another of them turned to Mother. "We'll speak to you first," he said, "and your daughter after that. Then we want the rest of the household. Don't any of you try to leave." And they went into the parlour with Mother and shut the door.

They hadn't even bothered to guard the doors. They just assumed we would obey them. I was shaking as I walked back to my room, but it was not terror any more. It was rage. I mean – we have all been brought up to honour the Dragonate. They are the cream of the men of the Ten Worlds. They are supposed to be gallant and kind and dedicated and devote their lives to keeping us safe from Thrallers, not to speak of maintaining justice, law and order all over the Ten Worlds. Dragonate men swear that Oath of Alienation, which means they can never have homes or families like ordinary people. Up to then, I'd felt sorry for them for that. They give up so much. But now I saw they felt it gave them the right to behave as if the rest of us were not real people. To walk in as if they owned our house. To order Timas out of his own parlour. Oh I was angry!

I don't know how long Mother was in the parlour. I was so angry it felt like seconds until I heard flying feet and Neal hurried into my room. 'They want you now.'

I stood up and took some of my anger out on poor Neal. I said, "Do you still want to join the Dragonate? Swear that stupid Oath? Behave like you own the Ten Worlds?"

It was mean. Neal looked at the floor. "They said straight away," he said. Of course he wanted to join. Every boy does, particularly on Sveridge, where women own most of the land. I swept down the stairs, angrier than ever. All the doors in the hallway were open and our people were standing in them, staring. The two housemen were at the dining-room door, the cattlewoman and two farmhands were looking out of the kitchen, and the stableboy and the second shepherd were craning out of the pantry. I thought, They still will be my people some day! I refuse to be frightened! My fathers were in the doorway of the bookroom. Donal and Yan were in work-clothes and had obviously rushed in without taking their boots off. I gave them what I hoped was a smile, but only Timas smiled back. They all know! I thought as I opened the parlour door.

There were only five of them, sitting facing me across our

best table. Five was enough. All of them stood up as I came in. The room seemed full of towering green uniforms. It was not at all like I expected. For one thing, the media always shows Dragonate as fair and dashing and handsome, and none of these were. For another, the media had led me to expect uniforms with big silver panels. These were all plain green, and four of them had little silver stripes on one shoulder.

"Are you Sigrid's daughter Siglin?" asked the one who had opened all the doors. He was a bleached, pious type like my father Donal and his hair was dust-colour.

"Yes," I said rudely. "Who are you? Those aren't Dragonate uniforms."

"Camerati, lady," said one who was brown all over with wriggly hair. He was young, younger than my father Yan, and he smiled cheerfully, like Yan does. But he made my stomach go cold. Camerati are the crack force, cream of the Dragonate. They say a man has to be a genius even to be considered for it.

"Then what are you doing here?" I said. "And why are you all standing up?"

The one in the middle, obviously the chief one, said, "We always stand up when a lady enters the room. And we are here because we were on a tour of inspection at Holmstad anyway, and there was a Slaver scare on this morning. So we offered to take on civic duties for the regular Dragonate. Now if that answers your questions, let me introduce us all." He smiled too, which twisted his white, crumpled face like a demon mask. "I am Lewin, and I'm Updriten here. On your far left is Driten Palino, our recorder." This was the pious type, who nodded. "Next to him is Driten Renick of Law Wing." Renick was elderly and iron-grey, with one of those necks that look like a chicken's leg. He just stared. "Underdriten Terens is on my left, my aide and witness." That was brown-and-wriggly. "And beyond him is Cadet Alectis, who is travelling with us to Home Nine."

Alectis looked a complete baby, only a year older than me, with pink cheeks and sandy hair. He and Terens both bowed and smiled so politely that I nearly smiled back. Then I realised that they were treating me as if I was a visitor. In my own home! I bowed freezingly, the way Mother usually does to Orm.

"Please sit down, Siglin," Lewin said politely.

I nearly didn't, because that might keep them standing up too. But they were all so tall I'd already got a crick in my neck. So I sat grandly on the chair they'd put ready facing the table. "Thank you," I said. "You are a very kind host, Updriten Lewin." To my great joy, Alectis went bright red at that, but the other four simply sat down too. Pious Palino took up a memo block and poised his fingers over its keys. This seemed to be in case the recorder in front of Lewin went wrong. Lewin set that going. Wriggly Terens leaned over and passed me another little square box.

"Keep this in your hand," he said, "or your answers may not come out clearly."

I caught the words *lie detector* from his wriggly head as clearly as if he had said them aloud. I don't think I showed how very scared I was, but my hand made the box wet almost straight away.

"Court is open," Lewin said to the recorder. "Presiding Updriten Lewin." He gave a string of numbers and then said, "First hearing starts on charges against Siglin, of Upland Holding, Wormstow, North Sveridge on Home Eight, accused of being heg and heg concealing its nature. Questions begin. Siglin, are you clear what being heg is?" He crumpled one eyebrow upwards at me.

"No," I said. After all, no one has told me in so many words. It's just a thing people whisper and shudder at.

"Then you'd better understand this," Lewin said. He really was the ugliest and most outlandish of the five. Dragonate men are never posted to the world of their birth, and I thought

Lewin must come from one a long way off. His hair was black, so black it had blue lights, but, instead of being dark all over to match it, like wriggly Terens, he was a lot whiter than me and his eyes were a most piercing blue – almost the colour they make the sky on the media. "If the charges are proved," he said, "you face death by beheading, since that is the only form of execution a heg cannot survive. Renick – "

Elderly Renick swept sourly in before Lewin had finished speaking. "The law defines a heg as one with human form who is not human. Medical evidence of brain pattern or nerve and muscle deviations is required prior to execution, but for a first hearing it is enough to establish that the subject can perform one or more of the following: mind-reading, kindling fire or moving objects at a distance, healing or killing by the use of the mind alone, surviving shooting, drowning or suffocation, or enslaving or otherwise afflicting the mind of a beast or human."

He had the kind of voice that bores you anyway. I thought, Great gods! I don't think I can do half those things! Maybe I looked blank. Palino stopped clicking his memo block to say, "It's very important to understand why these creatures must be stamped out. They can make people into puppets in just the same way that the Slavers can. Foul." Actually, I think he was explaining to Alectis. Alectis nodded humbly. Palino said, definitely to me, "Slavers do it with those V-shaped collars. You must have seen them on the media. Quite foul."

"We call them Thrallers," I said. Foul or not, I thought, I'm the only one of me I've got! I can't help being made the way I am.

Lewin flapped his hand to shut Palino up and Renick went on again. "A heg is required by law to give itself up for execution. Any normal person who knowingly conceals a heg is likewise liable for execution." Now I knew why Mother had told me to keep Neal out of it.

Then it seemed to be Palino's turn. He said, "Personal details follow. How old are you – er – Sigrun?"

'Sig*lin*,' I said. "Fourteen last month."

Renick stretched out his chicken neck. "In this court's opinion, subject is old enough to have awakened as heg." He looked at Terens.

Terens said, "I witness. Girls awaken early, don't they?"

Palino, tapping away, said, "Mother, Sigrid, also of Upland Holding."

At which Lewin leaned forward. "Cleared by this court," he said. I was relieved to hear that. Mother is clever. She hadn't let them know she knew.

Palino said, "And your father is – ?"

"Timas, Donal and Yan," I said. I had to bite the inside of my cheek not to laugh at how annoyed he was by that.

"Great Tew, girl!" he said. "A person can't have three fathers!"

"Hold it, Palino," said Lewin. "You're up against local customs here. Men outnumber women three to one on Home Eight."

"In Home Eight law, a woman's child is the child of all her husbands equally," Renick put in. "No more anomalous than the status of the Ahrings on Seven really."

"Then tell me how I rephrase my question," Palino said waspishly, "in the light of the primitive customs of Home Eight."

I said, "There's no such place as Home Eight. This world is called Sveridge." Primitive indeed!

Palino gave me a pale glare. I gave him one back. Lewin cut in, smooth and humorous, "You're up against primitive Dragonate custom here, Siglin. We refer to all the worlds by numbers, from Albion, Home One, to Yurov, Home Ten, and the worlds of the Outer Manifold are Cath One, Two, Three and Four to us. Have you really no idea which of your mother's husbands is actually your father?"

After that they all began asking me. Being heg is inherited, and I knew they were trying to find out if any of my fathers was heg too. At length even Alectis joined in, clearing his throat and going very red because he was only a Cadet. "I know we're not supposed to know," he said, "but I bet you've tried to guess. I did. I found out in the end."

That told me he was Sveridge too. And he suddenly wasn't a genius in the Camerati any more, but just a boy. "Then I bet you wished you hadn't!" I said. "My friend Inga at Hillfoot found out, and hers turned out to be the one she's always hated."

"Well," said Alectis, redder still. "Er – it wasn't the one I'd hoped – "

"That's why I've never asked," I said. And that was true. I'd always hoped it was Timas till now. Donal is so moral, and Yan is fun, but he's under Donal's thumb even more than he's under Mother's. But I didn't want my dear old Timas in trouble.

"Well, a cell-test should settle it," Lewin said. "Memo for that, Palino. Terens, remind me to ask how the regular Dragonate usually deal with it. Now – Siglin, this charge was laid against you by a man known as Orm the Worm Warden. Do you know this man?"

"Don't I just!" I said. "He's been coming here and looking through our windows and giggling ever since I can remember! He lives on the Worm Reserve in a shack. Mother says he's a bit wrong in the head, but no one's locked him up because he's so good at managing dragons."

There! I thought. That'll show them you can't trust a word Orm says! But they just nodded. Terens murmured to Alectis, "Sveridge worm, *draco draco*, was adopted as the symbol of the Dragonate – "

"We *have* all heard of dragons," Palino said to him nastily.

Lewin cut in again. I suppose it was his job as presiding Updriten. "Siglin. Orm, in his deposition, refers to an incident in the Worm Reserve last Friday. We want you to tell us what happened then, if anything."

Grim's teeth! I thought. I'd hoped they'd just ask me questions. You can nearly always get round questions without lying. And I'd no idea what Orm had said. "I don't usually go to the Dragon Reserve," I said, "because of being Mother's heir. When I was born, the Fortune Teller said the dragons would take me." I saw Renick and Palino exchange looks of contempt at our primitive customs. But Mother had in a good Teller, and I believe it enough to keep away from the Reserve.

"So why did you go last Friday?" said Lewin.

"Neal dared me to," I said. I couldn't say anything else with a lie detector in my hands. Neal gets on with Orm, and he goes to the Reserve a lot. Up to Friday, he thought I was being silly refusing to go. But the real trouble was that Neal had been there all along, riding Barra beside me on Nellie, and now Lewin had made me mention Neal, I couldn't think how to pretend he hadn't been there. "I rode up behind Wormhill," I said, "and then over the Saddle until we could see the sea. That means you're in the Reserve."

"Isn't the Reserve fenced off at all?" Renick asked disapprovingly.

"No," I said. "Worms – dragons – can fly, so what's the point? They stay in because the shepherds bombard them if they don't, and we all give them so many sheep every month." And Orm makes them stay in, bad cess to him! "Anyway," I said, "I was riding down a kyle – that's what we call those narrow stony valleys – when my horse reared and threw me. Next thing I knew – "

"Question," said Palino. "Where was your brother at this point?"

He *would* spot that! I thought. "Some way behind," I said. Six feet, in fact. Barra is used to dragons and just stood stock-still. "This dragon shuffled head down with its great snout across the kyle," I said. "I sat on the ground with its great amused eye staring at me and listened to Nellie clattering away up the kyle. It was a youngish one, sort of brown-green, which is why I hadn't seen it. They can keep awfully still when they want to. And I said a rude word to it.

" 'That's no way to speak to a dragon!' Orm said. He was sitting on a rock on the other side of the kyle, quite close, laughing at me." I wondered whether to fill the gap in the story where Neal was by telling them that Orm always used to be my idea of Jack Frost when I was little. He used to call at Uplands for milk then, to feed dragon fledglings on, but he was so rude to Mother that he goes to Inga's place now. Orm is long and skinny and brown, with a great white bush of hair and beard, and he smells rather. But they must have smelt him in Holmstad, so I said, "I was scared, because the dragon was so near I could feel the heat off it. And then Orm said, 'You have to speak politely to this dragon. He's my particular friend. You give me a nice kiss, and he'll let you go.' "

I think Lewin murmured something like, "Ah, I thought it might be that!" but it may just have been in his mind. I don't know because I was in real trouble then, trying to pick my way through without mentioning Neal. The little box got so wet it nearly slipped out of my hand. I said, "Every time I tried to get up, Orm beckoned, and the dragon pushed me down with its snout with a gamesome look in its eye. And Orm cackled with laughter. They were both really having fun." This was true, but the dragon also pushed between me and Neal and mantled its wings when Neal tried to help. And Neal said some pretty awful things to Orm. Orm giggled and insulted Neal back. He called Neal a booby who couldn't stand up for himself against women. "Then," I said, "then Orm said I was the image of Mother at the same age — which isn't true: I'm bigger all over — and he said, 'Come on, kiss and be friends!' Then he skipped down from his rock and took hold of my arm — "

I had to stop and swallow there. The really awful thing was that, as soon as Orm had hold of me, I got a strong picture from his mind: Orm kissing a pretty lady smaller than me, with another dragon, an older, blacker one, looking on from the background. And I recognised the lady as Mother, and I was absolutely disgusted.

"So I hit Orm and got up and ran away," I said. "And Orm shouted at me all the time I was running up the kyle and catching Nellie, but I took no notice."

"Question," said Renick. "What action did the dragon take?"

"They – they always chase you if you run, I'd heard," Alectis said shyly.

"And this one appears to have been trained to Orm's command," Palino said.

"It didn't chase me," I said. "It stayed with Orm." The reason was that neither of them could move. I still don't know what I did – I had a picture of myself leaning back inside my own head and swinging mighty blows, the way you do with a pickaxe – and Neal says the dragon went over like a cart-load of potatoes and Orm fell flat on his back. But Orm could speak and he screamed after us that I'd killed the worm and I'd pay for it. But I was screaming too, at Neal, to keep away from me because I was heg. That was the thing that horrified me most. Before that I'd tried not to think I was. After all, for all I knew, everyone can read minds and get a book from the bookcase without getting up from their chair. And Neal told me to pull myself together and think what we were going to tell Mother. We decided to say that we'd met a dragon in the Reserve and I'd killed it and found out I was heg. I made Neal promise not to mention Orm. I couldn't bear even to think of Orm. And Mother was wonderfully understanding, and I really didn't realise that I'd put her in danger as well as Neal.

Lewin looked down at the recorder. "Dragons are a pre-served species," he said. "Orm claims that you caused grievous bodily harm to a dragon in his care. What have you to say to that?"

"How could I?" I said. Oh I was scared. "It was nearly as big as this house."

Renick was on to that at once. "Query," he said. "Prevarication?"

"Obviously," said Palino, clicking away at his block.

"We haven't looked at that dragon yet," Terens said.

"We'll do that on our way back," Lewin said, sighing rather. "Siglin, I regret to say there is enough mismatch between your account and Orm's, and enough odd activity on that brain-measure you hold in your hand, to warrant my taking you to Holmstad Command Centre for further examination. Be good enough to go with Terens and Alectis to the van and wait there while we complete our inquiries here."

I stood up. Everything seemed to drain out of me. I could lam them like I slammed that dragon, I thought. But Holmstad would only send a troop out to see why they hadn't come back. And I put my oldest dress on for nothing! I thought as I walked down the hallway with Terens and Alectis. The doors were all closed. Everyone had guessed. The van smelt of clean plastic and it was very warm and light because the roof was one big window. I sat between Terens and Alectis on the back seat. They pulled straps round us all – safety straps, but they made me feel a true prisoner.

Afer a while, Terens said, "You could sue Orm if the evidence doesn't hold up, you know." I think he was trying to be kind, but I couldn't answer.

After another while, Alectis said, "With respect, Driten, I think suspects should be told the truth about the so-called lie detector."

"Alectis, I didn't hear you say that," Terens said. He pretended to look out of the window, but he must have known I knew he had deliberately thought *lie detector* to me as he passed me the thing. They're told to. Dragonate think of everything. I sat and thought I'd never hated anything so much as I hated our kind, self-sacrificing Dragonate, and I tried to take a last look at the stony yard, tipped sideways on the hill, with our square stone house at the top of it. But it wouldn't register somehow.

Then the front door opened and the other three came out, bringing Neal with them. Behind them, the hall was full of our people, with Mother in front, just staring. I just stared too, while Palino opened the van door and shoved Neal into the seat beside me. "Your brother has admitted being present at the incident," he said as he strapped himself in beside Neal. I could tell he was pleased.

By this time, Lewin and Renick had strapped themselves into the front seat. Lewin drove away without a word. Neal looked back at the house. I couldn't. "Neal – ?" I whispered.

"Just like you said," Neal said, loudly and defiantly. "Behaving as if they own the Ten Worlds. I wouldn't join now if they begged me to!" Why did I have to go and say that to him? "Why did *you* join?" Neal said rudely to Alectis.

"Six brothers," Alectis said, staring ahead.

The other four all started talking at once. Lewin asked Renick the quickest way to the Reserve by road and Renick said it was down through Wormstow. "I hope the dragons eat you!" Neal said. This was while Palino was leaning across us to say to Terens, "Where's our next inspection after this hole?" And Terens said, "We go straight on to Arkloren on Nine. Alectis will get to see some other parts of the Manifold shortly." Behaving as if we didn't exist. Neal shrugged and shut up.

The Dragonate van was much smoother and faster than a farm van. We barely bounced over the stony track that loops down to Hillfoot, and it seemed no time before we were speeding down the better road, with the rounded yellowish Upland Hills peeling past on either side. I love my hills, covered with yellow ling that only grows here on Sveridge, and the soft light of the sun through our white and grey clouds. Renick, still making conversation, said he was surprised to find the hills so old and worn down. "I thought Eight was a close parallel with Seven?" he said.

Lewin answered in a boring voice, "I wouldn't know. I haven't seen Seven since I was a Cadet."

"Oh, the mountains are much higher and greener there," Renick said. "I was posted in Camberia for years. Lovely spot."

Lewin just grunted. Quite a wave of homesickness filled the van. I could feel Renick thinking of Seven and Alectis not wanting to go to Nine. Terens was remembering boating on Romaine when he was Neal's age. Lewin was thinking of Seven, in spite of the grunt. We were coming over Jiot Fell already then, with the Giant Stones standing on top of the world against the sky. A few more turns in the road would bring us out above Wormstow where Neal and I went – used to go – to school. What about me? I was thinking. I'm homesick for life. And Neal. Poor Mother.

Then the air suddenly filled with noise, like the most gigantic sheet being torn.

Lewin said, "What the – ?" and we all stared upwards. A great silvery shape screamed overhead. And another of a fatter shape, more blue than silver, screamed over after it, both of them only just inside the clouds. Alectis put up an astonished pointing arm. "Thraller! The one behind's a Slaver!"

"What's it doing *here*?" said Terens. "Someone must have slipped up."

"Ours was a stratoship!" said Palino. "What's going on?"

A huge ball of fire rolled into being on the horizon, above the Giant Stones. I felt Lewin slam on the brakes. "We got him!" one of them cried out.

"The Slaver got ours," Lewin said. The brakes were still yelling like a she-worm when the blast hit.

I lose the next bit. I start remembering again a few seconds later, sitting up straight with a bruised lip, finding the van round sideways a long way on down the road. In front of me, Renick's straps had broken. He was lying kind of folded against the windscreen. I saw Lewin pull himself upright and pull at Renick. And stop pulling quickly. My ears had gone deaf, because I could only hear Lewin as if he was very far off.

" – hurt in the back?"

Palino looked along the four of us and shouted, "Fine! Is Renick – ?"

"Dead," Lewin shouted back. "Neck broken." He was jiggling furiously at buttons in the controls. My ears started to work again and I heard him say, "Holmstad's not answering. Nor's Ranefell. I'm going back to Holmstad. Fast."

We set off again with a roar. The van seemed to have lost its silencer and it rattled all over, but it went. And how it went. We must have done nearly a hundred down Jiot, squealing on the bends. In barely minutes, we could see Wormstow spread out below, old grey houses and new white ones, and all those imported trees that make the town so pretty. The clouds over the houses seemed to darken and go dense.

"Uh-oh!" said Terens.

The van jolted to another yelling stop. It was not the clouds. Something big and dark was coming down through the clouds, slowly descending over Wormstow. Something enormous. "What *is* that?" Neal and Alectis said together.

"Hedgehog," said Terens.

"A slaveship," Palino explained, sort of mincing the word out to make it mean more. "Are – are we out of range here?"

"I most thoroughly hope so," Lewin said. "There's not much we can do with hand weapons."

We sat and stared as the thing came down. The lower it got, the more Renick's bent-up shape was in my way. I kept wishing Lewin would do something about him, but nobody seemed to be able to think of anything but that huge descending ship. I saw why they call them hedgehogs. It was rounded above and flat beneath, with bits and pieces sticking out all over like bristles. Hideous somehow. And it came and hung squatting over the roofs of the houses below. There it let out a ramp like a long black tongue, right down into the Market Square. Then another into High Street, between the rows of trees, breaking a tree as it passed.

As soon as the ramps touched ground, Lewin started the van and drove down towards Wormstow.

"No, stop!" I said, even though I knew he couldn't. The compulsion those Slavers put out is really strong. Some of it shouts inside your head, like your own conscience through an amplifier, and some of it is gentle and creeping and insidious, like Mother telling you gently to come along now and be sensible. I found I was thinking, Oh well, I'm sure Lewin's right. Tears rolled down Alectis's face, and Neal was sniffing. We had to go to the ship, which was now hanging a little above us. I could see people hurrying out of houses and racing to crowd up the ramp in the Market Square. People I knew. So it must be all right, I thought. The van was having to weave past loose horses that people had been riding or driving. That was how I got a glimpse of the other ramp, through trees and the legs of a horse. Soldiers were pouring down it, running like a muddy river, in waves. Each wave had a little group of kings, walking behind it, directing the soldiers. They had shining crowns and shining Vs on their chests and walked mighty, like gods.

That brought me to my senses. "Lewin," I said. "Those are Thrallers and you're *not* to do what they say, do you hear?" Lewin just drove round a driverless cart, towards the Market Square. He was going to be driving up that ramp in a second. I was so frightened then that I lammed Lewin – not like I lammed the dragon, but in a different way. Again it's hard to describe, except that this time I was giving orders. Lewin was to obey *me*, not the Thrallers, and my orders were to drive away *at once*. When nothing seemed to happen, I got so scared that I seemed to be filling the whole van with my orders.

"Thank you," Lewin said, in a croaking sort of voice. He jerked the van around into Worm Parade and roared down it, away from the ship and the terrible ramps. The swerve sent the van door open with a slam and, to my relief, the body of poor Renick tumbled out into the road.

But everyone else screamed out, "No! What are you doing?" and clutched their heads. The compulsion was far, far worse if you disobeyed. I felt as if layers of my brain were being peeled off with hot pincers. Neal was crying, like Alectis. Terens was moaning. It hurt so much that I filled the van frantically with more and more orders. Lewin made grinding sounds, deep in his throat, and kept on driving away, with the door flapping and banging.

Palino took his straps undone and yelled, "You're going the wrong way, you damn cariarder!" I couldn't stop him at all. He started to climb into the front seat to take the controls away from Lewin. Alectis and Neal both rose up too and shoved him off Lewin. So Palino gave that up and scrambled for the open flapping door instead. Nobody could do a thing. He just jumped out and went rolling in the road. I didn't see what he did then, because I was too busy giving orders, but Neal says he simply scrambled up and staggered back towards the ship and the ramp.

We drove for another horrible half-mile, and then we must have got out of range. Everything suddenly went easy. It was like when somebody lets go the other end of a rope you're both pulling, and you go over backwards. Wham. And I felt too dim and stunned to move.

"Thank the gods!" I heard Terens more or less howl.

"It's Siglin you should be thanking," Lewin said. "Alectis, climb over to the front and shut that door. Then try and raise Holmstad again."

Neal says the door was too battered to shut. Alectis had to hold it with one hand while he worked the broadcaster with the other. I heard him saying that Holmstad still didn't answer through the roaring and rattling the van made when Lewin put on speed up the long looping gradient of Wormjiot. We hadn't nearly got up to the Saddle, when Terens said, "It's going! Aren't they quick!" I looked back, still feeling dim and horrible, in time to see the squatting hedgehog rise up inside the clouds again.

"Now you can thank the gods," Lewin said. "They didn't think we were worth chasing. Try medium wave, Alectis." There is an outcrop of ragged rock near the head of Wormjiot. Lewin drove off the road and stopped behind it while Alectis fiddled with knobs.

Instead of getting dance music and cookery hints, Alectis got a voice that fizzled and crackled. "This is Dragonate Fanejiot, Sveridge South, with an emergency message for all Dragonate units still in action. You are required to make your way to Fanejiot and report there soonest." It said that about seven times, then it said, "We can now confirm earlier reports that Home Nine is in Slaver hands. Here is a list of bases on Home Eight that have been taken by Slavers." It was a long list. Holmstad came quite early on it, and Ranefell about ten names after that.

Lewin reached across and turned it off. "Did someone say we slipped up?" he said. "That was an understatement."

"Fanejiot is two thousand flaming miles from here!" Terens said. "With an ocean and who knows how many Slavers in between!"

"Well put," said Lewin. "Did Palino's memo block go to the Slavers with him?"

It was lying on the back seat beside Neal. Neal tried to pretend it wasn't, but Alectis turned round and grabbed it as Neal tried to shove it on the floor. I was lying back in my straps, feeling grey and thinking, We could get away now. I'd better lam them all again. But all I did was lie there and watch Neal and Alectis having an angry tug-of-war. Then watch Lewin turn round and pluck the block away from the pair of them.

"Don't be a fool," he said to Neal. "I've already erased the recorder. And if I hadn't had Renick and Palino breathing righteously down our necks, I'd never have recorded anything. It goes against the grain to take in children."

Lewin pressed the *erase* on the memo block and it gave out a satisfied sort of gobble. Neither of the other two said anything, but I could feel Alectis thinking how much he had always hated Palino. Terens was looking down at Wormstow through a fieldglass and trying not remember a boy in Cadets with him who had turned heg and given himself up. I felt I wanted to say thank you. But I was too shy to do anything but sit up and look at Wormstow too, between the jags of the rock. Even without a fieldglass, I could see the place throbbing like a broken anthill with all the Slaver troops.

"Getting ready to move out and mop up the countryside," Terens said.

"Yes, and that's where most people live," Lewin said. "Farms and holdings in the hills. What's the quickest way to the Dragon Reserve?"

"There's a track on the right round the next bend," said Neal. "Why?"

"Because it's the safest place I can think of," Lewin said.

Neal and I looked at one another. You didn't need to be heg to tell that Neal was thinking, just as I was, that this was a bit much. They were supposed to help all those people in the holdings. Instead, they thought of the safest place and ran there! So neither of us said that the track was only a bridle path, and we didn't try to warn them not to take the van into the Reserve. We just sat there while Lewin drove it uphill, and then lumping and bumping and rattling up the path. The path gave out in the marshy patch below the Saddle, but Lewin kept grinding and roaring on, throwing up peat in squirts, until we tipped downhill again and bounced down a yellow fellside. We were in the Reserve by then. The ling was growing in lurid green

136

patches, black at the roots, where dragons had burnt it in the mating season. They fight a lot then.

We got some way into the Reserve. The van gave out clanging sounds and smelt bad, but Lewin kept it going by driving on the most level parts. We were in a wide stony scoop, with yellow hills all round, when the smell got worse and the van just stopped. Alectis let go of the door. "Worms – dragons," he said, "don't like machines, I've heard."

"Now he tells us!" said Terens, and we all got out. We all looked as if we had been in an accident – I mean, I know we had in a way, but we looked worse than I'd expected: sort of ragged and pale and shivery. Lewin turned his foot on a stone, which made him clutch his chest and swear. Neither of the other two even asked if he was all right. That is the Dragonate way. They just set out walking. Neal and I went with them, thinking of the best place to dodge off up a kyle, so that we could run home and try and warn Mother about the Slavers.

"Where that bog turns into a stream – I'll say when," Neal was whispering, when a dragon came over the hill into the valley and made straight for us.

"Stand still!" said Alectis. Lewin and Terens each had a gun in their hand without seeming to have moved. Alectis didn't, and he was white.

"They only eat moving prey," Neal said, because he was sorry for him. "Make sure not to panic and run and you're fine."

I was sorry for Alectis too, so I added, "It's probably only after the van. They love metal."

Lewin crumpled his face at me and said "Ah!" for some reason.

The dragon came quite slowly, helping itself with its spread wings and hanging its head rather. It was a bad colour, sort of creamy through the brown-green. I thought it might be one of the sick ones that turn man-eater, and I tried to brace myself and stop feeling so tired and shaky so that I could lam it. But

Neal said, "That's Orm's dragon! You didn't kill it after all!"

It *was* Orm's dragon. By this time, it was near enough for me to see the heat off it quivering the air, and I recognised the gamesome, shrewd look in its eye. But since it had every reason to hate me, that didn't make me feel much better. It came straight for me too. We all stood like statues. And it came right up to me and bent its neck, and laid its huge brown head on the ling in front of my feet, where it puffed out a sigh that made Lewin cough and gasp another swearword. It had felt me coming, the dragon said, and it was here to say sorry. It hadn't meant to upset me. It had thought it was a game.

That made me feel terrible. "I'm sorry too," I said. "I lost my head. I didn't mean to hurt you. That was Orm's fault."

Orm was only playing too, the dragon said. Orm called him Huffle, and I could too if I liked. Was he forgiven? He was ashamed.

"Of course I forgive you, Huffle," I said. "Do you forgive me?"

Yes. Huffle lifted his head up and went a proper colour at once. Dragons are like people that way.

"Ask him to fetch Orm here," Lewin said urgently.

I didn't want to see Orm, and Lewin was a coward. "Ask him yourself," I said. "He understands."

"Yes, but I don't think he'd do it for me," Lewin said.

"Then, will you fetch Orm for Lewin?" I asked Huffle.

He gave me a cheeky look. Maybe. Presently. He sauntered away past Terens, who moved his head back from Huffle's rattling right wing, looking as if he thought his last hour had come, and went to have a look at the van. He put out a great clawed foot, in a thoughtful sort of way, and tore the loose door off it. Then he tucked the door under his right front foreleg and departed, deliberately slowly, on three legs, helping himself with his wings, so that rocks rattled and flapped all along the valley.

Alectis sat down rather suddenly. But Lewin made him leap

up again and help Terens get the broadcaster out of the van before any more dragons found it. They never did get it out. They were still working and waggling at it to get it loose, and Lewin was standing over Neal and me, so that we couldn't sneak off, when we heard that humming kind of whistle that you get from a dragon in flight. We whirled round. This dragon was a big black one, coasting low over the hill opposite and gliding down the valley. They don't often fly high. It came to ground with that grinding of stones and leathery slap of wings closing that always tells you a dragon is landing. It arched its black neck and looked at us disdainfully.

Orm was sitting on its back looking equally disdainful. It was one of those times when Orm looks grave and grand. He sat very upright, with his hair and beard combed straight by the wind of flying, and his big pale eyes hardly looked mad at all. Neal was the only one of us he deigned to notice. "Good afternoon, Neal Sigridsson," he said. "You keep bad company. Dragonate are not human."

Neal was very angry with Orm. He put my heart in my mouth by saying, quite calmly, "Then in that case, I'm the only human here." With that dragon standing glaring! I've been brought up to despise boys, but I think that is a mistake.

To my relief, Orm just grinned. "That's the way, boy," he said. "Not a booby after all, are you?"

Then Lewin took my breath away by going right up to the dragon. He had his gun, of course, but that wouldn't have been much use against a dragon. He went so near that the dragon had to turn its head out of his way. "We've dropped the charges," he said. "And you should never have brought them."

Orm looked down at him. "You," he said, "know a thing or two."

"I know dragons don't willingly attack humans," Lewin said. "I always read up on a case before I hear it." At this, Orm put on his crazy look and made his mad cackle. "Stop that!" said Lewin. "The Slavers have invaded. Wormstow's full of Slaver troops and we need your help. I want to get everyone from the outlying farms into the Reserve and persuade the dragons to protect them. Can you help us do that?"

That took my breath away again, and Neal's too. We did a quick goggle at one another. Perhaps the Dragonate was like it was supposed to be after all!

Orm said, "Then we'd better get busy," and slid down from the dragon. He still towered over Lewin. Orm is huge. As soon as he was down, the black dragon lumbered across to the van and started taking it to bits. That brought other dragons coasting whistling in from all sides of the valley, to crunch to earth and hurry to the van too. In seconds, it was surrounded in black and green-brown shapes the size of haybarns. And Orm talked, at the top of his voice, through the sound of metal tearing, and big claws screaming on iron, and wings clapping, and angry grunts when two dragons happened to get hold of the same piece of van. Orm always talks a lot. But this time, he was being particularly garrulous, to give the dragons time to lumber away with their pieces of van, hide them and come back. "They won't even do what Orm says until they've got their metal," I whispered to Terens, who got rather impatient with Orm.

Orm said the best place to put people was the high valley at the centre of the Reserve. "There's an old she-drake with a litter just hatched," he said. "No one will get past her when she's feared for her young. I'll speak to her. But the rest are to promise me she's not disturbed." As for telling everyone at the farms where to come, Orm said, the dragons could do that, provided Lewin could think of a way of sending a message by them. "You see, most folk can't hear a dragon when it speaks," he said. "And some who can hear – " with a nasty look at me – "speak back to wound." He was still very angry with me. I kept on the other side of Terens and Alectis when the dragons all came swooping back.

Terens set the memo block to *repeat* and tapped out an official message from Lewin. Then he tore off page after page with the same thing on it. Orm handed each page to a dragon, saying things like, "Take this to the fat cow up at Hillfoot." Or, "Drop this on young vinegar lady at Crowtop – hard." Or, "This is for Dopey at High Jiot, but don't give it to her, give it to her youngest husband or they'll never get moving."

Some of the things he said made me laugh a lot. But it was only when Alectis asked what was so funny and Neal kicked my ankle, that I realised I was the only one who could hear the things Orm said. Each dragon, as it got its page, ran down the valley and took off, showering us with stones from the jump they gave to get higher in the air than usual. Their wings boom when they fly high. Orm took off on the black dragon last of all, saying he would go and warn the she-drake.

Lewin crumpled his face ruefully at the few bits of van remaining, and we set off to walk to the valley ourselves. It was a long way. Over ling slopes and up among boulders in the kyles we trudged, looking up nervously every so often when fat bluish Slaver fliers screamed through the clouds overhead. After a while, our dragons began booming overhead too, seawards to roost. Terens counted them and said every one we had sent seemed to have come back now. He said he wished he had wings. It was sunset by the time we reached the valley. By that time, Lewin was bent over, holding his chest and swearing every other step. But everyone was still pretending, in that stupid Dragonate way, that he was all right. We came up on the cliffs, where the kyle winds down to the she-drake's valley, and there was the sunset lighting the sea and the towers of rock out there, and the waves crashing round the rocks, where the young dragons were flying to roost – and Lewin actually pretended to admire the view. "I knew a place like this on Seven," he said. "Except there were trees instead of dragons. I can't get used to the way Eight doesn't have trees."

He was going to sit down to rest, I think, but Orm came

up the kyle just then. Huffle was hulking behind him. "So you got here at last!" Orm said in his rudest way.

"We have," said Lewin. "Now would you mind telling me what you were playing at bringing those charges against Siglin?"

"You should be glad I did. You'd all be in a slaveship now if I hadn't," Orm said.

"But you weren't to know that, were you?" Terens said.

"Not to speak of risking being charged yourself," added Lewin.

Orm leant on his hand against Huffle, like you might against a wall. "She half killed this dragon!" he said. "That's why! All I did was ask her for a kiss and she screams and lays into poor Huffle. My own daughter, and she tries to kill a dragon! And I thought, Right, my lady, then you're no daughter of mine any more! and I flew Huffle's mother straight into Holmstad and laid charges. I was that angry! My own father tended dragons, and his mother before him. And my daughter tried to kill one! You wonder I was angry?"

"Nobody *told* me!" I said. I had that draining-away feeling again. I was quite glad when Terens took hold of my elbow and said something like, "Steady, steady!"

"Are you telling the truth?" Neal said.

"I'm sure he is," Lewin said. "Your sister has his eyes."

"Ask Timas," said Orm. "He married your mother the year after I did. He can take being bossed about. I can't. I went back to my dragons. But I suppose there's a record of that?" he said challengingly to Lewin.

"And the divorce," said Lewin. "Terens looked it up for me. But I expect the Slavers have destroyed it by now."

"And she never told you?" Orm said to me. He wagged his shaggy eyebrows at me almost forgivingly. "I'll have a bone to pick with her over that," he said.

Mother arrived just as we'd all got down into the valley. She looked very indomitable, as she always does on horseback, and all our people were with her, down to both our shepherds. They had carts of clothes and blankets and food. Mother knew the valleys as well as Orm did. She used to meet Orm there when she was a girl. She set out for the Reserve as soon as she heard the broadcast about the invasion, and the dragon we sent her met them on the way. That's Mother for you. The rest of the neighbours didn't get there for some hours after that.

I didn't think Mother's face – or Timas's – could hold such a mixture of feelings as they did when they saw Neal and me and the Dragonate men all with Orm. When Orm saw Mother, he folded his arms and grinned. Huffle rested his huge chin on Orm's shoulder, looking interested.

"Here she comes," Orm said to Huffle. "Oh, I do love a good quarrel!"

They had one. It was one of the loudest I'd ever heard. Terens took Neal and me away to help look after Lewin. He turned out to have broken some ribs when the blast hit the van, but he wouldn't let anyone look even until I ordered him to. After that, Neal, Alectis and I sat under our haycart and talked, mostly about the irony of Fate. You see, Neal has always secretly wished Fate had given him Orm as a father, and I'm the one that's got Orm. Neal's father is Timas. Alectis says he can see the likeness. We'd both gladly swap. Then Alectis confessed that he'd been hating the Dragonate so much that he was thinking of running away – which is a serious crime. But now the Slavers have come, and there doesn't seem to be much of a Dragonate any more, he feels quite different. He admires Lewin.

Lewin consented to rest while Terens and Mother organised everyone into a makeshift camp in the valley, but he was up and about again the next day, because he said the Slavers were bound to come the day after, when they found the holdings were deserted. The big black she-drake sat in her cave at the head of the kyle, with her infants between her forefeet, watching groups of people rushing round to do what Lewin said, and didn't seem to mind at all. Huffle said she'd been bored and bad-tempered up to then. We made life interesting. Actually that she-drake reminds me of Mother. Both of them made me give them a faithful report of the battle.

I don't think the Slavers knew about the dragons. They just knew that there was a concentration of people in here, and they came straight across the Reserve to get us. As soon as the dragons told Orm they were coming, Lewin had us all out hiding in the hills in their path, except for Mother and Timas and Inga's mother and a few more who had shotguns. They had to stay and guard the little kids in the camp. The rest of us had any weapon we could find. Neal and Alectis had bows and arrows. Inga had her airgun. Donal and most of the farmers had scythes. The shepherds all had their slingshots. I was in the front with Lewin, because I was supposed to stop the effect of the Slavers' collars. Orm was there too, although nobody had ever admitted in so many words that Orm might be heg. All Orm did was to ask the dragons to keep back, because we didn't want *them* enslaved by those collars.

And there they came, a huddle of sheep-like troops, and then another huddle, each one being driven by a cluster of kingly Slavers, with crowns and winking V-shaped collars. And there again we all got that horrible guilty compulsion to come and give ourselves up. But I don't think those collars have any effect on dragons. Half of us were standing up to walk into the Slavers' arms, and I was ordering them as hard as I could not to, when the dragons smelt those golden crowns and collars. There was no holding them. They just whirred down over our heads and took those Slavers to pieces for the metal. Lewin said, "Ah!" and crumpled his face in a grin like a fiend's. He'd thought the dragons might do that. I think he may really be a genius, like they say Camerati are. But I was so sick at that, and then again at the sight of nice people like Alectis and Yan killing the sheep-like troops, that I'm not going to talk about it any more. Terens says I'm not to go when the Slavers come next. Apparently I broadcast the way I was feeling, just like the Slavers do, and even the dragons felt queasy. The she-drake snorted at that. Mother said, "Nonsense. Take travel pills and behave as my daughter should."

Anyway, we have found out how to beat the Slavers. We have no idea what is going on in the other of the ten Worlds, or even in the rest of Sveridge, but there are fifty more Worm Reserves around the world, and Lewin says there must be stray Dragonate units too who might think of using dragons against Slavers. We want to move out and take over some of the farms again soon. The dragons are having far too much fun with the sheep. They keep flying over with woolly bundles dangling from their claws, watched by a gloomy crowd of everyone's shepherds. "Green dot," the shepherds say. "The brutes are raiding Hightop now." They are very annoyed with Orm, because Orm just gives his mad cackle and lets the dragons go on.

Orm isn't mad at all. He's afraid of people knowing he's heg – he still won't admit he is. I think that's why he left Mother and Mother doesn't admit she was ever married to him. Not that Mother minds. I get the feeling she and Orm understand one another rather well. But Mother married Donal, you see, after Timas. Donal, and Yan too, have both told me that the fact that I'm heg makes no difference to them – but you should see the way they both look at me! I'm not fooled. I don't blame Orm for being scared stiff Donal would find out he was heg. But I'm not sure I shall ever like Orm, all the same.

I am putting all this down on what is left of Palino's memo block. Lewin wanted me to, in case there is still some History yet to come. He has made his official version on the recorder. I'm leaning the block on Huffle's forefoot. Huffle is my friend now. Leaning on a dragon is the best way to keep warm on a chilly evening like this, when you're forced to camp out in the Reserve. Huffle is letting Lewin lean on him too, beyond Neal, because Lewin's ribs still pain him. There is a lot of leaning-space along the side of a dragon. Orm has just stepped across Huffle's tail, into the light, chortling and rubbing his hands in his most irritating way.

"Your mother's on the warpath," he says. "Oh, I do love a good quarrel!"

And here comes Mother, ominously upright, and with her arms folded. It's not Orm she wants. It's Lewin. "Listen, you," she says. "What the dickens is the Dragonate thinking of, beheading hegs all these years? They can't help what they are. And they're the only people who can stand up to the Thrallers."

Orm is cheated of his quarrel. Lewin looked up, crumpled into the most friendly smile. "I do so agree with you," he said. "I've just said so in my report. And I'd have got your daughter off somehow, you know."

Orm is cackling like the she-drake's young ones. Mother's mouth is open and I really think that, for once in her life, she has no idea what to say.

Crusader Damosel

Crusader Damosel

Vera Chapman

When Adela learnt that her father was to go to the Holy Land, taking her and her mother with him, she was delighted. Her mother, Dame Blanche, was less delighted, but there was not much choice in the matter. Sir Brian de Bassecourt, of Stoke Bassecourt in the county of Kent, had been ordered by the Abbot to go on the Crusade, or else build an expensive chantry for the abbey — for Sir Brian had killed a monk. He hadn't really meant to kill the monk, he said, but when he found him half way up the stairs to Dame Blanche's bower, he had given him a little push down, and — the man had broken his neck. The Abbot acquitted him of wilful murder, but ordered that he should either build a chantry or go on the Crusade. Sir Brian wasn't a rich man, so although the Crusade might cost a good deal of money, the chantry would cost far more. Besides, there were advantages, as he pointed out to Dame Blanche.

"Just think — we get all our sins forgiven, all of them — yours too, and Adela's. And if we should die on the journey — "

Dame Blanche gave a shriek.

"*If* we should, we'd all go to heaven at once — no Purgatory at all. Think of that!"

"I'd rather not think of that," said Dame Blanche.

"Don't, then, my dear — never mind. There's other things. Almost everyone that goes out to Outremer comes back with a fortune. There's plunder, and ransoms — there's even lands and castles for the picking up. *And* we'd be sure to find a husband for Adela, which is more than we'll do here."

So Dame Blanche went about her preparations, tearfully at first, and later with zeal and fervour – and Adela watched the preparations with mounting excitement.

Adela was fifteen, and had never been outside Stoke Basse-court, where they lived in a humdrum little farmhouse dignified by the name of Manor, which Duke William had bestowed on Sir Brian's great-grandfather. Adela had a fine Norman profile, jet-black hair, and blue eyes inherited from a Saxon grand-mother. She was a bold girl, something of a tomboy, a good rider, and afraid of nothing she had met so far. But attractive as she was, she might as well go into a convent and be done with it, in that dull little corner. She'd never find a husband there.

So, after an overwhelming fuss and bother of preparation, they set out – Sir Brian in armour on his big charger, Dame Blanche in a mule litter, Adela on a palfrey. She had devised herself a dress like that invented by Queen Eleanor some seventy years before, when she and all her ladies went on the First Crusade with King Louis, before she became Queen of England. Well-cut leather breeches, discreetly covered by a long, voluminous divided skirt, so full and flowing that no one could see that the wearer sat easily astride on a man's saddle underneath all that brocade. There was also a light corselet of soft leather, shaped so as to enhance the figure very discreetly, and covered with a silken surcoat. In that outfit, with a hooded cape for the rain, Adela sat proudly and confidently on her pretty black mare.

The first rallying point was at Wrotham, for the Kentish levies. Here the Crusaders made their vows and "took the Cross – ". Sir Brian had a bold red cross, made of two stripes of red cloth, stitched to his mantle, while he took the Crusader's Oath in the church.

Adela wanted to be enrolled as a Crusader too. She saw at least two imposing ladies going up and receiving the Cross. "Why can't I?" she asked Sir Brian. "*They* can."

"Oh, yes, my dear, they do let ladies take the Cross, but only if they bring their own retinue of fighting men, as those two ladies are doing. I'm afraid my small following is barely a quota for one – besides that, you are under age."

But the noble words of the Crusader's Oath stayed in Adela's mind and haunted her. She wove daydreams about riding out to help King Guy to defend Jerusalem, with a long sword at her side, fighting to keep the heathen from regaining the Holy Sepulchre, the holiest spot on earth.

Somehow the milling crowd got across the Channel, and in the fields of France a long caravan formed, and slowly made its straggling way across Europe. It was an astonishing assembly – knights and noblemen with their soldiers, bands of volunteers from the country trudging with their bows, monks and clerics of every order, pilgrims, peddlers, hucksters and sutlers, wives and families of fighting men – and, of course, a number of dubious ladies who travelled with the wagons and were discreetly known as "baggage". Then there were smiths and cooks, with their furnaces and cauldrons, and flocks of sheep and herds of cattle to provide meat on the hoof – and Lord-knows-what besides. It was like a slowly moving town. Every day saw them strung out along the road, all in their accustomed order, with marshals riding up and down the line to keep them together. At night there could be the most astonishing variety of resting places. Sometimes they would reach a town or a castle, and then some of them at least (particularly the ladies, such as Adela and her mother) would be guests in comfort – or in more or less discomfort, as the luck was. Sometimes the company would halt in the open country, and make camp – everybody would pitch their tents, and once you got used to this and got organized, it wasn't bad at all. When a camp was made, it was a good opportunity to go up and down the lines and call on one's friends. Blanche did a good deal of visiting, with Adela beside her, rather overwhelmed with the newness of it all, and for the time being, diffident and a little withdrawn. Sir Brian brought young knights to their tent and presented them, ceremoniously, to Blanche and Adela. They were fine to look at, but Adela could find nothing to say to them.

Every morning began solemnly with Mass, either in the church of the town where they happened to be, or in a great pavilion set up with an altar and all the holy adornments – the knights and ladies devoutly kneeling on the grass outside. (But Dame Blanche took care to have a cushion.) It was one morning half way through France, when Mass was being celebrated in the pavilion, and all the company was ranged in order outside, that Adela looked over her right shoulder, and saw a phalanx of men, standing foursquare together, in straight rows. All were in armour, and over the armour a white tunic and a long white mantle, emblazoned with the red cross. Their helmets were round, and cut straight across the top, like round towers. Something grim and resolute marked these men out from the rest. Adela ran her eyes along their faces, such of them as she could see. Mostly bearded, greyish, lined, some of them scarred. But one – he was young, bright-eyed. Something about him said to Adela: "This is the one."

She had turned half round – very naughtily – and for the life of her she could not keep herself from fixing her eyes on his face. And he looked at her for one moment – dark brown his eyes were – and a flash of understanding passed between them. Then Dame Blanche was pinching Adela's arm quite painfully, and jerking her round. Adela returned to her devotions – but she hardly knew what she was doing.

At the end of Mass, Adela stole a discreet glimpse over her shoulder – but now the crowd in general turned to see the men in white mantles, frowning and aloof, marching away in disciplined ranks. She tried in vain to see the face she had noticed.

"Adela," her mother said, "you mustn't look at those men.

Don't you know what they are? Those are the Knights Templars."

"Are they? Well, what's wrong with them?"

"Nothing *wrong* with them – but don't you understand, they mustn't look at women, or even let women look at them. They are under a vow of poverty, obedience, and – chastity. You keep your eyes away from them, my dear."

But Adela had looked once too often already.

The Templars, part of whose duty it was to protect pilgrims, and the relatives and dependents of Crusaders, on their way to the Holy Land, now constituted themselves a guard to the company. Strung out at intervals, they patrolled the borders of the road, as well as going ahead and also covering the rear. They changed their positions often – and so one day Adela saw that face again, and then again, and found out from some of the servants that his name was Hugo Des Moulins, and that in spite of his French name, he was an English knight from Sussex. She looked him in the face, but the first time he answered her look with a kind of breathlessness, and the second time with a frown of anxiety, almost of pain. She knew she ought not to let her mind dwell on him, but how could she help it? And as they continued on their way, and reached Venice, and took ship (a dreadful passage it was) to Acre, her case grew more and more desperate. Until at last, at Acre, as soon as they were settled into their humble quarters in the great stony fortress, she felt she must take action. So, as soon as she knew where that lady would be quartered, she sought out the Abbess of Shaston.

The Abbess of Shaston was a remarkable woman. She knew a wonderful great deal about a great many things – people came to her to be cured of illnesses, and of heartaches – to resolve doubts, and points of law, and settle quarrels; to seek love, or to be delivered from love; she was sought by women who wished to have babies, and, it was whispered, by those who did not. She could not be called a midwife nor a leech, for such occupations would be beneath the dignity of an Abbess; but it was thought that she knew more than all the wise-women and all the doctors together. She went back and forth to the Holy Land as it pleased her, and it was said that she knew the secrets of the Saracens as well as of the Christians. She was certainly not a witch – nobody dared say such a thing, for she had high connections. She obeyed no authority lower than the Pope's – if his, seeing that she was perhaps his cousin. She had a strange beauty of her own and was very stately. Adela sought her out, taking with her the little jewel-box she always carried with her, containing such modest jewelry as she possessed. She opened this, and left it lying open before the Abbess.

"Put those things away, child," said the Abbess. "Now tell me. You're in love, of course?"

So Adela told her.

"A Templar? That's difficult. Why did it have to be a Templar, you silly girl? You know he can't marry you. Do you want to be his paramour?"

Adela blushed. "Oh, but Templars don't have paramours."

"Don't they, then? – There's a lot you don't know about Templars. – But that wouldn't do for you, nor for him, I think. What do you want, then?"

"Can't a Templar ever be absolved from his vows?"

"Oh, yes, he can. The Pope can dispense his vow. I'd see it done myself – the Pope would do it for me." She spoke with airy assurance. "Only – the petition must come from him, not from anyone else. He himself must ask for it. Would he do that – for you?"

"He doesn't know me," said Adela with her eyes downcast.

"No. – Oh, but he does, though. He dreams of you."

'How – how on earth do you know?"

"Never mind how – but I know. You and he know each other quite well, on the Other Side of the Curtain. But that's no good for earthly matters."

"What do you mean – the Other Side of the Curtain?"

"The other side of life and being. Even beyond dreams. Out of the body. You and he meet together, night after night, while your dreams hang a misleading curtain before your mortal minds."

Adela felt as if a great window was opened before her, full of beauty and wonder.

"Oh, if only I could know – if only I could remember! Could you not send me through the Curtain in my waking mind, or make it so that I remembered?"

"My child, I believe I could. But you must attend and do exactly as I say."

So then she gave Adela certain instructions, and taught her certain words and certain signs. And once again she waved aside Adela's jewel-box.

So that night, Adela, lying on her bed wide awake, and having done all that the Abbess told her, felt herself rise out of her body, like slipping a hand out of a glove. She looked down at herself lying peacefully asleep on the bed, and then she stepped over herself, and was lightly out of doors and across the night and into a moonlit orchard, where Hugo was waiting for her.

"Welcome, my dear companion," he said, and clasped both her hands, but did not kiss her. It was enough for her, so far – just to feel his happy fellowship.

"I knew you would come," he said. "You always do."

"Yes," she answered, feeling quite sure that they had known each other quite well for a long time. "But this time I shall know what I am doing, and remember it afterwards."

"I wish I did," he said. "I never remember anything when I am awake. I don't know even that I know you."

"What do you call me – here?" she asked.

"Why – Adal, I think," he answered.

"And am I a boy or a girl?"

"A boy, of course – no, a girl – oh, to be sure, I don't know," and he laughed in confusion. "But come on – the trumpets are sounding – we must ride against the infidel."

By his side was a horse, saddled and ready, and she got up behind him. It seemed that they were both armoured and accoutred in the Templars' armour, and she had a long sword by her side. She remembered the device on the Templars' seal – two knights riding on one horse.

They galloped out of the orchard, and it was daylight. Before them lay a wide plain, and far off a little compact city on a hill, which she knew must be Jerusalem. Behind them rode the squadron of the Templars, but she could not see them clearly because they were behind her. Suddenly, as they rode toward the City, there rose up before them a host of men; on their heads were small red turbans with golden crescents.

"Oh, what are these?" exclaimed Adela.

"Paynims, Saracens – have no fear of them – charge for the Cross!" And he drew his sword and galloped into the thick of them. She drew her sword too, but passed it into her left hand so that, as he slashed on the right she could slash on the left. In the body which she now seemed to wave, her left arm was as good as her right.

They hewed at the Saracens, who fought fiercely and shouted, but fell as they slashed them, without any blood – they seemed to be made of something like soft wood, or wax, and never bled, nor did their expressionless faces show any pain. More and more came up on them, but they hewed them all down, and rushed on through them with a fierce delight. Behind them came the other Crusaders but never overtook them. At one moment Hugo drew rein, and Adela was able to look behind them – there were a few of the Crusaders fallen, but over each one hovered a fine white-winged angel, just like those in the church paintings at home – gently drawing the man's soul out of his body, and carrying it upward.

The Holy City was nearer now, and shone with gold; on a pinnacle in the midst Our Lady stood, in a robe of blue, with the Holy Child in her arms. As the Crusaders fought their way towards the City, Our Lady smiled at Hugo and Adela and flung a handful of rose petals.

And then Adela was suddenly awake, and it was all a dream – or was it? The tips of her fingers smelt of roses.

There were galleries all round the great courtyard, and there Adela, her mother, and all the ladies of the company, were seated on the chairs to watch a spectacle. Down below, the courtyard was thronged with armed men. With pomp and pageantry, a procession entered below. Count Raymond himself, with all his peers, glittering with metal and coloured silks, and a tall swordsman by his side, and men with a brazier. Adela supposed the brazier was to keep Count Raymond warm out there.

Then were led in a long line of tall, dignified men, in long white robes and turbans. Their arms were tied, and the foot soldiers led them along. Their faces were sallow but pale, and their eyes dark, and all had beards, some black, some grey. They held themselves with sorrowful composure, and reminded Adela of pictures she had seen of Christian martyrs.

"Oh, who are these?" she asked.

"Paynims, child – Saracens, Mussulmans and heathens. These are the enemy."

"Oh – " But these were not in the least like the fierce men in the dream.

The first was led before Count Raymond in his chair. Now, Adela thought, he will loose his bonds and set him free. The paynim man made a low obeisance – Count Raymond gave a sign to the man with the sword – the sword fell, and the paynim's head toppled horribly to the ground. Indeed these were not like the men in the dream who did not bleed . . .

Another and another. . . There were some whose hands were chopped off . . .

"They don't feel anything, those paynims," said Dame Blanche. "They'd serve our own men the same if they caught them. Anyway they've refused baptism. Now this one will be a different punishment, look – "

"Let me go – I don't feel well," Adela said, shuddering, and escaped to her room, where she cried for hours.

It was some nights before she could get "through the Curtain" to Hugo again, but when she did, she told him about it, and all her horror and revulsion. And he looked serious and worried, and said, "How can we understand? All we know, when we are awake is that we must obey and fight. But I know – I have felt it too."

But then the fierce Saracens crept up on them, and once again they had to fight their way through them. And this time they broke right through the Saracen army, and came to the golden walls of the Holy City – and the gates stood open, and they went in. There was nobody to be seen there – all stood deserted, all the houses of gold, with their windows of jewels – but from somewhere, high up, a sound of heavenly music and joyful singing filled the air. From every part of the city could be seen the pinnacle where Our Lady stood.

"Come," said Hugo, "we must seek the Sepulchre of the Lord," and they went on through the golden streets, but somewhere the ways diverged, and Adela looked round for Hugo and he was not there. She went on, calling for him, and found herself outside the City on the other side, looking back at the walls.

And there before her, but facing the City, was the host of the Saracens – those same tall, turbaned, white-robed men, with pale faces and dark beards. They were armed and on horses, and galloping, galloping towards the City. Out against them came a horde of men, just like those she had fought against with Hugo but these had round red caps on their heads with silver crosses on them. And the Saracens charged into them, hewing and slicing off heads, arms and legs as before; and as before, the men fell without bleeding and with no sign of pain. Before the Saracens, as they fought, stood the Holy City, but on the pinnacle where Adela had seen Our Lady, was a tall tree full of flowers. Some of the Saracens fell, and over each one hovered a beautiful girl, with butterfly wings and clothed in rainbow silks, who drew out his soul and carried it aloft.

Two Saracens closed up beside her.

"Come, lady," they said, "we welcome you with all honour." They led her away from the battle, to a richly decorated tent where sat Saladin himself on silken cushions. He smiled and bade her welcome, and as she thought of the tall men slaughtered in the castle yard, her eyes filled with tears.

"Lady of the Giaours," he said, "if we all pitied our enemies, there would be no wars."

"And would not that be a good thing?" she said with the boldness of a dream.

"Ah, who knows? But we know that Allah made soldiers to fight. What else would they do?"

He made her sit on cushions by his side, and sip a strange sweet drink, and he told her a password which she was to remember. Over and over he said it – and she woke up saying it. In the moment of waking she wrote it down, in a sort of fashion, in such letters as she knew, just so that she should not forget it.

Everything was astir in the castle and town of Acre. "We shall have to move as soon as we can," said Sir Brian. "Get boats and be off tomorrow early. It isn't safe here. Saladin's forces are between us and Tiberias. We're cut off. Tiberias is besieged, with Count Raymond's wife and family in it. Some say the army is to march on Tiberias – some say not. I know what *we'll* do. Get packed."

So the rest of the day was full of bustle. But Adela, whose heart was heavy with foreboding, went to sleep early.

*

When she slipped out of her body, and went in search of Hugo, she knew there was a difference. She did not find herself in the moonlit orchard – she was not in the magical world of visions, but hovering over and wandering through the real world, like a ghost, unseen. She was watching the army of the Crusaders on the march, through the night, the Templars leading. Hugo was there, on his horse, but not riding gallantly. They were none of them riding gallantly. They laboured through the night on tired horses, and drooped in their saddles. She heard them talking.

"Why on earth did we have to leave Sephoria? Plenty of water in Sephoria, and a good defensive position. But no – before we'd time even to water the horses – "

"And after marching all day – hardly time for a mouthful to drink, and God! I'm thirsty . . ."

"They say the Commanders quarrelled. Count Raymond, like a sensible man, said stay in Sephoria, with the water, and wait a bit – though, mind you, it's *his* wife and children who are in Tiberias. He said it was a trap to get us to move out. And King Godfrey listened to him, didn't he?"

"Yes, but then Count Gerard came in, and said Raymond was a traitor and had sold out to the Saracens. So King Guy got in a panic and ordered us to march on Tiberias at once, before we'd had any rest."

"What can you do, when your Commanders disagree? – Oh, what would I give for a drink. Never mind ale or wine – just water."

"If we can get through to Galilee, there's plenty of water."

"And all the Saracens between us and Galilee. The horses will flounder first."

"What's this place we're making for – the top of that hill?"

"They call it Hattin – the Horns of Hattin – the Horns of Hattin – "

She moved throgh the ranks and hovered over Hugo, trying to enter his mind. But all that came across to her was thirst, thirst, thirst – and the oppressive weight of his armour, the heat inside it, the weakness of the body that had sweated all day and was now drained dry. The grey-faced old Templars rode beside him, bidding him cheer up, for the more the suffering the greater the glory. He listened dull-eyed.

She woke, dry-throated, crying out, "Water, water – the Horns of Hattin, the Horns of Hattin . . ."

She knew what she had to do. Quietly she slipped out of bed and dressed in her riding breeches and corselet, but without the skirt, and threw a hooded mantle over her. Stealthily she slipped out to the horse-lines, found her own black mare, saddled her, and before she mounted, slung on her saddle two small casks full of water. It was as much as she could require the mare to carry.

The sentry at the door barred her way.

"Oh, please – " she said.

"Oh, a lady. By heaven, the Lady Adela – "

"Soldier," she said, "you know why people sometimes have reasons to slip out alone – "

Certainly he did – with half the Castle engaged in love-affairs.

"Surely – but *you*, Lady Adela – I'd never have thought *you* – "

In the dark he could not see her blush.

"All right, my lady – not a word from me. But take care of yourself, won't you?" He let her past.

Then she rode like the wind towards Tiberias.

From daybreak to noon she rode, and that noon was fiercely hot. It was July, and the grass was dry and the earth was splitting. Once in sheer exhaustion she dismounted, drank from a wayside spring and let the mare drink, and rested a short time. She could not have eaten if she had had food with her.

Then she went on eastwards, and as she went she could smell burning grass. Nothing unusual in that – the grass caught fire very easily at that season. But now the smoke was denser – soon it was a choking smother. As she came up a hill, and saw Galilee below her, she also saw the battle. It raged fiercely over the plateau – the Horns of Hattin! The army of the Cross, fighting fiercely, fighting desperately against the vast, over-whelming army of the Saracens. As they fought, the smoke from the grass-fire, blowing away from the Saracens, covered the Crusaders in its stifling, throat-drying fog.

The foot-soldiers had broken and fled. Most of the horses lay exhausted on the ground, and the knights were falling one by one, or lying, helpless heaps of clashing metal, at their enemies' feet. This was no battle of bloodless men – far from it. Adela was spared nothing of the blood and horror.

Alone among the rest stood the Templars and the Hospitallers, grouped around the black-and-white banner, isolated in the field like the last sheaf to be reaped. They were laying about them fiercely, and Hugo was amongst them – but they were failing. As she watched she saw him fall.

Without a moment's hesitation she spurred forward, forcing the unwilling mare to face the smoke. But there was rough cliff in front of her, and a drop – no way down. She had to go round, and the only way she could go led her in a curve to the opposite side of the battlefield. She found herself dashing into the lines of the Saracens. Hands reached up to catch her bridle-reins.

"Oh, let me go!" she exclaimed, not at all sure if they understood her language. "I must get to him. I must save life – save life, do you understand?" It seemed the battle was over – the Saracens were coming back from the field, leading prisoners. Then Adela remembered the password she had learnt from Saladin in her dream, and spoke it.

The men fell back in astonishment, and let her through.

Down that grim hillside she went, the smoke still all about

her. She tried to remember the place where she had seen Hugo fall by the black-and-white standard. The worst was having to pass the other men, wounded, dying, ghastly, who cried to her from the ground for water. Some of them were too parched to cry out. Some seemed to be unwounded – it was only the heat and the smoke and the drought that had killed them. But she could not spare any water at all. There were one or two with still enough strength to scramble to their feet and try to snatch the water-barrels. But she beat them off with her riding-whip – they had not much strength after all and could not run after her.

And at last she found him.

He lay on a horrible heap of dead men, and he did not move. She dismounted, and dragged him aside to a clean patch of ground, and bathed his face, and trickled water into his mouth, and freed him from his armour – she had to take his dagger to cut its lacings, and even when she had unfastened it, the metal was still hot to the touch. She flung each piece away from him. He began to stir, opened his eyes, and then was able to swallow the water she held to his lips. She laid a wet kerchief over his nostrils against the smoke. And when at last he showed enough signs of life, she helped him on to her mare, and mounted behind him, holding him, and so rode slowly and carefully away from that dreadful place, once again like two Templars on one horse. She went boldly through the camp of the Saracens, and spoke that password. The Saracens buzzed in amazement, and some of them sent messengers to tell Saladin, but they let them through.

And after a long time they halted by the sweet shores of Galilee, and she laid him with his back propped against a sycamore tree, and let him drink again. And then he took notice of her at last.

"Adal," he said. "My good comrade. But I thought truly that we had been through Purgatory together, and were entering Paradise. But now I know that you are a woman."

"Are you glad or sorry?" she said.

"Oh, I'm glad, I'm glad!" he cried. "And yet – what am I saying? My vow – the Templars – "

Very gently she told him how the Templars and the Hospitallers lay on the battlefield. He crossed himself, and wept. Then he held out his arms to her as if she had been his mother.

"And now – but what shall we do, my love, what shall we do?"

"I know what we must do," she said. "We'll go to the Abbess of Shaston. She'll make everything right for us."

Cry Wolf

Cry Wolf

Pat McIntosh

I heard his voice before I turned in at the archway by the inn, indistinct through the thick walls, with a clipped accent I did not recognize. The one that answered had the local accent, as thick as the local cider; as I rode through the archway the first voice spoke again.

"But the slate is up at the door. Are you certain there are no rooms?"

"Her be forgetful to tak un down." The Amyner struck a light and set it to a lantern, which sputtered into life as the third of the three men in the yard turned to look at me.

"Hello," he said. "You after a room too? I think we're out of luck."

This one was clearly from my own part of the world, and he took me for a boy. In the lantern light, hair and moustache glinted red.

"Be no rooms," said the ostler, as if he was prepared to go on repeating it.

The redhead stepped to his horse's head and gathered up the reins, saying, "Wolf, let's go and see if the gate-ward'll let us out. There was a good spot a mile or so back."

The inn door flew open and a volley of sound poured out. Then a girl shot down the wooden steps to land sprawling in the yard, and the inn-wife appeared in the doorway flourishing a broom and still screeching curses.

"Let me see thy sour-apple face again!" she shouted. "Just once more in my clean inn, thee gall-weevil leaf-blighted barren strumpet! And if that city trash come nosing round here again, the constables I'll set on him. Out!"

The girl, already at the archway, turned and shrieked something indistinct but venomous, then left hastily as the inn-wife made to come down the steps. She watched the empty archway for a moment, then turned back into the inn with a satisfied air.

"Applesweet," called the redhead. She paused, and turned ponderously, peering into the lamplight. The redhead returned his reins to the man called Wolf and went forward, "Mind me, applesweet? Changed thee have not, saving better. Knew thy voice on the first word, that I did."

The dialect of Amyn sat oddly on his Westlands tongue but the inn-wife appeared to think otherwise. With a shriek of delight she cast herself down the steps at him; he caught her, staggering, and patted her ample bottom.

"Barlach!" she exclaimed. "Truly it be thee?"

"Is that you forget me so quick? Truly me – no, not here, shock himself you will. Has thee room for himself, applesweet?"

She cast a quick glance beyond him at the man called Wolf, straightened, and bobbed a curtsy.

"Got a lovely room, now she'm left. Two beds, and both clean sheets, it has. Come thee and see," she said to the redhead, and started up the steps onto the inn. He came back to where the man called Wolf was still holding the reins of both their horses.

"Well?" he said. "I'm provided for – " He grinned in the lamplight. "D'you want to share?" he said to me.

I stared at him. I knew my answer, of course. Any member of the Order, said the rules, who shall wittingly and willingly share a room, a bed, or a blanket with a man shall be held excommunicate until suitable expiation . . . I looked at the mounted man, and he pushed back his hood and smiled at me. In the lamplight his face was pale and diamond-shaped, and his eyes, smiling, drew the heart out of me. Blinded, I smiled back, and nodded.

"Fine," said the redhead. "You see to the horses, then."

I dismounted, and led Dester and my packhorse into the stable, wondering whether I had run mad. I had been sane enough when I rode in at the archway, and now here I was, Thula, warrior of the Order of the Moon as Alkris, sworn to remain virgin and eschew the company of men, about to share a room with one. I put my horses in the stalls the ostler pointed to, and unlashed my saddlebags from Dester's saddle. There was enough money in them to buy a half share in the inn.

"Well, friend?" said the man called Wolf. I turned, and he was looking at me with those disturbing eyes. I moved toward the door, and slipped on rotted straw. He put out a quick hand to steady me, and at his touch the world swirled and went dark about me.

I lay flat – in a bed, perhaps – and about me were hooded figures, faceless in the light of a spider-lamp that glimmered faintly on the wooden bowl before my face. I must drink or choke on the bitter liquid it held; I raised my hand to push it away, without success, and panic rose in my throat as I saw my hand. Not square-fingered and short-nailed, but long and thin, taper-nailed, a scar across the knuckles . . .

"Easy," said the man called Wolf. "How long since you ate?"

I pulled away from him. The vision had passed, but not the feeling of panic, and I was trembling.

"I'm all right," I said. "Dizzy for a moment. I need a drink."

We crossed the yard in silence, I with my thoughts in turmoil. We are taught to regard such visions as having meaning, but what should this one tell me . . . ?

The room was a good one, although not so good as the inn-wife claimed; she was insisting that the High King of the Westlands himself slept in it frequently when we arrived.

"Gonseir the Usurper?" said Barlach. "It looks it,

applesweet. Wolf, that's three crescents. If we pay two and the youngster pays one – "

"I should pay one and a half." I objected.

"The Wolf gets the bigger bed." Barlach said. "He'd never get into this one. Got a crescent?"

"Please," I said, embarrassed. "I can't – "

"Fair's fair," Barlach argued. "If you like to share the other bed, you can – "

"Barlach," said the Wolf quietly. The redhead turned to look at him, said, "Oh, all right," and accepted my one-and-a-half crescents. The inn-wife, paid, leered lovingly at Barlach and puffed off down the stairs. I put my saddlebags down on the small bed and looked around. Fresh water and a basin stood on the table between the beds.

"Ale before supper, Barlach?" asked the Wolf. He had removed cloak and hood and stood clad in black; a single heavy black plait swung as he turned his head, and his eyes gleamed pale under dark brows.

"I've a thirst like a lime kiln," said the redhead. The Wolf turned to me, one eyebrow raised. I shook my head.

"I'll wash first," I said. "I'll follow you down."

As they left, I realized for the first time their relative heights. Barlach was smaller than me, six inches or so, which made him five feet three at the most, but broader and heavier, solidly made; the Wolf was a foot taller than his friend and the leanest man I had ever seen. They made a strange pair.

The door closed behind them and I turned to the ewer and basin. What was I doing, I wondered. Had I indeed run mad? I was now excommunicate; moonlight falling on me would kill me; I must not pray to the Lady – I ought to be on my knees shaking and weeping and begging to First Star to intercede for me . . . Instead I was calmly washing the dust off my face and wondering what the tall man with the light eyes would say if he knew I was a girl. And what he would do.

I looked at the door. Firmly shut. And I was covered in

dust. I decided to risk a proper wash, and pulled off my padded tunic and, with another glance at the door, my shirt and the linen band that goes under it. The cool water was blissful on my throat and shoulders; I reached for the soap and began to remove the rest of the dust.

I was finished and rinsed and reaching for my linen towel when hasty feet sounded along the corridor. I grabbed at the towel as the door burst open.

"Wolf, have you got – " began the redhead, and halted. He stared at me, took in what he had seen, and stepped inside. I felt the slow tide of colour rise in my face and spread down my neck. Helplessly I stared back at him, almost mesmerized.

"Devern's golden ball," he said, closing the door behind him. "Well, now, gorgeous. You're on the wrong track. The Wolf's under an oath, he'll have no use for you. Why not make do with me?"

I had never seen anything like his expression. I clutched the folds of linen against me and said with difficulty.

"Please – it wasn't like that! I don't – I mustn't – "

"Or were you planning to knife him in the night?" He stared at me, frowning. Then the frown cleared and the other, more alarming expression returned. "No, you weren't. Come on, then," he said, trying to coax me taking a step forward. I retreated, though my knees threatened to give way. Unarmed and half-naked I was awash with panic.

Again feet came along the corridor, light and hasty. The door flung open and the Wolf appeared. He glanced swiftly at me, at Barlach and back; frowning, he stepped in and closed the door. Panic died before despair; I had been mistaken in him, and here was my end, force and ignominy and falling on my sword.

Then his glance sharpened. Comprehension dawned. He took Barlach by the shoulder and swung him around, turning himself to face the door.

"Let you dress, madam," he said quietly. Heart pounding,

knees trembling, I rubbed myself half-dry and obeyed, wrestling with clinging linen and dust-caked wool. At last I said,

"You can turn around now."

My voice sounded small in my own ears. He released Barlach and turned to face me, and I found myself going scarlet again.

"I will sleep in the stables," he said harshly, and moved to lift his saddlebag. "Best you leave before us in the morning. I will not ask your name, lest this come to the ears of your superiors."

His tone had shaken me, but he could not maintain it, and his eyes did not match it. I had fallen from grace already, what was a little more?

"I want to ride with you," I said. He stared at me, his face going rigidly expressionless. Barlach produced an appalling snigger.

"I've told you, sweetheart," he said. "The Wolf has no use for you. Why not make do with me – ?"

The Wolf dropped the saddlebags and struck him backhanded. He sat down on the kist behind the door, rubbing his mouth and looking startled: the Wolf turned to me and said, still without expression, "We are not for such as you. I am – I am under judgment on a matter of league with Darkness and Barlach – " He halted, and glanced over his shoulder at the redhead, who smiled deprecatingly.

"You should see the village where we lived for six months," I said.

"Your shield-sister is dead?" he said, more gently. I nodded and there was another pause. The Barlach came to his feet.

"Oh, hell's teeth, let's go and eat," he said. "I'm hungry."

The Wolf looked at him, and back at me.

"Aye," he said. "Let us eat."

I came forward to obey. I could argue in the morning. Barlach looked me up and down and snorted, disapproving.

"I like 'em well covered, anyway," he said.

We ate at one end of the long table in the public room. It was stuffy, full of Amyner peasants, and noisy, but a row of empty bowls showed that the other guests had already eaten well. Barlach disappeared shortly, to help the inn-wife at the tap of the great cider barrel in the corner; to judge by the sounds that reached us now and then, he was little help. We two left at the table ate stew with thick barley bread. The Wolf, finishing first, sat in silence, looking at his hands clasped on the table. They were as pale as his face, with no line at the cuffs of his shirt such as I had on each wrist; they were long and thin, taper-nailed, and as he reached for his cider-mug I saw the long scar across the knuckles.

Something lurched inside me, I stared, transfixed; then, finding him looking at me with faint concern, I said the first thing that came into my head.

"The scar on your hand – troll?"

He looked down at it and shook his head, half smiling.

"Na, not that one. This was a troll." He touched his upper arm as if it were still tender, and I recalled that he had not used that arm all evening. There was a a tear in his shirtsleeve, clumsily mended, and a bloodstain partly washed out. "A week since," he added, feeling the silence. "Perhaps three days' hard ride." There was another pause; I finished my stew. "You know trolls?"

"Trolls killed Fenala," I said. "I got the trolls."

"Where was that?"

"A long way. North of Rhawn Dys – other side of the Mountains."

"You have crossed the Mountains alone?" he said.

"Well I wasn't alone when I set out," I said. He quirked one eyebrow and looked interested, so I told him the story of how I crossed the Mountains. Bits of it made him laugh; once or twice he made a dry comment that made me laugh. Behind me the taproom filled with villagers, cider fumes and noise, but isolated in its centre we continued to talk of the Mountains, of merchants, of the trading road through the Isthmus to the Southlands . . .

Then the Wolf, who could see the tap and the crowd around it, broke across something I was saying.

"Madam," he said softly, "in a moment there will be fighting. When I say the word, go quickly and stay in our room. Open only to Barlach or to me. Is that clear?"

"I can use a knife," I said. He looked at me like a man not used to being disobeyed.

"Battle, even with trolls, is one thing," he said. "A drunken brawl is another." His glance went beyond me again. "Go now. Quickly." He got to his feet and without staying to see that I obeyed made his way quietly through the crowd about the tap. A silence fell, in which I heard Barlach's voice.

"Let go of me, pig-feet," he said clearly.

"Tak they filthy hands off of she," said an Amyner voice, "or mak thee I will."

"Let go of me first," said Barlach.

"What business is it of thine, brother?" said the inn-wife shrilly. "Is that I gave thee leave to meddle wi' my doings?"

"Be quiet, woman," said the Amyner voice. "Now tak thy hands off of she, thee city trash, afore I mak thee."

The Wolf had reached them now, and seemed about to join in the discussion when a man by the door shouted:

"Werewolf!"

The Wolf stiffened. My heart began to thump unpleasantly – I had once before seen a shapeshifter taken, but that was in an Eastlands city, and the Peacekeepers had arrived before blood was shed. Here anything might –

"Where be werewolf?" demanded somebody. "Where?"

"There! Him i' the black tunic!"

Over the heads of the crowd the Wolf's narrow black-clad

shoulders were rigid. I stared, and the men nearest him laid hands on him. Those farther away backed away a little, and I saw Barlach come up in a rush to help his friend. Someone clipped him on the side of the head with a cider mug, and he went down, and the man by the door shouted,

"Kill the filthy shapeshifter!"

"He be no werewolf!" the inn-wife protested. "Know him I do, all on us do!"

"He bear the marks," said the man. He was marked himself, a livid birthmark like a horse-track on one cheek, and his eyes were wild and burning. Cloth ripped, and somebody swore, and as the crowd fell back again the Wolf stood passive in the hands of his captors, tunic and shirt torn to the waist. Everyone knows the marks of the werewolf: hair on the back and none on the chest, different teeth, the extra nipples down the belly like a wolf. They made no attempt to count his teeth. I saw the meaning of his nickname, and a chill wave of horror washed through me.

"Kill the filthy shapeshifter!" someone shouted. They all took up the cry. I should have left, but I stayed where I was, shaking. I had left my young charge with a werefalcon in the Mountains, but a bird was a bird. A wolf killed people. They told tales – especially in the north, nearer to the Wolf-land – things I had heard jumped to my mind. And I had nearly shared a room with that . . .

"Hang the brute!" someone yelled. The man near the door seemed to have vanished. I got to my feet and slid to the door, and through it, and ran along the passage and up the stairs and into the room. Mother of mares, what an escape! I might have been torn to pieces while I slept!

Common sense took over. In the first place, being torn to pieces was likely to wake one; in the second, he had ordered me out of a possible brawl. Not trying to reason out why this made a difference, I went back to the door and opened it. Voices rose in ciderous discord, arguing about what to do with him.

They could not hang him, Grum's cow had eaten the rope. They could not burn him, for fear of firing the thatch this dry weather. Knifing only worked with a silver blade, everyone knew that.

Someone suggested, drowning, and they all took that up. Hope leapt in me. They must open the gates to take him down to the river, and in the mood they were in they would not close them. With much shouting they settled on that, and I left the door and hastily stuffed soap-box and linen towel into my saddlebag. The Wolf's heavy fur cloak and hood, their bag, was that everything – ?

In the dark stable, Dester snorted at me, and nudged an enquiring muzzle into my hand. At any other time I would have cursed into Outer Darkness any ostler who left him to eat his supper around his bit; now I only prayed that all four horses were yet bridled, and almost wept with relief to find it so. It can be hard to bit and bridle a strange horse in haste. Their two were easily identified, the ugly black the Wolf had ridden and a nappy half-broken chestnut who threatened to bite as I clapped his saddle on his back. I tightened the girths with trembling fingers; the packhorse, my gift from Fenist the Falcon, grumbled sleepily and tried to blow himself out, but I thumped him in the ribs and he subsided. Gathering up the four sets of reins, I led the horses out across the yard.

As I came to the archway the rabble of villagers poured past in the street; it had taken them until now to find cords enough to bind him, and as he passed I saw by moonlight the knots and tangles about his arms. I could not tell if he had seen me but it mattered little. As they battled loudly with the gates, I led the horses out and tied them up before the inn.

Inside all was deserted. The inn-wife sobbed in the distance, and in the taproom Barlach lay in a gaudy heap on the floor, cider dark in his hair. I shook him, but he showed no sign of rousing, so I grabbed the back of his orange tunic and tugged.

He slithered across the floor, limp and amazingly heavy, rushes piling up before him. Mother of mares, I prayed, let his tunic hold, for I like him, no matter what he said to me, and he is the Wolf's friend.

The tunic held, while I towed him across to the door, and somehow down the steps to where the horses shied away, snorting. My packhorse seemed the best steed; something gave me strength to lift him across the pack-saddle before the horse could avoid me. I lashed him on with the unused stirrup-leathers from my saddlebag and mounted Dester, four sets of reins wound around my hand. The gates at the end of the silent street stood wide open. I turned the beasts, and nudged Dester forward with my knees.

We came forth at the canter, into the open beyond the fence. Down yonder, away to the right was a group of men shouting and splashing in the moonlit river. I drew my sword with my free hand and shouted a war-cry, and we bore down on the gaggle of villagers like an army – four horses, one unconscious man, and a frightened war-maid. Many of the Amyners scattered, leaving something dark in the river, I let go the other horses' reins and two of them shied off, frightened by the shouting, but the ugly black one the Wolf had ridden chased the few Amyners who tried to stand ground. I halted Dester in the water and leaned down.

He was beyond struggles, lying limply in a foot of water. I reached for him, trying to get some purchase on arm or shoulder, and his black horse left off chasing peasants and to my surprise splashed into the river, bent his head and got the slack of the Wolf's tunic in his teeth and heaved. I grabbed at the limp body as it came up dripping moonlight, and getting some purchase in the ropes about his arms dragged him across my saddle-bow. No time to see to him now: the peasants, seeing the avenging army to be but one rider and three uncontrolled horses, were returning. I shouted, and flourished my sword, and turning Dester's head for the road kicked him in the ribs.

The other horses, seeing him running, came after, and we went off down the road like the Wild Hunt.

A mile from the village I first noticed the ravens. The urgency was wearing off, and we were doing a hand-canter, so that I had time to look around; and there were three birds flapping along near us, wheeling across the moon, quite plainly ravens. I wondered vaguely what ravens should be doing out at this hour, but my attention was for the Wolf, who was beginning to stir across my knees. I touched his arm, meaning to say something reassuring, and through torn wet linen my fingers found cold and clammy skin. Once again the world swirled and went dark about me.

I faced a man, one who though seated I could discern to be tall, who regarded me with piercing eyes from under a broad-brimmed hat. Gems hung bright from the hat, catching the light of the candle-crown I knew was over my head, and a slow voice spoke, and I felt myself answer.

Then I snatched my hand away, and I was on Dester's back, a half-drowned man across my knees, with the strange feeling that the man in the gem-hung hat knew all the paths of my mind and how I trod them . . .

There was a good place to stop. I turned Dester and walked him down onto the grassy slope between the stream and the road. The Wolf's black horse spoke to the other beasts, or so it seemed, for in response to its half-threatening snicker they wheeled off the road and stood obediently waiting to be tethered for the night. I unloaded my two prizes, and tethered the beasts hastily, not letting them drink yet. Barlach, when I checked him, was twitching slightly; I covered him with his own blanket against the dew, and turned to the Wolf.

He was wholly unconscious again, soaked to the skin, cold and clammy to the touch as I cut the ropes away. Fresh blood spotted his sleeve over the troll-wound, but it seemed to me the first thing was to warm him. I got the dry wood out of my pack-saddle and began to build a fire.

By the time the water boiled he was rousing. I put various herbs to infuse in the pan, this and that against fevers and chills, and when he groaned I lifted it from the fire and poured some into my pewter mug. Setting it near him I knelt beside him and, without thinking, put my hand on his cheek to turn his head. He groaned again, and his eyes opened, and his gaze met mine.

This time, more than ever, I was not myself. I was sitting in a high wooden chair, carved and uncomfortable, facing the tall man with the piercing eyes, who sat in another such chair. Between us, to left and right, were long tables and men seated behind them, watching us. The man before me was speaking, eyeing me closely from under his gem-hung hat, but I could not understand the words. Then he said, "You who are accused, the first test, for tainting of thought, intent and memory, gave no result. The second test, for tainting of purpose, gave no result. This test will show if you are tainted by Darkness in blood, bone and sinew, and by the writing in the nail. Do you submit to this final test?"

I nodded, because I had obeyed when this truly happened.

"The test is carried out within a Ring of Feeling," he said, and the words echoed in my head, ring-of-feeling, ring-of-feeling — the swirling happened again, and there were chalked lines about me and a gleaming and glowing in the air. I saw this and knew it illusion, there was only chalk on the marble floor; but I felt raw, mind and body, not hurting but as if anything that did hurt would be too much to bear, like a crab without a shell. The man in the hat said, "Hold out your left hand."

I did so, and hands took it; it was pale and long-fingered, and they twitched it expertly into position on a slab of marble, and before I fully realized what came next the hinged chopper cracked down on my little finger. It went through bone and muscle cleanly, someone caught the severed joint in a little silver bowl, and my hand was allowed to swing free, down inside the glowing ring. A demon of pain, fearsome even in memory, devoured hand and arm, and darkness covered me.

A series of images. A dwarf, strangely dressed, mixing this and

178

that in little bowls on a table before the man in the hat. Two rats, a white and a black, in a cage before my feet, one eating boiled flesh, the other refusing his share. A sickening smell, and the stomach-churning, sudden knowledge that this was my flesh, the scraps of muscle from the severed joint. The same with the bone ... The dwarf working over another little bowl, stirring with a glass rod, heating it over a tiny brazier, adding wine vinegar and water-of-sulphur. The phrase rose in my mind again: the Writing in the Nail.

The dwarf facing me.

"You had a brush with Darkness," he said. "Six weeks since." The words echoed in my mind; my hand hurt, and the world looked strange.

"We were here," said Barlach's voice. *"Talking to Gonseir the Bastard."*

I saw indistinctly the man with the birthmark whom I had seen in the inn, his eyes furious, the birthmark pulsing redly.

Then my sight cleared, and I was kneeling over the Wolf, staring down at him in the moonlight. My left hand resting on his cheek had four whole fingers attached to it.

"You went away," he said. I drew a shaking breath, and let it go. Whatever it meant, that was a dream. This was reality — two hurt men to see to, and this one soaking wet.

"I was afraid you'd think that," I said. I raised his head and lifted the cup which was still scalding hot. "Try and drink this, it's hot."

He drank a little, then rolled over on all fours, stomach heaving. I set down the cup and held his head, and he retched till his belly was empty and then subsided against me shivering. I found I was holding his left hand in mine; it was long-fingered, pale in the moonlight, and the last joint of the little finger was missing. *The wound was still tarred over.*

It came to me with a lurch. These visions had no meaning for me — they were his, memories rather than dreams, of some sort of trial. What had he said? "I am under judgment on a matter of league with Darkness." Mother of mares, no wonder his judges had wanted the Oracular Joint!

I pushed him down on the turf and reached for the cup again. He drank obediently and said, "I mind I was in the water."

"You were," I said. "I thought you were drowned. I frightened the men with the flat of my sword, but that horse of yours chased them off – like a dog after rabbits. They were more scared of it than of me."

He laughed, almost light-headedly.

"Squirrel is wise," he said. "Wise as the Wizard's ravens."

"We've got three of those," I said. "Ravens I mean."

"Ravens?" he said quickly.

"Yes," I said. "Flapping round us all the way here. They've gone now, but – "

"Ravens!" he muttered. "The message. It must be – !" He stared about him at the silent sky. "You are certain? They were not owls?"

"I saw them against the moon," I said.

Mother of mares, the Moon! I had broken the Rules, should have run mad by now, riding about in the moonlight like this – and yet I had prayed to her, and she had answered. Or at least Barlach's tunic had held. Were my teachers all wrong, was I specially favoured – ?

I realized the Wolf was shivering.

"You should change," I said. "I'll be down by the river. Shout if you need me."

Barlach groaned beyond the fire. The Wolf jumped, and turned and peered at the redhead, still lying inert under his blanket.

"It's Barlach," I explained. "He's not hurt, except for a bang on the head."

"Can you do everything?" he asked. His tone of rueful amusement made my face burn.

"I'm scared of thunder," I said. He laughed at that, and began getting to his feet. The torn tunic fell open, and I remembered why it had been torn.

"I'll be down by the stream," I repeated, and went off across the short turf.

Down by the water I found a flat stone to sit on, and for some time stared at the black-and-silver water without seeing it. All the things that had happened this evening went round and round in my head, images of Barlach, the peasants crowding about the pool, the Wolf's bare chest in the moonlight, and over all his compelling eyes by lamplight in the yard. I liked him, I was drawn to him, when he smiled I would be his bond-servant for life, but he was a werewolf, half animal, a shapeshifter – my nurse's tales danced in my mind.

Then suddenly all the spinning images fell into a pattern. The moon had showed me all these; she had lit my way out of the inn-yard, she had given me light by the river, and now she had reminded me what this man was. I was being given a choice: to go with him, follow my liking, forsake the training of my youth; or ride away and leave him and go with the moonlight. For the first time in my life, I found the moonlight cheerless.

But supposing, against all better judgment, I did as I wanted and rode with him. If the rules are broken, how shall the Order survive? I would be in the displeasure of the Moon, that I had served since I was seven years old ... And anyway, he had refused my earlier request: maybe he would refuse this one. Suddenly I decided I would not speak. I would go up the bank, and collect my horses, and ride on before they left, never seeing him again. I would go down to Maer-Cuith and tell them at the Temple that Fenala was dead; they would find me another girl to ride with, and we would go out and combat evil under the moon ...

Twigs snapped. I turned, and he stood against the stars; I rose to my feet, and the moon came out. I had been so engrossed in my thoughts I had not noticed the clouds coming up.

"You'll be all right here," I said. "I'll go on now, my horse should be rested."

"I assure you," he said, and his voice was smiling. "I stopped eating little girls for breakfast when I left my mother's country."

"That's not – " I began, and stopped guiltily.

"For one thing," he pursued drily, "I dislike meat first thing in the morning."

I couldn't help it, I giggled.

"I prefer a light breakfast myself," I agreed. He sat down as if his legs had given way, and my voice said of its own accord, "I never met a werewolf before. I didn't think – " I regained control and changed that to, "When the man with the birth-mark shouted 'Werewolf' – "

"Birthmark?" he said quickly.

"Yes, the man by the door." I thought quickly. "No, he kept out of your sight. Six feet, dark hair, wild eyes, a mark like a horseshoe on his cheek." I drew it on my own cheek to make it clear, and he took a long unsteady breath.

"Gonseir," he said. "Gonseir the Bastard. My loving cousin."

"Gonseir?" I said. There was a short silence. Then I said "He was in your dream. The third one."

He glanced at me, unsurprised.

"I felt your fear, when Barlach surprised you," he said. "Clear across the yard, I felt it. My dream, lady – if you saw that, you saw that I have been on trial," he said, as if the words tasted bad. "My cousin, who is High King of the Westlands, can think of no better way to be rid of me than to impeach me before the Order of White Sorcery on a charge of league with Darkness." He shivered, his hands working together. I saw that he was rubbing at the damaged finger as if there were a ring missing from it. "By the laws of the Order, if I am innocent, he must submit to the same trial, but he thought it worth the attempt."

"And you are innocent?" I said. Try as I might I could not keep the question out of my voice. He nodded.

"I know myself to be innocent. But my cousin is less than sane, and he has many resources, and speech with him can mark one like a brush with Darkness. They were to decide today."

"But surely," I said, "if he tried to get you the other way just now, the judgment must be for you?"

"The ravens will tell me," he said, and his voice was weary. I suddenly remembered my decision. I moved to go past him saying.

"I wish you luck. The moon shine on you."

He put up his hand and caught my wrist. His fingers went right around it. I stared down at him, and he said. "I have an oath on me as binding as yours. I would not harm you."

The Moon came out – when had it gone in? – and in the same moment Barlach called from the fire. I slipped from his slackened grasp and went up the bank. By the time he followed me, Barlach was sitting up cursing and feeling his head, which was not broken despite all he said.

"I think he'll live." I said over his shoulder to the Wolf. "His tongue isn't damaged, anyway."

"No bones broken, small brother?" said the Wolf.

"Only my head," said the redhead. "Devern's brass ball, if I ever drink Amyn cider again – " He was silent, staring before him. The Wolf turned, and I likewise, as a second and a third raven flopped down to join the one on the turf.

"Greetings to the emissary of the Wizard," said the Wolf, and went down on one knee. The first bird waddled forward and ducked its head in a travesty of a bow.

"My son," it said, "Gonseir's charges against you stand not proven."

The second bird joined it, and in the same outlandish accents recited, "Wherever this finds you, make all haste to join me."

The third raven came clumsily across the grass and halted at the Wolf's knee. "Gonseir is suspended," it said. "Take your ring and walk in light."

Gold glittered on its leg. The Wolf lifted it gently, his hands trembling, and worked the ring over its claw. It croaked, and bit him, but at length he set it free and held up the ring. Getting to his feet he slid the ring onto his damaged finger and turned to us.

"Walk in light," he said. Barlach scrambled up and sprang at him, hugging him and then punching him in the ribs so that he swayed.

"Careful," I said. "He was nearly drowned."

"Drowned?" said Barlach blankly. "Hey – how'd we get here, anyway?"

"We were brought," said the Wolf, one arm still across Barlach's shoulders, "by the lady whose name we still do not know."

"Thula," I said.

"Thula," he repeated. "What way do you ride, Thula? We must make all speed westwards, since the Wizard summons me."

Barlach groaned, and muttered somthing about the Wizard, but I stared at the Wolf. Here was my decision, made and unmade in my head a dozen times, being taken for me. All the sanctuaries and holy places of the Westlands lay south from here, not west. They rode on an errand with no place for me. South down the moon's path was my road.

"South," I said, and my voice cracked. He looked at me a long moment, while Barlach stared from one to the other of us. Then he bent his head.

"So be it," he said. "Let us break the fire."

But when the fire was broken, the horses watered, all made ready to leave, he came to me where I tested Dester's girth.

"Thula," he said, and his hand was held out. "It is in my heart that we shall meet again, and before too long. I do not know our plans, and only the Moon knows what comes to you, but the Bunch of Grapes in Maer-Cuith is a good place."

"A good place for what?" I said. The clasp of his hand made my heart thump, but when that wore off he was saying.

"Have you a coin? Any coin will do."

"What for?" I asked, searching my pockets. "If you're planning to go back and pay the reckoning – "

"Na!" He was laughing. "Only, there is this I wish to give you, and I do not wish to cut the friendship."

I found a half-copper crescent, and gave him it, and he put in my hand a dagger, a good one, blue Southron steel with a shagreen hilt. He closed my hands over it, and bent and kissed my closed fingers, and swinging about went and mounted his horse.

"Come, Barlach," he said, and they moved off, crossed the road, set off westward in the moonlit countryside. I watched them until the Moon changed shape and wavered and spilled over, and he did not look back.

Black God's Kiss

Black God's Kiss

C. L. Moore

They brought in Joiry's tall commander, struggling between two men-at-arms who tightly gripped the ropes which bound their captive's mailed arms. They picked their way between mounds of dead as they crossed the great hall toward the dais where the conqueror sat, and twice they slipped a little in the blood that spattered the flags. When they came to a halt before the mailed figure on the dais, Joiry's commander was breathing hard, and the voice that echoed hollowly under the helmet's confines was hoarse with fury and despair.

Guillaume the conqueror leaned on his mighty sword, hands crossed on its hilt, grinning down from his height upon the furious captive before him. He was a big man, Guillaume, and he looked bigger still in his spattered armour. There was blood on his hard, scarred face, and he was grinning a white grin that split his short, curly beard glitteringly. Very splendid and very dangerous he looked, leaning on his great sword and smiling down upon fallen Joiry's lord, struggling between the stolid men-at-arms.

"Unshell me this lobster," said Guillaume in his deep, lazy voice. "We'll see what sort of face the fellow has who gave us such a battle. Off with his helmet, you."

But a third man had to come up and slash the straps which held the iron helmet on, for the struggles of Joiry's commander were too fierce, even with bound arms, for either of the guards to release their hold. There was a moment of sharp struggle; then the straps parted and the helmet rolled loudly across the flagstones.

Guillaume's white teeth clicked on a startled oath. He stared.

Joiry's lady glared back at him from between her captors, wild red hair tousled, wild lion-yellow eyes ablaze.

"God curse you!" snarled the lady of Joiry between clenched teeth. "God blast your black heart!"

Guillaume scarcely heard her. He was still staring, as most men stared when they first set eyes upon Jirel of Joiry. She was tall as most men, and as savage as the wildest of them, and the fall of Joiry was bitter enough to break her heart as she stood snarling curses up at her tall conqueror. The face above her mail might not have been fair in a woman's head-dress, but in the steel setting of her armour it had a biting, sword-edge beauty as keen as the flash of blades. The red hair was short upon her high, defiant head, and the yellow blaze of her eyes held fury as a crucible holds fire.

Guillaume's stare melted into a slow smile. A little light kindled behind his eyes as he swept the long, strong lines of her with a practised gaze. The smile broadened, and suddenly he burst into full-throated laughter, a deep bull bellow of amusement and delight.

"By the Nails!" he roared. "Here's welcome for the warrior! And what forfeit d'ye offer, pretty one, for your life?"

She blazed a curse at him.

"So? Naughty words for a mouth so fair, my lady. Well, we'll not deny you put up a gallant battle. No man could have done better, and many have done worse. But against Guillaume – " He inflated his splendid chest and grinned down at her from the depths of his jutting beard. "Come to me, pretty one," he commanded. "I'll wager your mouth is sweeter than your words."

Jirel drove a spurred heel into the shin of one guard and twisted from his grip as he howled, bringing up an iron knee into the abdomen of the other. She had writhed from their grip and made three long strides toward the door before Guillaume caught her. She felt his arms closing about her from behind, and lashed out with both spiked heels in a futile assault upon his leg armour, twisting like a maniac, fighting with her knees and spurs, straining hopelessly at the ropes which bound her arms. Guillaume laughed and whirled her round, grinning down into the blaze of her yellow eyes. Then deliberately he set a fist under her chin and tilted her mouth up to his. There was a cessation of her hoarse curses.

"By Heaven, that's like kissing a sword-blade," said Guillaume, lifting his lips at last.

Jirel choked something that was mercifully muffled as she darted her head sidewise, like a serpent striking, and sank her teeth into his neck. She missed the jugular by a fraction of an inch.

Guillaume said nothing, then. He sought her head with a steady hand, found it despite her wild writhing, sank iron fingers deep into the hinges of her jaw, forcing her teeth relentlessly apart. When he had her free he glared down into the yellow hell of her eyes for an instant. The blaze of them was hot enough to scorch his scarred face. He grinned and lifted his ungauntleted hand, and with one heavy blow in the face he knocked her halfway across the room. She lay still upon the flags.

Jirel opened her yellow eyes upon darkness. She lay quiet for a while, collecting her scattered thoughts. By degrees it came back to her, and she muffled upon her arm a sound that was half curse and half sob. Joiry had fallen. For a time she lay rigid in the dark, forcing herself to the realization.

The sound of feet shifting on stone near by brought her out of that particular misery. She sat up cautiously, feeling about her to determine in what part of Joiry its liege lady was imprisoned. She knew that the sound she had heard must be the sentry, and by the dank smell of the darkness that she was underground. In one of the little dungeon cells, of course. With careful quietness she got to her feet, muttering a curse as her head reeled for an instant and then began to throb. In the utter dark she felt around the cell. Presently she came to a little wooden stool in a corner, and was satisfied. She gripped one leg of it with firm fingers and made her soundless way around the wall until she had located the door.

The sentry remembered, afterward, that he had heard the wildest shriek for help which had ever rung in his ears, and he remembered unbolting the door. Afterward, until they found him lying inside the locked cell with a cracked skull, he remembered nothing.

Jirel crept up the dark stairs of the north turret, murder in her heart. Many little hatreds she had known in her life, but no such blaze as this. Before her eyes in the night she could see Guillaume's scornful, scarred face laughing, the little jutting beard split with the whiteness of his mirth. Upon her mouth she felt the remembered weight of his, about her the strength of his arms. And such a blast of hot fury came over her that she reeled a little and clutched at the wall for support. She went on in a haze of red anger, and something like madness burning in her brain as a resolve slowly took shape out of the chaos of her hate. When that thought came to her she paused again, mid-step upon the stairs, and was conscious of a little coldness blowing over her. Then it was gone, and she shivered a little, shook her shoulders and grinned wolfishly, and went on.

By the stars she could see through the arrow-slits in the wall it must be near to midnight. She went softly on the stairs, and she encountered no one. Her little tower room at the top was empty. Even the straw pallet where the serving-wench slept had not been used that night. Jirel got herself out of her armour alone, somehow, after much striving and twisting. Her doeskin shirt was stiff with sweat and stained with blood. She tossed it disdainfully into a corner. The fury in her eyes had cooled now to a contained and secret flame. She smiled to herself as she slipped a fresh shirt of doeskin over her tousled red head and donned a brief tunic of link-mail. On her legs she buckled the greaves of some forgotten legionary, relic of the not long past days when Rome still ruled the world. She thrust a dagger through her belt and took her own long two-handed sword bare-bladed in her grip. Then she went down the stairs again.

She knew there must have been revelry and feasting in the great hall that night, and by the silence hanging so heavily now she was sure that most of her enemies lay still in drunken slumber, and she experienced a swift regret for the gallons of her good French wine so wasted. And the thought flashed through her head that a determined woman with a sharp sword might work some little damage among the drunken sleepers before she was overpowered. But she put that idea by, for Guillaume would have posted sentries to spare, and she must not give up her secret freedom so fruitlessly.

Down the dark stairs she went, and crossed one corner of the vast central hall whose darkness she was sure hid wine-deadened sleepers, and so into the lesser dimness of the rough little chapel that Joiry boasted. She had been sure she would find Father Gervase there, and she was not mistaken. He rose from his knees before the altar, dark in his robe, the starlight through the narrow window shining upon his tonsure.

"My daughter!" he whispered. "My daughter! How have you escaped? Shall I find you a mount? If you can pass the sentries you should be in your cousin's castle by daybreak."

She hushed him with a lifted hand.

"No," she said. "It is not outside I go this night. I have a more perilous journey even than that to make. Shrive me, father."

He stared at her.

"What is it?"

She dropped to her knees before him and gripped the rough cloth of his habit with urgent fingers.

"Shrive me, I say! I go down into hell tonight to pray the devil for a weapon, and it may be I shall not return."

Gervase bent and gripped her shoulders with hands that shook.

"Look at me!" he demanded. "Do you know what you're saying? You go – "

"Down!" She said it firmly. "Only you and I know that passage, father – and not even we can be sure of what lies beyond. But to gain a weapon against that man I would venture into perils even worse than that."

"If I thought you meant it," he whispered, "I would waken Guillaume now and give you into his arms. It would be a kinder fate, my daughter."

"It's that I would walk through hell to escape," she whispered back fiercely. "Can't you see? Oh, God knows, I'm not innocent of the ways of light loving – but to be any man's fancy, for a night or two, before he snaps my neck or sells me into slavery – and above all, if that man were Guillaume! Can't you understand?"

"That would be shame enough," nodded Gervase. "But think, Jirel! For that shame there is atonement and absolution, and for that death the gates of heaven open wide. But this other – Jirel, Jirel, never through all eternity may you come out, body or soul, if you venture – down!"

She shrugged.

"To wreak my vengeance upon Guillaume I would go if I knew I should burn in hell forever."

"But Jirel, I do not think you understand. This is a worse fate than the deepest depths of hell-fire. This is – this is beyond all the bounds of the hells we know. And I think Satan's hottest flames were the breath of paradise, compared to what may befall there."

"I know. Do you think I'd venture down if I could not be sure? Where else would I find such a weapon as I need, save outside God's dominion?"

"Jirel, you shall not!"

"Gervase, I go! Will you shrive me?" The hot yellow eyes blazed into his, lambent in the starlight.

After a moment he dropped his head. "You are my lady. I will give you God's blessing, but it will not avail you – there."

She went down into the dungeons again. She went down a long way through utter dark, over stones that were oozy and odorous with moisture, through blackness that had never known the light of day. She might have been a little afraid at other times, but that steady flame of hatred burning behind her eyes was a torch to light the way, and she could not wipe from her memory the feel of Guillaume's arms about her, the scornful press of his lips on her mouth. She whimpered a little, low in her throat, and a hot gust of hate went over her.

In the solid blackness she came at length to a wall, and she set herself to pulling the loose stones from this with her free hand, for she would not lay down the sword. They had never been laid in mortar, and they came out easily. When the way was clear she stepped through and found her feet upon a downward-sloping ramp of smooth stone. She cleared the rubble away from the hole in the wall, and enlarged it enough for a quick passage; for when she came back this way – if she did – it might well be that she would come very fast.

At the bottom of the slope she dropped to her knees on the cold floor and felt about. Her fingers traced the outline of a circle, the veriest crack in the stone. She felt until she found the ring in its center. That ring was of the coldest metal she had ever known, and the smoothest. She could put no name to it. The daylight had never shone upon such metal.

She tugged. The stone was reluctant, and at last she took

194

her sword in her teeth and put both hands to the lifting. Even then it taxed the limit of her strength, and she was strong as many men. But at last it rose, with the strangest sighing sound, and a little prickle of goose-flesh rippled over her.

Now she took the sword back into her hand and knelt on the rim of the invisble blackness below. She had gone this path once before and once only, and never thought to find any necessity in life strong enough to drive her down again. The way was the strangest she had ever known. There was, she thought, no such passage in all the world save here. It had not been built for human feet to travel. It had not been built for feet at all. It was a narrow, polished shaft that cork-screwed round and round. A snake might have slipped in it and gone shooting down, round and round in dizzy circles – but no snake on earth was big enough to fill that shaft. No human travellers had worn the sides of the spiral so smooth, and she did not care to speculate on what creatures had polished it so, through what ages of passage.

She might never have made that first trip down, nor anyone after her, had not some unknown human hacked the notches, which made it possible to descend slowly; that is, she thought it must have been a human. At any rate, the notches were roughly shaped for hands and feet, and spaced not too far apart; but who and when and how she could not even guess. As to the beings who made the shaft, in long-forgotten ages – well, there were devils on earth before man, and the world was very old.

She turned on her face and slid feet-first into the curving tunnel. That first time she and Gervase had gone down in sweating terror of what lay below, and with devils tugging at their heels. Now she slid easily not bothering to find toeholds, but slipping swiftly round and round the long spirals with only her hands to break the speed when she went too fast. Round and round she went, round and round.

It was a long way down. Before she had gone very far the

curious dizziness she had known before came over her again, a dizziness not entirely induced by the spirals she whirled around, but a deeper, atomic unsteadiness as if not only she but also the substances around her were shifting. There was something queer about the angles of those curves. She was no scholar in geometry or aught else, but she felt intuitively that the bend and slant of the way she went were somehow outside any other angles or bends she had ever known. They led into the unknown and the dark, but it seemed to her obscurely that they led into deeper darkness and mystery than the merely physical, as if, though she could not put it clearly even into thoughts, the peculiar and exact lines of the tunnel had been carefully angled to lead through poly-dimensional space as well as through the underground – perhaps through time, too. She did not know she was thinking such things; but all about her was a blurred dizziness as she shot down and round, and she knew that the way she went took her on a stranger journey than any other way she had ever travelled.

Down, and down. She was sliding fast, but she knew how long it would be. On that first trip they had taken alarm as the passage spiralled so endlessly and with thoughts of the long climb back had tried to stop before it was too late. They had found it impossible. Once embarked, there was no halting. She had tried, and such waves of sick blurring had come over her that she came near to unconsciousness. It was as if she had tried to halt some inexorable process of nature, half finished. They could only go on. The very atoms of their bodies shrieked in rebellion against a reversal of the change.

And the way up, when they returned, had not been difficult. They had had visions of back-breaking climb up interminable curves, but again the uncanny difference of those angles from those they knew was manifested. In a queer way they seemed to defy gravity, or perhaps led through some way outside the power of it. They had been sick and dizzy on the return, as on the way down, but through the clouds of that confusion it had seemed to them that they slipped as easily up the shaft as they had gone down; or perhaps that, once in the tunnel, there was neither up nor down.

The passage levelled gradually. This was the worst part for a human to travel, though it must have eased the speed of whatever beings the shaft was made for. It was too narrow for her to turn in, and she had to lever herself face down and feet first, along the horizontal smoothness of the floor, pushing with her hands. She was glad when her questing heels met open space and she slid from the mouth of the shaft and stood upright in the dark.

Here she paused to collect herself. Yes, this was the beginning of the long passage she and Father Gervase had travelled on that long-ago journey of exploration. By the veriest accident they had found the place, and only the veriest bravado had brought them thus far. He had gone on a greater distance than she – she was younger then, and more amenable to authority – and had come back white-faced in the torchlight and hurried her up the shaft again.

She went on carefully, feeling her way, remembering what she herself had seen in the darkness a little farther on, wondering in spite of herself, and with a tiny catch at her heart, what it was that had sent Father Gervase so hastily back. She had never been entirely satisfied with his explanations. It had been about here – or was it a little farther on? The stillness was like a roaring in her ears.

Then ahead of her the darkness moved. It was just that – a vast, imponderable shifting of the solid dark. Jesu! This was new! She gripped the cross at her throat with one hand and her sword-hilt with the other. Then it was upon her, striking like a hurricane, whirling her against the walls and shrieking in her ears like a thousand wind-devils – a wild cyclone of the dark that buffeted her mercilessly and tore at her flying hair and raved in her ears with the myriad voices of all lost things crying in the night. The voices were piteous in their terror and loneliness. Tears came to her eyes even as she shivered with nameless dread, for the whirlwind was alive with a dreadful instinct, an animate thing sweeping through the dark of the underground; an unholy thing that made her flesh crawl even though it touched her to the heart with its pitiful little lost voices wailing in the wind where no wind could possibly be.

And then it was gone. In that one flash of an instant it vanished, leaving no whisper to commemorate its passage. Only in the heart of it could one hear the sad little voices wailing or the wild shriek of the wind. She found herself standing stunned, her sword yet gripped futilely in one hand and the tears running down her face. Poor little lost voices, wailing. She wiped the tears away with a shaking hand and set her teeth hard against the weakness of reaction that flooded her. Yet it was a good five minutes before she could force herself on. After a few steps her knees ceased to tremble.

The floor was dry and smooth underfoot. It sloped a little downward, and she wondered into what unplumbed deeps she had descended by now. The silence had fallen heavily again, and she found herself straining for some other sound than the soft padding of her own boots. Then her foot slipped in sudden wetness. She bent, exploring fingers outstretched, feeling without reason that the wetness would be red if she could see it. But her fingers traced the immense outline of a footprint – splayed and three-toed like a frog's, but of monster size. It was a fresh footprint. She had a vivid flash of memory – that thing she had glimpsed in the torchlight on the other trip down. But she had had light then, and now she was blind in the dark, the creature's natural habitat . . .

For a moment she was not Jirel of Joiry, vengeful fury on the trail of a devilish weapon, but a frightened woman alone in the unholy dark. That memory had been so vivid . . . Then she saw Guillaume's scornful, laughing face again, the little beard dark along the line of his jaw, the strong teeth white with his laughter; and something hot and sustaining swept over her like a thin flame, and she was Joiry again, vengeful and resolute. She went on more slowly, her sword swinging in a semi-circle before every third step, that she might not be surprised too suddenly by some nightmare monster clasping her in smothering arms. But the flesh crept upon her unprotected back.

The smooth passage went on and on. She could feel the cold walls on either hand, and her upswung sword grazed the roof. It was like crawling through some worm's tunnel, blindly under the weight of countless tons of earth. She felt the pressure of it above and about her, overwhelming, and found herself praying that the end of this tunnel-crawling might come soon, whatever the end might bring.

But when it came it was a stranger thing than she had ever dreamed. Abruptly she felt the immense, imponderable oppression cease. No longer was she conscious of the tons of earth pressing about her. The walls had fallen away and her feet struck a sudden rubble instead of the smooth floor. But the darkness that had bandaged her eyes was changed too, indescribably. It was no longer darkness, but void; not an absence of light, but simple nothingness. Abysses opened around her, yet she could see nothing. She only knew that she stood at the threshold of some immense space, and sensed nameless things about her, and battled vainly against that nothingness which was all her straining eyes could see. And at her throat something constricted painfully.

She lifted her hand and found the chain of her crucifix taut and vibrant around her neck. At that she smiled a little grimly, for she began to understand. The crucifix. She found her hand shaking despite herself, but she unfastened the chain and dropped the cross to the ground. Then she gasped.

All about her, suddenly as the awakening from a dream, the nothingness had opened out into undreamed-of distances. She stood high on a hilltop under a sky spangled with strange stars. Below she caught glimpses of misty plains and valleys with mountain peaks rising far away. And at her feet a ravening circle of small, slavering, blind things leaped with clashing teeth.

They were obscene and hard to distinguish against the darkness of the hillside, and the noise they made was revolting. Her sword swung up of itself, almost, and slashed furiously at the little dark horrors leaping up around her legs. They died squashily, splattering her bare thighs with unpleasantness, and after a few had gone silent under the blade the rest fled into the dark with quick, frightened pantings, their feet making a queer splashing noise on the stones.

Jirel gathered a handful of the coarse grass which grew there and wiped her legs of the obscene splatters, looking about with quickened breath upon this land so unholy that one who bore a cross might not even see it. Here, if anywhere, one might find a weapon such as she sought. Behind her in the hillside was the low tunnel opening from which she had emerged. Overhead the strange stars shone. She did not recognize a single constellation, and if the brighter sparks were planets they were strange ones, tinged with violet and green and yellow. One was vividly crimson, like a point of fire. Far out over the rolling land below she could discern a mightly column of light. It did not blaze, nor illuminate the dark about. It cast no shadows. It simply was a great pillar of luminance towering high in the night. It seemed artificial – perhaps man-made, though she scarcely dared hope for men here.

She had half-expected, despite her brave words, to come out upon the storied and familiar red-hot pave of hell, and this pleasant, starlit land surprised her and made her more wary.

The things that built the tunnel could not have been human. She had no right to expect men here. She was a little stunned by finding open sky so far underground, though she was intelligent enough to realize that however she had come, she was not underground now. No cavity in the earth could contain this starry sky. She came of a credulous age, and she accepted her surroundings without too much questioning, though she was a little disappointed, if the truth were known, in the pleasantness of the mistily starlit place. The fiery streets of hell would have been a likelier locality in which to find a weapon against Guillaume.

When she had cleansed her sword on the grass and wiped her legs clean, she turned slowly down the hill. The distant column beckoned her, and after a moment of indecision she turned toward it. She had no time to waste, and this was the likeliest place to find what she sought.

The coarse grass brushed her legs and whispered round her feet. She stumbled now and then on the rubble, for the hill was steep, but she reached the bottom without mishap, and struck out across the meadows toward that blaze of faraway brilliance. It seemed to her that she walked more lightly, somehow. The grass scarcely bent underfoot, and she found she could take long sailing strides like one who runs with wings on his heels. It felt like a dream. The gravity pull of the place must have been less than she was accustomed to, but she only knew that she was skimming over the ground with amazing speed.

Travelling so, she passed through the meadows over the strange, coarse grass, over a brook or two that spoke endlessly to itself in a curious language that was almost speech, certainly not the usual gurgle of earth's running water. Once she ran into a blotch of darkness, like some pocket of void in the air, and struggled through gasping and blinking outraged eyes. She was beginning to realize that the land was not so innocently normal as it looked.

On and on she went, at that surprising speed, while the meadows skimmed past beneath her flying feet and gradually the light drew nearer. She saw now that it was a round tower of sheeted luminance, as if walls of solid flame rose up from the ground. Yet it seemed to be steady, nor did it cast any illumination upon the sky.

Before much time had elapsed, with her dreamlike speed she had almost reached her goal. The ground was becoming marshy underfoot, and presently the smell of swamps rose in her nostrils and she saw that between her and the light stretched a belt of unstable ground tufted with black reedy grass. Here and there she could see dim white blotches moving. They might be beasts, or only wisps of mist. The starlight was not very illuminating.

She began to pick her way carefully across the black, quaking morasses. Where the tufts of grass rose she found firmer ground, and she leaped from clump to clump with that amazing lightness, so that her feet barely touched the black ooze. Here and there slow bubbles rose through the mud and broke thickly. She did not like the place.

Halfway across, she saw one of the white blotches approaching her with slow, erratic movements. It bumped along unevenly, and at first she thought it might be inanimate, its approach was so indirect and purposeless. Then it blundered nearer, with that queer bumpy gait, making sucking noises in the ooze and splashing as it came. In the starlight she saw suddenly what it was, and for an instant her heart paused and sickness rose over-whelmingly in her throat. It was a woman – a beautiful woman whose white bare body had the curves and loveliness of some marble statue. She was crouching like a frog, and as Jirel watched in stupefaction she straightened her legs abruptly and leaped as a frog leaps, only more clumsily, falling forward into the ooze a little distance beyond the watching woman. She did not seem to see Jirel. The mud-spattered face was blank. She blundered on through the mud in awkward leaps. Jirel watched until the woman was no more than a white wandering blur in the dark, and above the shock of that sight pity was rising, and uncomprehending resentment against whatever had brought so lovely a creature into this — into blundering in frog leaps aimlessly through the mud, with empty mind and blind, staring eyes. For the second time that night she knew the sting of unaccustomed tears as she went on.

The sight, though had given her reassurance. The human form was not unknown here. There might be leathery devils with hoofs and horns, such as she still half expected, but she would not be alone in her humanity; though if all the rest were as piteously mindless as the one she had seen — she did not follow that thought. It was too unpleasant. She was glad when the marsh was past and she need not see any longer the awkward white shapes bumping along through the dark.

She struck out across the narrow space which lay between her and the tower. She saw now that it was a building, and that the light composed it. She could not understand that, but she saw it. Walls and columns outlined the tower, solid sheets of light with definite boundaries, not radiant. As she came nearer she saw that it was in motion, apparently spurting up from some source underground as if the light illuminated sheets of water rushing upward under great pressure. Yet she felt intuitively that it was not water, but incarnate light.

She came forward hesitantly, gripping her sword. The area around the tremendous pillar was paved with something black and smooth that did not reflect the light. Out of it sprang the uprushing walls of brilliance with their sharply defined edges. The magnitude of the thing dwarfed her to infinitesimal size. She stared upward with undazzled eyes, trying to understand. If there could be such a thing as solid, non-radiating light, this was it.

She was very near under the mighty tower before she could see the details of the building clearly. They were strange to her – great pillars and arches around the base, and one stupendous portal, all molded out of the rushing, prisoned light. She turned toward the opening after a moment, for the light had a tangible look. She did not believe she could have walked through it even had she dared.

When that tremendous portal arched over her she peered in, affrighted by the very size of the place. She thought she could hear the hiss and spurt of the light surging upward. She was looking into a mighty globe inside, a hall shaped like the interior of a bubble, though the curve was so vast she was scarcely aware of it. And in the very centre of the globe floated a light. Jirel blinked. A light, dwelling in a bubble of light. It glowed there in midair with a pale, steady flame that was somehow alive and animate, and brighter than the serene illumination of the building, for it hurt her eyes to look at it directly.

She stood on the threshold and stared, not quite daring to venture in. And as she hesitated a change came over the light. A flash of rose tinged its pallor. The rose deepened and darkened until it took on the colour of blood. And the shape underwent strange changes. It lengthened, drew itself out narrowly, split at the bottom into two branches, put out two tendrils from the top. The blood-red paled again, and the light somehow lost its brilliance, receded into the depths of the thing that was forming. Jirel clutched her sword and forgot to breathe, watching. The light was taking on the shape of a human being – of a woman – of a tall woman in mail, her red hair tousled and her eyes staring straight into the duplicate eyes at the portal . . .

"Welcome," said the Jirel suspended in the centre of the globe, her voice deep and resonant and clear in spite of the distance between them. Jirel at the door held her breath, wondering and afraid. This was herself, in every detail, a mirrored Jirel – that was it, a Jirel mirrored upon a surface which blazed and smouldered with barely repressed light, so that the eyes gleamed with it and the whole figure seemed to hold its shape by an effort, only by that effort restraining itself from resolving into pure, formless light again. But the voice was not her own. It shook and resounded with a knowledge as alien as the light-built walls. It mocked her. It said,

"Welcome! Enter into the portals, woman!"

She looked up warily at the rushing walls about her. Instinctively she drew back.

"Enter, enter!" urged that mocking voice from her own mirrored lips. And there was a note in it she did not like.

"Enter!" cried the voice again, this time a command.

Jirrel's eyes narrowed. Something intuitive warned her back, and yet – she drew the dagger she had thrust in her belt and with a quick motion she tossed it into the great globe-shaped hall. It struck the floor without a sound, and a brilliant light flared up around it, so brilliant she could not look upon what was happening; but it seemed to her that the knife expanded, grew large and nebulous and ringed with dazzling light. In less time than it takes to tell, it had faded out of sight as if the very atoms which composed it had flown apart and dispersed in the golden glow of that mighty bubble. The dazzle faded with the knife, leaving Jirel staring dazedly at the bare floor.

That other Jirel laughed, a rich, resonant laugh of scorn and malice.

"Stay out, then," said the voice. "You've more intelligence than I thought. Well what would you here?"

Jirel found her voice with an effort.

"I seek a weapon," she said, "a weapon against a man I so hate that upon earth there is none terrible enough for my need."

"You so hate him, eh?" mused the voice.

"With all my heart!"

"With all your heart!" echoed the voice, and there was an undernote of laughter in it that she did not understand. The echoes of that mirth ran round and round the great globe. Jirel felt her cheeks burn with resentment against some implication in the derision which she could not put a name to. When the echoes of the laugh had faded the voice said indifferently.

"Give the man what you find at the black temple in the lake. I make you a gift of it."

The lips that were Jirel's twisted into a laugh of purest mockery; then all about that figure so perfectly her own the light flared out. She saw the outlines melting fluidly as she turned her dazzled eyes away. Before the echoes of that derision had died, a blinding formless light burned once more in the midst of the bubble.

Jirel turned and stumbled away under the mighty column of the tower, a hand to her dazzled eyes. Not until she had reached the edge of the black, unreflecting circle that paved the ground around the pillar did she realize that she knew no way of finding the lake where her weapon lay. And not until then did she remember how fatal it is said to be to accept a gift from a demon. Buy it, or earn it, but never accept the gift. Well – she shrugged and stepped out upon the grass. She must surely be damned by now, for having ventured down of her own will into this curious place for such a purpose as hers. The soul can be lost but once.

She turned her face up to the strange stars and wondered in what direction her course lay. The sky looked blankly down upon her with its myriad meaningless eyes. A star fell as she watched, and in her superstitious soul she took it for an omen, and set off boldly over the dark meadows in the direction where the bright streak had faded. No swamps guarded the way here, and she was soon skimming along over the grass with that strange, dancing gait that the lightness of the place allowed her. And as she went she was remembering, as from long ago in some other far world, a man's arrogant mirth and the press of his mouth on hers. Hatred bubbled up hotly within her and broke from her lips in a little savage laugh of anticipation. What dreadful thing awaited her in the temple in the lake, what punishment from hell to be loosed by her own hands upon Guillaume? And though her soul was the price it cost her, she would count it a fair bargain if she could drive the laughter from his mouth and bring terror into the eyes that mocked her.

Thoughts like these kept her company for a long way upon her journey. She did not think to be lonely or afraid in the uncanny darkness across which no shadows fell from that mighty column behind her. The unchanging meadows flew past underfoot, lightly as meadows in a dream. It might almost have been that the earth moved instead of herself, so effortlessly did she go. She was sure now that she was heading in the right direction, for two more stars had fallen in the same arc across the sky.

The meadows were not untenanted. Sometimes, she felt presences near her in the dark, and once she ran full-tilt into a nest of little yapping horrors like those on the hilltop. They lunged up about her with clicking teeth, mad with a blind ferocity, and she swung her sword in frantic circles, sickened by the noise of them lunging splashily through the grass and splattering her sword with their deaths. She beat them off and went on fighting her own sickness, for she had never known anything quite so nauseating as these little monstrosities.

She crossed a brook that talked to itself in the darkness with that queer murmuring which came so near to speech, and a few strides beyond it she paused suddenly feeling the ground tremble with the rolling thunder of hoofbeats approaching. She stood still, searching the dark anxiously, and presently the earth-shaking beat grew louder and she saw a white blur flung wide across the dimness to her left, and the sound of hoofs deepened and grew. Then out of the night swept a herd of snow-white horses. Magnificently they ran, manes tossing, tails streaming, feet pounding a rhythmic, heart-stirring roll along the ground. She caught her breath at the beauty of their motion. They swept by a little distance away, tossing their heads, spurning the ground with scornful feet.

But as they came abreast of her she saw one blunder a little and stumble against the next and that one shook his head bewilderedly; and suddenly she realized that they were blind – all running so splendidly in a deeper dark than even she groped through. And she saw, too, their coats were rough-ened with sweat, and foam dripped from their lips, and their nostrils were flaring pools of scarlet. Now and again one stumbled from pure exhaustion. Yet they ran, frantically, blindly through the dark, driven by something outside their comprehension.

As the last one of all swept by her, sweat-crusted and staggering, she saw him toss his head high, spattering foam, and whinny shrilly to the stars. And it seemed to her that the sound was strangely articulate. Almost she heard the echoes of a name – "Julienne Julienne!" – in that high, despairing sound. And the incongruity of it, the bitter despair, clutched at her heart so sharply that for the third time that night she knew the sting of tears.

The dreadful humanity of that cry echoed in her ears as the thunder died away. She went on, blinking back the tears for that beautiful blind creature, staggering with exhaustion, calling a girl's name hopelessly from a beast's throat into the blank darkness wherein it was forever lost.

Then another star fell across the sky, and she hurried ahead, closing her mind to the strange, incomprehensible pathos that made an undernote of tears to the starry dark of this land. And the thought was growing in her mind that, though she had come into no brimstone pit where horned devils pranced over flames, yet perhaps it was after all a sort of hell through which she ran.

Presently in the distance she caught a glimmer of something bright. The ground dipped after that and she lost it, and skimmed through a hollow where pale things wavered away from her into the deeper dark. She never knew what they were, and was glad. When she came up onto higher ground again she saw it more clearly, an expanse of dim brilliance ahead. She hope it was a lake, and ran more swiftly.

It *was* a lake – a lake that could never have existed outside some obscure hell like this. She stood on the brink doubtfully, wondering if this could be the place the light-devil had meant. Black, shining water stretched out before her, heaving gently with a motion unlike that of any water she had ever seen before. And in the depths of it, like fireflies caught in ice, gleamed myriad small lights. They were fixed there immovably, not stirring with the motion of the water. As she watched, something hissed above her and a streak of light split the dark air. She looked up in time to see something bright curving across the sky to fall without a splash into the water, and small ripples of phosphorescence spread sluggishly toward the shore, where they broke at her feet with the queerest whispering sound, as if each succeeding ripple spoke the syllable of a word.

She looked up, trying to locate the origin of the falling lights, but the strange stars looked down upon her blankly. She bent and stared down into the centre of the spreading ripples, and where the thing had fallen she thought a new light twinkled through the water. She could not determine what it was, and after a curious moment she gave the question up and began to cast about for the temple the light-devil had spoken of.

After a moment she thought she saw something dark in the centre of the lake, and when she had stared for a few minutes it gradually became clearer, an arch of darkness against the starry background of the water. It might be a temple. She strolled slowly along the brim of the lake, trying to get a closer view of it, for the thing was no more than a darkness against the spangles of light, like some void in the sky where no stars shine. And presently she stumbled over something in the grass.

She looked down with startled yellow eyes, and saw a strange, indistinguishable darkness. It had solidity to the feel but scarcely to the eye, for she could not quite focus upon it. It was like trying to see something that did not exist save as a void, a darkness in the grass. It had the shape of a step, and when she followed with her eyes she saw that it was the beginning of a dim bridge stretching out over the lake, narrow and curved and made out of nothingness. It seemed to have no surface, and its edges were difficult to distinguish from the lesser gloom surrounding it. But the thing was tangible – an arch carved out of the solid dark – and it led out in the direction she wished to go. For she was naïvely sure now that the dim blot in the centre of the lake was the temple she was searching for. The falling stars had guided her, and she could not have gone astray.

So she set her teeth and gripped her sword and put her foot upon the bridge. It was rock-firm under her, but scarcely more than a foot or so wide, and without rails. When she had gone a step or two she began to feel dizzy; for under her the water heaved with a motion that made her head swim, and the stars twinkled eerily in its depths. She dared not look away for fear of missing her footing on the narrow arch of darkness. It was like walking a bridge flung across the void, with stars underfoot and nothing but an unstable strip of nothingness to bear her up. Halfway across, the heaving of the water and the illusion of vast, constellated spaces beneath and the look her bridge had of being no more than empty space ahead, combined to send her head reeling; and as she stumbled on, the bridge seemed to be wavering with her, swinging in gigantic arcs across the starry void below.

Now she could see the temple more closely, though scarcely more clearly than from the shore. It looked to be no more than an outlined emptiness against the starcrowded brilliance behind it, etching its arches and columns of blankness upon the twinkling waters. The bridge came down in a long dim swoop to its doorway. Jirel took the last few yards at a reckless run and stopped breathless under the arch that made the temple's vague doorway. She stood there panting and staring about narrow-eyed, sword poised in her hand. For though the place was empty and very still she felt a presence even as she set her foot upon the floor of it.

She was staring about a little space of blankness in the starry lake. It seemed to be no more than that. She could see the walls and columns where they were outlined against the water and where they made darknesses in the star-flecked sky, but where there was only dark behind them she could see nothing. It was a tiny place, no more than a few square yards of emptiness upon the face of the twinkling waters. And in its centre an image stood.

She stared at it in silence, feeling a curious compulsion growing within her, like a vague command from something outside herself. The image was of some substance of nameless black, unlike the material which composed the building, for even in the dark she could see it clearly. It was a semi-human figure, crouching forward with out-thrust head, sexless and strange. Its one central eye was closed as if in rapture, and its mouth was pursed for a kiss. And though it was but an image and without even the semblance of life, she felt unmistakably the presence of something alive in the temple, something so alien and innominate that instinctively she drew away.

She stood there for a full minute, reluctant to enter the

place where so alien a being dwelt, half-conscious of that voiceless compulsion growing up within her. And slowly she became aware that all the lines and angles of the half-seen building were curved to make the image their centre and focus. The very bridge swooped its long arc to complete the centring. As she watched, it seemed to her that through the arches of the columns even the stars in lake and sky were grouped in patterns which took the image for their focus. Every line and curve in the dim world seemed to sweep round toward the squatting thing before her with its closed eye and expectant mouth.

Gradually the universal focusing of lines began to exert its influence upon her. She took a hesitant step forward without realizing the motion. But that step was all the dormant urge within her needed. With her one motion forward the compulsion closed down upon her with whirlwind impetuosity. Helplessly she felt herself advancing, helplessly with one small, sane portion of her mind she realized the madness that was gripping her, the blind, irresistible urge to do what every visible line in the temple's construction was made to compel. With stars swirling around her she advanced across the floor and laid her hands upon the rounded shoulders of the image – the sword, forgotten, making a sort of accolade against its hunched neck – and lifted her red head and laid her mouth blindly against the pursed lips of the image.

In a dream she took that kiss. In a dream of dizziness and confusion she seemed to feel the iron-cold lips stirring under hers. And through the union of that kiss – warm-blooded woman with image of nameless stone – through the meeting of their mouths something entered into her very soul; something cold and stunning; something alien beyond any words. It lay upon her shuddering soul like some frigid weight from the void, a bubble holding something unthinkably alien and dreadful. She could feel the heaviness of it upon some intangible part of her that shrank from the torch. It was like the weight of remorse or despair, only far colder and stranger and – somehow – more ominous, as if this weight were but the egg from which things might hatch too dreadful to put even into thoughts.

The moment of the kiss could have been no longer than a breath's space, but to her it was timeless. In a dream she felt the compulsion falling from her at last. In a dim dream she dropped her hands from its shoulders, finding the sword heavy in her grasp and staring dully at it for a while before clarity began its return to her cloudy mind. When she became completely aware of herself once more she was standing with slack body and dragging head before the blind, rapturous image, that dead weight upon her heart as dreary as an old sorrow, and more coldly ominous than anything she could find words for.

And with returning clarity the most staggering terror came over her, swiftly and suddenly – terror of the image and the temple of darkness, and the coldly spangled lake and of the whole, wide, dim, dreadful world about her. Desperately she longed for home again, even the red fury of hatred and the press of Guillaume's mouth and the hot arrogance of his eyes again. Anything but this. She found herself running without knowing why. Her feet skimmed over the narrow bridge lightly as a gull's wings dipping the water. In a brief instant the starry void of the lake flashed by beneath her and the solid earth was underfoot. She saw the great column of light far away across the dark meadows and beyond it a hilltop rising against the stars. And she ran.

She ran with terror at her heels and devils howling in the wind her own speed made. She ran from her own curiously alien body, heavy with its weight of inexplicable doom. She passed through the hollow where pale things wavered away, she fled over the uneven meadows in a frenzy of terror. She ran and ran, in those long light bounds the lesser gravity allowed her, fleeter than a deer, and her own panic choked in her throat and that weight upon her soul dragged at her too drearily for tears. She fled to escape it, and could not; and the ominous certainty that she carried something too dreadful to think of grew and grew.

For a long while she skimmed over the grass, tirelessly, wing-heeled, her red hair flying. The panic died after a while, but that sense of heavy disaster did not die. She felt somehow that tears would ease her, but something in the frigid darkness of her soul froze her tears in the ice of that grey and alien chill.

And gradually, through the inner dark, a fierce anticipation took form in her mind. Revenge upon Guillaume! She had taken from the temple only a kiss, so it was that which she must deliver to him. And savagely she exulted in the thought of what that kiss would release upon him, unsuspecting. She did not know, but it filled her with fierce joy to guess.

She had passed the column and skirted the morass where the white, blundering forms still bumped along awkwardly through the ooze, and was crossing the coarse grass toward the nearing hill when the sky began to pale along the horizon. And with that pallor a fresh terror took hold upon her, a wild horror of daylight in this unholy land. She was not sure if it was the light itself she so dreaded, or what that light would reveal in the dark stretches she had traversed so blindly – what unknown horrors she had skirted in the night. But she knew instinctively that if she valued her sanity she must be gone before the light had risen over the land. And she redoubled her efforts, spurring her wearying limbs to yet more skimming speed. But it would be a close race, for already the stars were blurring out, and a flush of curious green was broadening along the sky, and around her the air was turning to a vague, unpleasant grey.

She toiled up the steep hillside breathlessly. When she was halfway up, her own shadow began to take form upon the rocks, and it was unfamiliar and dreadfully significant of something just outside her range of understanding. She averted her eyes from it, afraid that at any moment the meaning might break upon her outraged brain.

She could see the top of the hill above her, dark against the paling sky, and she toiled up in frantic haste, clutching her sword and feeling that if she had to look in the full light upon the dreadful little abominations that had snapped around her feet when she first emerged she would collapse into screaming hysteria.

The cave-mouth yawned before her, invitingly black, a refuge from the dawning light behind her. She knew an almost irresistible desire to turn and look back from this vantage-point across the land she had traversed, and gripped her sword hard to conquer the perverse longing. There was a scuffling in the rocks at her feet, and she set her teeth in her underlip and swung viciously in brief arcs, without looking down. She heard small squeakings and the splashy sound of feet upon the stones, and felt her blade shear thrice through semi-solidity, to the click of little vicious teeth. Then they broke and ran off over the hillside, and she stumbled on, choking back the scream that wanted so fiercely to break from her lips.

She fought that growing desire all the way up to the cave-mouth, for she knew that if she gave way she would never cease shrieking until her throat went raw.

Blood was trickling from her bitten lip with the effort at silence when she reached the cave. And there, twinkling upon the stones, lay something small and bright and dearly familiar. With a sob of relief she bent and snatched up the crucifix she had torn from her throat when she came out into this land. And as her fingers shut upon it a vast, protecting darkness swooped around her. Gasping with relief, she groped her way the step or two that separated her from the cave.

Dark lay like a blanket over her eyes, and she welcomed it gladly, remembering how her shadow had lain so awfully upon the hillside as she climbed, remembering the first rays of savage sunlight beating upon her shoulders. She stumbled through the blackness, slowly getting control again over her shaking body and labouring lungs, slowly stilling the panic that the dawning day had roused so inexplicably within her. And as that terror died, the dull weight upon her spirit became strong again. She had all but forgotten it in her panic, but now the impending and unknown dreadfulness grew heavier and more oppressive in the darkness of the underground, and she groped along in a dull stupor of her own depression, slow with the weight of the strange doom she carried.

Nothing barred her way. In the dullness of her stupor she scarcely realized it, or expected any of the vague horrors that peopled the place to leap out upon her. Empty and unmenacing, the way stretched before her blindly stumbling feet. Only once did she hear the sound of another presence – the rasp of hoarse breathing and the scrape of a scaly hide against the stone – but it must have been outside the range of her own passage, for she encountered nothing.

When she had come to the end and a cold wall rose up before her, it was scarcely more than automatic habit that made her search along it with groping hand until she came to the mouth of the shaft. It sloped gently up into the dark. She crawled in, trailing her sword, until the rising incline and lowering roof forced her down upon her face. Then with toes and fingers she began to force herself up the spiral, slippery way.

Before she had gone very far she was advancing without effort, scarcely realizing that it was against gravity she moved. The curious dizziness of the shaft had come over her, the strange feeling of change in the very substance of her body, and through the cloudy numbness of it she felt herself sliding round and round the spirals, without effort. Again, obscurely,

216

she had the feeling that in the peculiar angles of this shaft was neither up nor down. And for a long while the dizzy circling went on.

When the end came at last, and she felt her fingers gripping the edge of that upper opening which lay beneath the floor of Joiry's lowest dungeons, she heaved herself up warily and lay for a while on the cold floor in the dark, while slowly the clouds of dizziness passed from her mind, leaving only that onimous weight within. When the darkness had ceased to circle about her, and the floor steadied, she got up dully and swung the cover back over the opening, her hands shuddering from the feel of the cold, smooth ring which had never seen daylight.

When she turned from this task she was aware of the reason for the lessening in the gloom around her. A guttering light outlined the hole in the wall from which she had pulled the stones – was it a century ago? The brilliance all but blinded her after her long sojourn through blackness, and she stood there awhile, swaying a little, one hand to her eyes, before she went out into the familiar torchlight she knew waited her beyond. Father Gervase, she was sure, anxiously waiting her return. But even he had not dared to follow her through the hole in the wall, down to the brink of the shaft.

Somehow she felt that she should be giddy with relief at this safe homecoming, back to humanity again. But as she stumbled over the upward slope toward light and safety she was conscious of no more than the dullness of whatever unreleased horror it was which still lay so ominously upon her stunned soul.

She came through the gaping hole in the masonry into the full glare of torches awaiting her, remembering with a wry inward smile how wide she had made the opening in anticipation of flight from something dreadful when she came back that way. Well, there was no flight from the horror she bore within her. It seemed to her that her heart was slowing, too, missing a beat now and then and staggering like a weary runner.

She came out into the torchlight, stumbling with exhaustion, her mouth scarlet from the blood of her bitten lip and her bare greaved legs and bare sword-blade foul with the deaths of those little horrors that swarmed around the cave-mouth. From the tangle of red hair her eyes stared out with a bleak, frozen, inward look, as of one who has seen nameless things. That keen, steelbright beauty which had been hers was as dull and fouled as her sword-blade, and at the look in her eyes Father Gervase shuddered and crossed himself.

They were waiting for her in an uneasy group – the priest anxious and dark, Guillaume splendid in the torchlight, tall and arrogant, a handful of men-at-arms holding the guttering lights and shifting uneasily from one foot to the other. When she saw Guillaume the light that flared up in her eyes blotted out for a moment the bleak dreadfulness behind them, and her slowing heart leaped like a spurred horse, sending the blood riotously through her veins. Guillaume, magnificent in his armour, leaning upon his sword and staring down at her from his scornful height, the little black beard jutting. Guillaume, to whom Joiry had fallen. Guillaume.

That which she carried at the core of her being was heavier than anything else in the world, so heavy she could scarcely keep her knees from bending, so heavy her heart laboured under its weight. Almost irresistibly she wanted to give way beneath it, to sink down and down under the crushing load, to lie prone and vanquished in the ice-gray, bleak place she was so dimly aware of through the clouds that were rising about her. But there was Guillaume, grim and grinning, and she hated him so very bitterly – she must make the effort. She must, at whatever cost, for she was coming to know that death lay in wait for her if she bore this burden long, that it was a two-edged weapon which could strike at its wielder if the blow were delayed too long. She knew this through the dim mists that were thickening in her brain, and she put all her strength into the immense effort it cost to cross the floor toward him. She stumbled a little and made one faltering step and then another, and dropped her sword with a clang as she lifted her arms to him.

He caught her strongly, in a hard, warm clasp, and she heard his laugh triumphant and hateful as he bent his head to take the kiss she was raising her mouth to offer. He must have seen, in that last moment before their lips met, the savage glare of victory in her eyes, and been startled. But he did not hesitate. His mouth was heavy upon hers.

It was a long kiss. She felt him stiffen in her arms. She felt a coldness in the lips upon hers, and slowly the dark weight of what she bore lightened, lifted, cleared away from her cloudy mind. Strength flowed back through her richly. The whole world came alive to her once more. Presently she loosed his slack arms and stepped away, looking up into his face with a keen and dreadful triumph upon her own.

She saw the ruddiness of him draining away, and the rigidity of stone coming over his scarred features. Only his eyes remained alive, and there was torment in them, and understanding. She was glad – she had wanted him to understand what it cost to take Joiry's kiss unbidden. She smiled thinly into his tortured eyes, watching. And she saw something cold and alien seeping through him, permeating him slowly with some unnameable emotion which no man could ever have experienced before. She could not name it, but she saw it in his eyes – some dreadful emotion never made for flesh and blood to know, some iron despair such as only an unguessable being from the grey, formless void could ever have felt before – too hideously alien for any human creature to endure. Even she shuddered from the dreadful, cold bleakness looking out of his eyes, and knew as she watched that there must be many emotions and many fears and joys too far outside man's comprehension for any being of flesh to undergo, and live. Greyly she saw it spreading through him, and the very substance of his body shuddered under that iron weight.

And now came a visible, physical change. Watching, she was aghast to think that in her own body and upon her own soul she had borne the seed of this dreadful flowering, and did not wonder that her heart had slowed under the unbearable weight of it. He was standing rigidly with arms half bent, just as he stood when she slid from his embrace. And now great shudders began to go over him, as if he were wavering in the torchlight, some grey-faced wraith in armour with torment in his eyes. She saw the sweat beading his forehead. She saw a trickle of blood from his mouth, as if he had bitten through his lip in the agony of this new, incomprehensible emotion. Then a last shiver went over him violently, and he flung up his head, the little curling beard jutting, ceilingward and the muscles of his strong throat corded, and from his lips broke a long, low cry of such utter, inhuman strangeness that Jirel felt coldness rippling through her veins and she put up her hands to her ears to shut it out. It meant something – it expressed some dreadful emotion that was neither sorrow nor despair nor anger, but infinitely alien and infinitely sad. Then his long legs buckled at the knees and he dropped with a clatter of mail and lay still on the stone floor.

They knew he was dead. That was unmistakable in the way he lay. Jirel stood very still, looking down upon him, and strangely it seemed to her that all the lights in the world had gone out. A moment before he had been so big and vital, so magnificent in the torchlight – she could still feel his kiss upon her mouth, and the hard warmth of his arms . . .

Suddenly and blindingly it came upon her what she had done. She knew now why such heady violence had flooded her whenever she thought of him – knew why the light-devil in her own form had laughed so derisively – knew the price she must pay for taking a gift from a demon. She knew that there was no light anywhere in the world, now that Guillaume was gone.

Father Gervase took her arm gently. She shook him off with an impatient shrug and dropped to one knee beside Guillaume's body, bending her head so that the red hair fell forward to hide her tears.

The Contributors

Jane Yolen
American Jane Yolen has written many novels and short stories on fantastic and fairy-tale themes, including her *Pit Dragon* trilogy.

Tanith Lee
Tanith Lee became well known in the 1970s as a writer of children's fantasy and as a writer of heroic fantasy and science fiction.

Pat McIntosh
Pat McIntosh wrote fantasy stories for *Anduril*, a specialist fantasy magazine or 'fanzine', in the 1970s.

Robin McKinley
American Robin McKinley's first novel *Beauty* was a retelling of the story of Beauty and the Beast. *The Blue Sword* was the first book about her fantasy world of *Damar* (modelled on the British Raj); her second *Damar* book, *The Hero and the Crown* won the USA Newbery Medal for the best children's book of the year. The *Damar* Chronicles feature strong heroines questing for adventure and romance.

Diana Wynne Jones
Diana Wynne Jones published her first children's fantasy in 1973 and now commands a wide readership among children and adults. Most of her stories are fantasies; the one chosen for this collection is a rare example of her science fiction work.

Vera Chapman

Vera Chapman recently celebrated her 91st birthday. Her life has been so busy that she did not take up writing seriously until her retirement. *Crusader Damosel* is one of a series of stories about the Abbess of Shaston.

C.L. Moore

Catherine Lucille Moore (1911-1987) was an important pioneer of heroic, feminist fantasy and women's science fiction. Writing first in the 1930s for fantasy and science fiction magazines, she created the space adventurer Northwest Smith, and the heroic warrior Jirel of Joiry, and brought to the male-dominated world of science fiction new emotional and psychological insights. She married Henry Kuttner, who had written enthusiastic fan letters to her without realising her female identity. They collaborated on many science fiction stories and novels.

Also in
Lions Tracks

To order direct from the publisher, just tick the titles you want and fill in the order form on the last page.

Lions Tracks